DEEP ALLEGIANCE

A NOAH WOLF THRILLER

DAVID ARCHER

RIGHTHOUSE

ISBN-13: 978-1-63696-117-0

ISBN-10: 1-63696-117-7

Cover design by: Damonza

Printed in the United States of America

www.righthouse.com

www.instagram.com/righthousebooks

www.facebook.com/righthousebooks

twitter.com/righthousebooks

PRAISE FOR THE NOAH WOLF SERIES

NOAH WOLF THRILLERS

PROLOGUE

Donald Jefferson would have been the first to acknowledge that he didn't spend a lot of time thinking about life. Most of the time, life just rolled by and he went along for the ride. Life is something that changed about as often as you thought about it, anyway. Donald thought it was beautiful, if somewhat frightening at times, and didn't give it a lot more thought than that.

Blatant, subtle, cold, amusing, incidental, sarcastic irony never ceased to entertain life's spectators because it never ceased to surprise them. For Donald Jefferson, the experience never failed to give him pause. He was not a superstitious man, but he was a suspicious one and he believed in irony. He believed in irony the same way some men believe in God, but more than that, he believed in irony the way some believed in paranormal activity, government conspiracies, or alien invasions.

While there were always a dozen or more people ready to stand up and argue the believing man's lack of proof or truth, Donald knew the believers were not altogether wrong. After all, he *was* part of a government conspiracy, the number two man and operations director for the Elimination and Eradication Agency. In that position, he dealt with a number of United States allied governments who occasionally had need of the agency's services and personnel, the acknowledged best in the field of assassination and espionage. E & E was so secret that it never allowed evidence of issued assignments to leave its offices, and occasionally had to leave their own people out in the cold in order to avoid discovery.

Working for E & E had made Donald realize that the religion of irony was a religion of give and take. It gave by putting him in a profession that ran through his blood, a profession he couldn't imagine not doing. It gave him the iron determination to make sure that the men and women he worked with, the men and women he had to send out to kill and infiltrate and destroy the lives of the enemies of America, were the best there could be at what they did.

It took by the way it brought Donald to the knowledge that he was responsible for the lives of people like Noah Wolf and his team, as well as many others. It took by requiring him to trust his own ability to perform his duties in a competent manner, and that trust wasn't something that came to him easily.

Part of those duties involved dealing with the people who were constantly requesting their assistance. In that capacity, Donald occasionally had to travel around the world to meet with diplomatic officials and others who had the authority to request E & E services. It was his job to determine whether those requests were viable enough to pass up the line to his superior, Allison Peterson, the director of the agency.

He constantly calculated every factor involved in each such meeting. This was a habit that was so deeply ingrained in his psyche that he rarely missed even the slightest detail.

It was because of this belief, this honed skill, this ability to read expressions and body language better than almost anyone else, that he'd made the discovery that sent him down another road of intrigue. But it was the *take* part of irony that prevented him from seeing the full picture sooner.

Donald Jefferson was walking into a trap.

Of course, there was no way he could have known that at the

time. His old friend Harold, the Austrian Ambassador to England, had asked him to come and visit for the purpose of arranging a liaison between Chechnya and E & E. The small country had many internal enemies, and some of them were so incorrigible that there was no way to remove them short of assassination, but they were also powerful and well-protected. It would take expertise such as E & E could offer to eradicate them, and Harold had been instrumental in arranging such liaisons in the past. In fact, it was Harold who had convinced the British government to allow the agency to operate in the U.K. when necessary.

Donald and Harold went way back. During the Middle East conflicts, the two of them had been involved in intelligence and had several occasions to work together. Afterward, when Harold went into the diplomatic services, the friendship they had developed became an asset to both of them.

Neither of them knew that Harold was one of many such men whose lives were manipulated and controlled by someone who considered himself the ultimate puppet master.

———

THE WEALTHY AND philanthropic Harold Ingemar's penthouse party was in full swing when Caleb Dawson stepped out of the elevator and smoothly showed his invitation to the doorman.

Inwardly, Dawson scoffed at calling the garish affair a *party*. He hated these things; the pointless yet pointed interactions that only added to the atmosphere of unreasoned privilege, and the arrogant belief of being untouchable. All in attendance were steadfastly ignoring the dirt and grime forty stories below, preferring to believe that the world was as they wished it to be. At one time, 'party' had meant casual clothes, loud music, the chance to act like a fool and be loved for it. This expensively catered event drew only those with expensive tastes in everything, people who had their fingers in everything else. These were the kind of people who thought themselves above everyone else, unreachable, even untouchable by the lower and baser parts of the world.

They were really nothing more than idiots. Dawson knew better than anyone that absolutely everyone was touchable.

As he strolled casually but directly across the room to the balcony doors, he tuned out the insignificant conversations and focused on identifying the number of people who were in attendance along with him. Dawson recognized some, but knew none would recognize him. That was how he worked. He didn't often associate with the others. He never stuck around long enough to do so. He never stuck around long enough to even be noticed.

Still in front of the balcony doors, Dawson stopped. Down the stairs to his right was a tall, athletic-looking man in his fifties. This was his target, Donald Jefferson. He was easily identifiable, even without the physical description. Though his serious face fit perfectly with the small group of tuxedoed gentlemen surrounding him, the confident and easy way he stood set him subtly apart.

Dawson held back a grin when he realized the Director himself was among the men Jefferson mingled with. Dawson was rarely given the opportunity to perform his skills right in front of his master.

He would make this interesting, for Spear's sake.

He didn't acknowledge the Director and the Director didn't acknowledge him. Caleb Dawson was the consummate professional, and anonymity was of value to both of them.

Watching Jefferson, Dawson smiled slightly. If all went well, he'd be free from this facade of a party in less than five minutes.

He tucked his invitation smoothly into his pocket and moved onto the balcony. It was empty and he was glad. He pulled a vape pen from his left pocket, its innocent appearance already deadly, loaded with the two centimeter dart that held the drug. From his other pocket, he took the fake battery that held the pressurized CO_2 charge that would launch the tiny dart. He felt an odd sense of pleasure as the pieces locked easily together. He had practice, and it all went together smoothly and soundlessly. There would be no issues.

Fixing the device in his hand, Dawson turned back toward the doors and the elite society to be found behind them, not even glancing at the spectacular London skyline.

When he stepped back into the room, he tracked Jefferson, seeing that he'd moved away from the balcony doors. Casually, Dawson lifted a glass of champagne from a strolling server and watched. Jefferson shifted nearer to the food table, seemingly also seeking a glass of champagne. Dawson sipped carefully. As he lowered the glass from his lips, the drug was fired unceremoniously into Jefferson's neck. His aim was perfect, and no one noticed a thing. Not a ripple of disturbance buzzed the other partygoers.

Jefferson's hand flew to his neck, rubbing at the spot. His eyes were wide, and the "Oh, no," that emerged from his lips was too soft to hear. Dawson couldn't help admiring the instant recognition that shone from his victim's eyes as he searched the room for his killer, realizing instantly what had happened even at a time when most others would have spent their last seconds clinging to denial.

The clarity only lasted a moment, dissipating rapidly as the drug took over.

Dawson's work was done.

Leaving his champagne on the table to his right, he returned to the elevators, ignoring Jefferson clutching his neck less than ten feet away.

The elegant old age-style elevator welcomed him with a friendly ding as he entered calmly and pushed the button to take him back down to the main lobby. He'd traveled only two floors down when he started to hear the screams. By the time he walked out through the building's front doors, a small crowd was gathering around Donald Jefferson's body on the parking lot's hard pavement.

Sirens could already be heard ringing in the distance.

Dawson ignored the first two cab drivers and he was ignored in turn, the drivers too distracted by all the noise and excitement to bother trying to pick up another fare. He slid into the back seat of the third taxi in the line, and the driver didn't even realize he'd picked up a fare for a few seconds.

The job had not taken anywhere near as long as he'd expected, after all, and it was a beautiful night. He'd always enjoyed some of the London night life, and so he decided to go and have a drink. With any luck, one of the girls he'd met the last time he was here would be around.

ONE

NOAH WOLF WAS ASLEEP AND DREAMING WHEN THE call came. This one was actually more like a memory, the kind of dream where the sounds and motions of the outside world merge so completely with the images of the mind that the line separating truth and the world of dreams is temporarily wiped away.

In the dream, he was still suffering the effects of his last mission, still afflicted with the emotions that had come flooding back into him as the result of the trauma he had gone through. It was terrifying for Noah to be having those feelings again after so many years, so this dream was as much a nightmare as anything else.

The phone woke him on its very first ring, and for a moment, he thought he was still in the hospital ward. His eyes searched the darkness of his bedroom, looking for any sign that he was still in that reality, but Noah is one of those whose dreams fade away quickly after he wakes.

He blinked and the phone rang again. He snatched it up and put it to his ear, the horror of the dream already forgotten.

"Camelot," he said.

"There is a plane waiting for you at Heathrow," Allison said. "Get your team on board and get here as quickly as you can. As soon as you arrive, Noah, I need to see you. Just you, Noah. Nobody else right now."

There was something in her voice that made asking questions seem like a very bad idea.

"We're on the way," Noah said. "I'll see you tomorrow."

Sarah roused herself as he started to climb out of bed. "Noah? What's going on?"

"Allison wants us back at Neverland," he said. "There's a plane waiting for us at Heathrow, and I'm supposed to see her tomorrow, as soon as we arrive. She said to come to her office alone, so the rest of you will be able to go out to the house and relax." He pulled on his jeans and started toward the door.

Sarah picked up her phone and hit the button to make it light up. "It's only three o'clock in the morning," she said. "What could be so important it couldn't wait until normal hours?"

"I don't know," Noah said, "but I'm going to find out." He stepped out into the hall and woke the others, letting them know that they needed to get up and pack quickly. He made it clear that he didn't know the answer to their questions, so they simply packed up and then headed for the airport.

———

BECAUSE OF THE time difference and the ten hour flight, it was just after seven a.m. when the plane touched down in Kirtland. The van, driven by a new recruit who they didn't recognize, was waiting for them at the airport, and dropped Noah off at the Brigadoon Investments building, the headquarters of E & E. The rest of them stayed in the van and headed out to Noah's house. They would relax there until he came back to tell them what was going on.

Noah rode up in the elevator and walked past the empty receptionist's desk. He opened the door without hesitation to see Allison sitting behind her own desk, and for the first time in many years, Noah found himself slightly surprised when he saw her.

Her face was red, especially around the eyes. Allison Peterson had been crying, and Noah hadn't even believed such a thing would be possible.

"Thank you for coming so quickly," she said. "Sit down, Noah." She tapped on the keyboard of her computer and the screen on the wall behind her snapped to life, showing a collage of photographs: a nondescript brown-haired man engaged in various activities.

Noah instantly memorized the man's face, even before Allison began speaking.

"The first thing I have to tell you is that Donald Jefferson is dead," she said.

Noah's expression did not change as he continued to stare at the photos displayed over her shoulder.

"What happened?" he asked. It was the same way he might ask why the coffee pot was empty.

"He was in London to meet with officials from one of the smaller European countries, to discuss the possibility of E & E helping them with some of their problems. He was attending a private party at the home of the Austrian ambassador that had more security than the President of the United States, and he should have been perfectly safe. Unfortunately, there are a few assassins out there who are almost as good as you. One of them got to Donald in the middle of the reception. He was injected with a drug, something that affected his mind within only a matter of seconds. It caused some sort of terror reaction, because he suddenly appeared frightened of everyone around him and jumped out a fortieth floor window as if he was trying to escape them."

"The killer would be the man on the screen behind you?" Noah asked.

"The man you're looking at is responsible for Donald's death, yes. No one knows his real name. He uses many identities. In this case, he was using the name Caleb Dawson."

"How did you identify him?" Noah asked.

"Security video, of course," Allison replied. "As I said, the affair had terrific security, including hidden video cameras just about everywhere. The footage was handed over to MI6, who shared it with our people over there." She sighed. "From what we have been able to learn, Dawson has for the past couple of years maintained an exclusive contract with a powerful underworld leader whom we know only by the name of Spear."

Spear, Noah thought, surprised that as he rolled the name through his mind, he still felt absolutely nothing. The name should have meant more; hearing the name of Donald's killer should have caused at least a desire to punish the individual, but Noah only considered him a threat that needed to be eliminated. Who in the world was Caleb Dawson, and who was this Spear? What possible motive could they have had for killing Donald?

"Spear," Noah said. "I don't think I've heard the name before. What can you tell me about him?"

"Spear is a manipulator," Allison replied. "All we know about him is that he is known for orchestrating terror events and assassinations that are designed to push governments into doing specific things. To give you an example, he is suspected of being behind the recent mass casualty attacks in Berlin that caused the German government to begin rounding up and deporting Muslim immigrants. That action has led to sanctions against Germany from almost every other nation and has crippled several parts of the German economy. As a result, Germany is now beholden to the rest of the European Union just to continue surviving as a nation."

Noah nodded. "What was Mr. Jefferson doing at the time of his death?"

"Donald was discussing the possibility of opening a liaison office in Chechnya when he was killed. Chechnya has a lot of internal strife, and some of the players are too powerful to touch through conventional means. Harold Ingemar, the Austrian ambassador, was an old friend of Donald's. The Chechnyan government approached him to act as a go-between, and he invited Donald to come and discuss the situation. In order to avoid having Donald go to the Chechnyan Embassy, Ingemar arranged a party at his own home and made sure the ambassador was there. Donald was supposed to speak with him, but never got the chance." She paused for a second, her eyes misty. "We believe the motive for his assassination was to prevent Chechnya from pursuing a relationship with our organization. Their ambassador has declined to continue the discussion."

"Do we have any idea where Dawson is now?"

"No," Allison said. "Sooner or later, however, he will be ordered to kill again and all of our intelligence agencies are scanning for information on when that might take place. I'm sending you and your team, Noah, to find and track this son of a bitch and identify Spear, who is actually responsible for Donald's death. I want you to get started as soon as you can, but not before the day after tomorrow. Donald's body will be arriving back here tomorrow, and his funeral is scheduled for the day after that."

"I'm curious, but why didn't you have his body brought back on the same plane with us?"

"Because there can be no association between you and him. Donald was known as part of our agency; given half a chance, some of our enemies would use the fact that you were on that plane to connect you and your team to the organization, as well. We can't risk that."

"You'll have identity kits and such ready for us by then?"

"Molly is going to be taking over for Donald," Allison said. "She'll be handling such things, so check with her tomorrow. She should have everything ready in plenty of time." She paused and looked at him for a moment. "Noah, Sarah is not going. I'm not risking my grandchild, and don't you dare say a word, by letting her go on this mission."

Noah nodded once, then got to his feet. "I'll take care of it," he said. "Mr. Jefferson was a good man."

A tear snaked its way down Allison's cheek. "He was that," she said. "And a lot more, besides."

Noah recognized the dismissal as he heard it. He got up and walked out of the office, then took the elevator down to the first floor. He wasn't surprised to find Doctor Nathan Parker sitting on the bench outside the front door.

"Doc," Noah said. "Are you waiting for me?"

"Of course," Parker said, getting slowly to his feet. "First, I knew you were going to need a ride out to your house, but there's also the fact that I want to discuss a couple of factors regarding your new mission." He got up off the bench and started toward the Cadillac parked at the curb. "Get in, son, I'm not going to waste a lot of time. We can talk on the way to your place."

Noah followed him and got into the car on the passenger side. Parker slid behind the wheel, started up the car and pulled away from the curb. He didn't say anything until they had passed the first intersection.

"Donald Jefferson was one of the finest men I've ever known. This world is not going to be the place it should be without him in it."

"I can agree with that assessment," Noah said.

"However, we must also remember that Donald was an experienced and capable agent in his own right. He was one of the most powerful men in the free world, being the right hand of the woman who can order the death of any human being for any reason she chooses. I don't believe there is anyone in the world who would not have considered Donald an extension of Allison Peterson, so had he ever suggested that someone needed to die, that suggestion would have been taken as an order by almost any intelligence operative of our country or its allies. Can you understand what I'm saying?"

"Sir, it sounds like you are implying that Donald may have been tempted to use that power from time to time?"

"He was a man, wasn't he? One of the curses about being in my position with this organization is that some of you people seem to think of me as your Father Confessor. Donald was one who made a point of catching up with me from time to time, so

I'm privy to a few things that even Allison may not know. While our intelligence does indicate that Spear is behind the assassination, I need you to be aware that there could be other factors involved. Some of those factors could exist within our own government."

"Mr. Jefferson had enemies, then," Noah said. "Do you have any reason to believe one of those was responsible for the assassination?"

"I don't even have a reason to believe the sun will come up tomorrow morning," Parker said, "not at my age. There is absolutely nothing certain in this world, Noah, other than the truth you see directly in front of your eyes at a given moment. Truth has a habit of mutating itself; it is always possible that, no matter what the evidence in front of you might suggest, there can be another explanation for any event you can imagine. All I'm trying to say to you is that, while I expect you to carry out your mission and eliminate Spear, you need to be aware that there could be other forces at work, as well."

"Very well, sir," Noah said. "I'll make a note of it and pay close attention to what's happening around us."

"You do that, Noah," Parker said. "And I want you to do yourself one more favor. My gut says you're going to need somebody on this mission who isn't on any intelligence radar. It needs to be somebody who can mold himself to whatever situation comes along. I know that you have absolute autonomy on planning your missions, but I'm going to make a suggestion and I hope you'll take it to heart."

"Please go ahead, sir," Noah said. "A suggestion from you is always going to be welcome."

Parker glanced over at him, then cut his eyes back to the road. "Gary Mitchell," he said. "Gary is the acting coach, I'm sure you remember him. He helped you prepare for a couple of missions in the past, I believe. Gary is a chameleon; he can be whoever he needs to be, even down to making incredibly complex alterations to his appearance. Take him along, and do your best to bring him back. He's a valuable asset in his regular job with us, but I think he may be even more valuable to you in this particular case."

"I'm sure it's going to be an infiltration mission," Noah said. "I think he may be quite valuable indeed."

They chatted about mundane things for the rest of the ride, and then Parker dropped Noah off at his country home. Noah walked in the house and found that everyone had gone back to sleep when they arrived, so he stripped down quickly and crawled into bed beside Sarah.

He was awakened a few hours later by the sound of Neil coming into the house from his trailer across the yard. As he sat up to begin getting dressed, Sarah rolled over and looked at him.

"I didn't even hear you come in," she said. "I never seem to be able to get any rest when I sleep on airplanes. I was so tired when we got here that I just flopped in the bed and was asleep in no time."

"That's all right," Noah said. "We should all take every opportunity to rest, especially with a mission hanging over our heads."

Sarah let out a sigh. "There's a mission, then? What is it this time?"

"Come on out into the living room," Noah said. "I need to tell everyone at the same time." He pulled on his jeans and tugged a T-shirt over his head, then walked out of the room in his bare feet. Sarah got up quickly and dressed herself, then followed and found them all in the kitchen, rather than the living room. Renée had made coffee, and they were all sitting around the table. Sarah got a cup for herself and sat down with them.

"All right," Neil said, "she's here. What's all this about? Why did we have to come back over here so soon?"

"Donald Jefferson is dead," Noah said. "He was assassinated in London the night before last. The assassin has been identified, and Allison believes she knows who was behind it. We are going to eliminate both of them."

There was silence at the table for several seconds, and then all of them tried to speak at once. At first, they all tried to deny what

Noah had said, but his calm demeanor told them he was telling the truth. When they finally came to the point of acceptance, each of them had something to say about Jefferson, and Noah simply let them talk until they were finished.

"We'll be meeting with Molly tomorrow, she'll be taking over Mr. Jefferson's duties. She'll have our identity kits and such ready for us by then." He looked at his wife. "You will be sitting this one out. I'm not taking you out on any more missions. Marco can drive, and so can I. In fact, we all can."

"Neil can't," Marco said, and Neil shot him a glare.

Sarah stared at Noah for a second, and then her face clouded up. "Now, you just wait a..."

"Allison agrees with me," Noah said. "I think you may be the precedent for a new rule, which will probably state that pregnant operatives do not go into the field."

Sarah sputtered, but gave up on arguing. "I'm not going to be happy about this," she said. "Remember what happened the last time you went out on a mission without me."

"That time he went without all of us," Neil said. "Don't worry, Sarah, we will take care of him."

"Of course we will," Jenny said. "We all have his back, Sarah."

A sigh escaped her as Sarah settled back into her chair. "I know you do," she said. "And I understand why I can't go, because of the baby. I just hate the idea of us being apart."

Noah took her hand and smiled at her. "I understand, babe."

———

THE FOLLOWING MORNING, Noah walked into Allison's office again, this time followed by Neil, Jenny, Marco and Renée. Molly was there waiting for them, looking slightly uncomfortable as she sat at the same spot Donald Jefferson had always occupied.

"The nature of this mission is different from many of your other missions in the past," Molly began. "You are to locate and engage Caleb Dawson, then maintain some form of surveillance on him until he leads you to Spear. At that point, your orders are to eliminate both of them. How you achieve the mission, of course, is entirely up to you, Noah, but I have your mission identities ready."

She picked up a large fabric shopping bag and reached inside it, producing a wallet, a watch and a cell phone in a plastic bag. "Noah, your identity for this mission is William Rogers. Your back story is that of a purchasing representative for a large tobacco company." She handed the bag over to him, and he began looking at the photos and other items inside the wallet. Most of them were mundane, probably even nonsensical, but they would lend credibility to the identity, should they be examined by police or other agencies.

Molly withdrew another bag and passed it to Neil. "Neil, you are Leonard Roth, CEO of Roth Technologies. The company produces security software for computers, and actually does exist. It's one of the front companies for E & E, so it was easy to insert you as its CEO."

She took a purse out of the bag and handed it to Jenny. "Jenny, your name is Jennifer Roth, and you are Leonard's wife. Your back story indicates that you were his high school sweetheart and that you are responsible for marketing for the company. Again, should anyone bother to check, both the website and the company staff will confirm your position."

Another purse went to Renée. "Renée, you are Abigail Willis. Your back story is that you are an effective executive assistant, working regularly for temporary agencies throughout the world. One of the jobs you held was actually for Roth Technologies, while they were expanding into Europe."

The final reach into the bag produced another plastic bag filled with wallet, cell phone, etc. "Marco, you are Jeremiah Duchesne. This takes advantage of your Cajun upbringing, so you can let your accent out again. Your back story makes you a former government agent from the United States, now occasionally involved in some shady deals. That identity might come in handy on this mission, and we have built an extensive record of various nefarious activities. You will find a list of them in the cell phone, so you need to scan through it and memorize as many as possible."

Each of them took a moment to examine what they had been given, and then Noah looked at Molly.

"What about Gary Mitchell?" he asked. "I had put in a request to have him assigned to the team for this mission."

"And it's been approved," Allison said. "He's being advised of that fact this morning, and will be waiting for you at R&D. He'll already have his identity kit."

"Which I'm basing on his real past," Molly said. "If he's checked out by the authorities, he will come up as an actor who is looking for work."

Noah nodded. "All right, then. How soon do we leave?"

"As soon as we get any information on where you can find Dawson," Allison said, and then she licked her lips. "Noah, we're having Donald's funeral in the morning, and I thought you would all want to be there."

"Of course we do," Noah said, and the rest nodded their agreement.

TWO

"Someday, in the near future, your grief will fade away. While today we lay the body of Donald Jefferson to rest, we know that Donald himself now sits at the right hand of Our Lord in the kingdom of Heaven, where we all will one day be reunited with him. And, despite the fact that he is no longer here with us in the flesh, he shall forever remain alive in our hearts."

Noah watched Donald's funeral from a distance, as always stoic and unmoved. He watched and listened as the minister's words faded away and Donald's family and friends moved back from the casket.

"Noah? What are you thinking about?" Donald asked him one night, when the two of them were alone. They were standing outside the headquarters building, leaving a meeting that had run late into the evening. Now, standing here watching Donald's body being lowered into the ground, Noah suddenly remembered the conversation, but it was almost like it was happening all over again.

The question managed to bring Noah out of his thoughts. The coolness of the air had settled around him without even being noticed. The street lights were blinking on around them, making it harder to see the stars up above. He turned to look at the ops director.

"I was thinking about whether I would ever make it to retirement," he said casually, knowing that Donald would be surprised.

"Why?" said Donald. "Why on Earth would you want to retire? Then you'd have to figure out what to do with yourself every day, and that's not easy for somebody who's been in our line of work."

"Maybe." He shrugged back. "Or maybe it wouldn't be all that hard."

"But why? You can't try to say you're getting old; hell, you're still in your twenties." Donald waited for Noah's usual grunt of acknowledgment, and Noah noted Donald's typical resort to sarcasm. It was Donald's way of deflecting feelings, and a trait Noah had always admired. It reminded him of the kind of banter Neil and Marco liked to engage in.

"Your last few missions may not have all gone off exactly as you planned, but you're still at the top of your game. Hell, Noah, you are the best there is at this job. It's who you are, you know that. E & E wouldn't be the same without you."

Some part of Noah's mind recognized that things had changed with Jefferson's death, and the imaginary conversation turned toward the present.

"It's not supposed to be the same. As a team leader, I know that when things change, you have to adapt. And you know that what works for me isn't always going to work for anybody else. How is my team supposed to cope, now that you're gone? Who's going to have our backs?"

Donald was shaking his head.

"It's not about how many of our missions come off successful," Noah tried to explain. His record of success had never been out of any need to be perfect, but Donald had always assumed that it was.

Noah decided to move to the heart of the matter. "Donald, my team has done more than any other team you've got. They need a break, and they deserve one." He felt compelled to clarify. "I'm not saying we need to leave E & E for good, there's always going to be *somewhere we can fit in, some way we can serve. I'm just saying that we've paid our dues. I'm saying that maybe it's time we had a chance at a future."*

"I know where this is coming from," Donald said. "This is about Sarah being pregnant."

"It's not just that, Donald. I wish I could say it was, but it's not."

"So adapt, isn't that what you've always done?"

"This is adapting," he countered carefully. "At the very least, my team is ready for a break."

"Not yet, Noah. You can't have one just yet," Donald said in his imagination, and there was something imploring in his face. "I'm counting on you. You're the only one who can make my sacrifice worthwhile."

Noah let out a sigh. "And you know that I won't let you down."

Donald smiled. "Now, that's the Noah Wolf I know and love."

The memory of Donald's voice in Noah's head, the conversation that ran through his mind, was so clear that he wanted to turn around to make sure Donald wasn't really standing behind him. He half expected the man to be waiting to tell him he'd faked his death as part of a mission, or something else just as crazy, but Noah kept his face forward. He knew there was no one standing at his back.

He gave a tight, determined nod toward Donald's casket, where it waited to be lowered into the ground. Whatever mourning Noah might need to do for Donald would have to be done later. Right now, he had a mission to complete. When that mission was finished, he might consider asking for that break.

After what he had recently been through, the thought of having a child grow up without either of his parents was something that left him feeling empty inside. There had to be a way to ensure it wouldn't happen to his child, as it had happened to him. No matter what happened, he had to make sure that Sarah never went out on a mission again.

It occurred to him that it might not be realistic to have such hopes, but Noah was one who believed that nothing was impossible. His life almost seemed to be some sort of a testament to that fact.

He came out of his reverie when he saw Donald's wife and daughter approaching. Elaine, Donald's daughter, had once been romantically involved with Moose Conway, a former team member who had given his life to protect Noah and Neil. Noah and Sarah still considered her a friend, so he prepared to express his condolences.

"Mrs. Donaldson," he said, "Elaine. I'm truly sorry for your loss."

Mrs. Donaldson gave him a sad smile and thanked him, but Elaine looked him in the eye.

"It's you, isn't it? Allison is sending you after whoever did this, am I right?" Elaine had sufficient security clearance to know the answer, but Noah wasn't certain about her mother. In the split second that he thought about that, he made a decision.

"That's correct," he said softly.

"In that case," Elaine said, her eyes hard, "I want to ask a favor. I want to ask you to make sure that person suffers. Can you do that for me?"

Noah nodded once. "I can, and I will."

Elaine looked at him for another couple of seconds, then turned and walked away without another word.

———

RETURNING to the house on the lake, especially after spending so much time at the estate in England, almost seemed nostalgic. The place on the lake was probably the only place in his entire life that he had actually thought of as home, and it was undoubtedly the place where he wanted to raise his child. Even if he did manage to get out of the assassination business, he knew that he would end up working with E & E in some way. It was certainly going to be a lot safer living near Neverland than anywhere else. Even the estate in England wasn't nearly as secure as the little town of Kirtland, Colorado.

He took his time wandering the premises with Sarah, refamiliarizing himself with it before turning to the task of calling in his team. The familiar, welcome surroundings gave him a sense of confidence as he sat down on the couch in the living room where they had spent so much time together. It was time to bring them together once more, and begin laying out the mission he was planning to avenge the assassination of Donald Jefferson.

For the moment, all he could do was wait for one of the intelligence agencies to find them a lead. Then it would be time to act, and he intended to act swiftly, but for now, he sent the rest of the team back to their homes. They could rest and relax until it came time to put the plan into action.

———

NEIL BLESSING HUNG up his phone and swallowed the last of the coffee he'd made after the funeral. Naturally, Allison wanted Team Camelot to handle the situation, to deal with the man who had killed Mr. Jefferson; that was understandable. It wasn't just because they were the best, but because she thought of Noah as more than just one of her agents, and the rest of the team was somehow included in that classification. They were family, not just employees, and that made Donald Jefferson something like their patriarch. If anyone was going to avenge his death, it should be the people closest to him.

Jenny had decided to get a nap after the funeral, but even as he got up from the table to go and wake her, she stepped out of the bedroom. The look on her face told him that she was hoping the call he had taken would mean it was time to do something. Unlike himself, she was ready to get back out into the field; sitting around caused her anxiety to build up, and she needed the thrill of a kill to abate it.

———

MARCO TURIN KICKED IDLY at the wrench next to his toe, shaking his head at the old Norton motorcycle he'd been working on the past few days. He had purchased it not long before their last trip to England, but hadn't had time to work on it until now. The damage he'd hoped was minimal was looking more and more like it was terminal. The thought didn't sit well with him. He had a hard time giving up on his toys.

Hell, he had a hard time giving up on anything.

Already his mind was spinning, considering what parts he had on hand and estimating the prices of the ones he'd need to find. He could strip the bike and rebuild it from the ground up, maybe even make some improvements over the original design. It would be a long project, but he could do it. He'd done it with the old Chevelle sitting behind his garage and the Mustang he'd bought with his first E & E paycheck. This was just another machine, even if it did have only two wheels. Marco loved working on old vehicles, and always had. It was one of several things he and Noah had in common.

Besides, tinkering always helped in the weeks before they went out on another mission, and he really needed something to fill that time. At the moment, Marco needed something that would keep him busy, so he wouldn't be thinking about what had happened to Noah his last time out.

It wasn't that he didn't enjoy the break times in between missions, but that last one had been the most terrible of all. They'd almost lost Noah forever, and that wasn't something Marco could handle thinking about.

E & E missions were different from the ones handled by other agencies or special forces groups. They were situations in which he could act, he could actively do something about a problem, which made it a lot different from the feeling of impotence he had while Noah was missing. On missions, Marco knew he could make a difference. Maybe not for himself, but for someone, he could make things better.

But now they had lost Mr. Jefferson. The man had been one of the most important fixtures of E & E that anyone could remember, ever since the agency had been created. He had been Allison's right-hand man, and his loss was going to be felt for a long time to come.

"Nothing I can do about that, either," he mumbled to himself. There was a bitterness in his voice that even he could hear.

He stared at the broken motorcycle again, and started making a list of the parts he was going to need.

The ringing of his phone was almost a relief, and he grabbed it quickly. He was even more pleased when he heard Noah's voice on the other end of the line, telling him it was time to go back to work.

He went into the house to clean up before telling Renée that they were going back out on a mission sooner than had been anticipated.

———

"DONALD JEFFERSON." Donald had held his hand out openly that day they first met, but Gary Mitchell had seen the wariness in his eyes. Wariness indicated secrecy, and an unwillingness or inability to trust others. In someone who was supposedly bringing funding to the project, the ability to keep a secret could be beneficial, but a lack of trust could cause problems.

On the other hand, it was the weariness in Donald's eyes that bothered Gary most. Wariness could give you an edge. Weariness, however, the kind of weariness Donald Jefferson was showing, was the kind that could cause you to make mistakes, slip up. It might have been a side effect of the wariness, but it was enough to make Gary a little nervous.

Gary decided then and there that if he ever saw that look in the mirror, it would be time for him to give up the acting school. It had been his dream for a long time, but too much of anything wasn't necessarily good, and could eventually lead to burnout.

"Gary Mitchell," he responded. He shook Jefferson's hand firmly, but let hesitation and curiosity surface in his voice. "Do you get involved in backing student theater groups very often?" he asked skeptically. His passion was found in the plays his acting class liked to put on, and he hated the thought that somebody might not take it seriously. Gary was a teacher, and teaching was something he could never give up completely.

"Not often," Donald answered. "But yours are no ordinary students. I've never seen a play performed better."

There it was, thought Gary, the flattery. He smiled, ready to play along. "I can take you on a tour backstage, if you'd like."

"I'd like that," said Donald. "As long as it's convenient. I don't want anything official."

If Jefferson wasn't here on official business, then Gary had to wonder what this was really all about. "We don't usually get very official around here, only when we take on anything by Shakespeare, I guess, so I think you're safe. Come on, I'll show you the sets my kids have built." Gary turned, walking up the steps to the stage.

Gary had never heard of Donald Jefferson before; the call, offering funding that could take the class well into the next level, had come out of nowhere that morning. It seemed like something that was too good to be true, but Gary was not a man to look a gift horse in the mouth. If Jefferson really wanted to put up money, Gary had every intention of accepting it. If not...

By the time he led Donald into the stage's wings, pointing out the backstage props so Donald wouldn't trip over them in the dark, the theater was mostly empty. Gary took a seat in one of the prop department's cushioned chairs, and started pulling off the mustache and beard he'd applied for his small part in this particular play.

Donald sat opposite, choosing the hard bench rather than the soft chair, and Gary waited. They were on Donald's time, so it was up to him to open the conversation.

"Gary." Donald hesitated, dragging a thumb across his chin. "I've come to ask your help with something, and I think I can trust you."

The curiosity was obvious in Gary's eyes. "I was under the impression, sir, that you were here to offer help rather than ask for it."

Jefferson smiled. "Perhaps I should say that I've come to ask if we can help one another. The funding I offered is yours, but I'm afraid there is a bit of a catch. It would involve you helping your government. Is that something you'd be willing to consider?"

Gary looked at him for a moment, then let a smile slowly spread across his own face. "I would certainly be willing to listen to what you have in mind," he said.

"Gary?"

Gary popped his head up toward his office door, trying to pretend he wasn't lost in a reverie from three years earlier. "Mr. Lawson. I'm sorry, I didn't hear you knock."

"Are you all right?" Wally Lawson asked. "You look like you've been here all night."

Gary closed the file he had been given about Donald Jefferson's assassination and leaned back, rubbing his hands over his eyes. "I'm fine. I just got caught up in something. Not anything big, though. What can I do for you?"

Wally opened the door wider and came in to lean on the desk. "Maybe that's a question I should be asking. Is there anything I can help you with?"

Gary shook his head, trying to clear the memory of Donald's voice from his mind. *Gary, I've come to ask your help with something, and I think I can trust you.* "I'm afraid not, sir, just a personal matter."

"You've got to take care of yourself, Gary. You're not always going to be a young man, you know. Someday you'll be old like me."

"You're not old, sir," Gary said with a grin. "Was there something you needed?" He hoped Mr. Lawson didn't dwell too much on the abrupt change of subject. Ever since he'd started working with E & E, the friendly R&D director had taken him under his wing, almost making him feel like part of his family. They even played on the R&D softball team together.

"Actually, yes," said Mr. Lawson, dropping a written phone message in front of him. "You got a call at the front desk. They tried to transfer it back, but you weren't picking up your phone. It seemed urgent."

Gary opened the folded paper, and then he swallowed. The message was about the mission. He had been asked to assist Noah Wolf with Donald Jefferson's assassination, going after the man who had killed him. The message told him to contact Noah ASAP; naturally, it was Team Camelot who would be going after Donald's killer, and it looked like the time had come at last.

He'd always wanted the chance to work with Noah. He hadn't really expected it to actually happen, though; the man was the agency's top field agent, and Gary wasn't really any sort of agent at all. And he'd definitely not expected it to come on a mission like this.

"Gary," Wally said, "I know what this is about. Don't worry, you'll do fine."

"It's not that I'm worried, not really," he explained. "I just want to do the absolute best job I can, to help them get this done. Whatever they need, I'll do it."

"Ah, yes," Wally said. He dropped a hand on Gary's shoulder. "As it happens, I know Noah pretty well. I have a feeling this might be a lot more than just helping them prepare."

Gary nodded, swallowing carefully again, noting the truth in the inventor's words. He stood up, rubbing his hands over his face. "Thank you, sir, and I know that. I'd better get going. I don't want to keep them waiting."

"Yes, that's probably not a good idea," Wally commented wryly. "Especially with a guy who could kill you without even a moment's hesitation."

Gary shrugged that comment off, focusing now on other things. If he was going to be of use on this mission, it would be best if he didn't look like walking death. He wondered if he would have time to run back to his place and grab a quick shower.

Hell with it, he thought. *What's he going to do, kill me for being late?*

THREE

JENNY AND NEIL SHOWED UP FIRST, BECAUSE THEY were living in the trailer that was just across the yard from Noah's house. Neil had spotted it when he was first assigned to Noah's team and had begged for the chance to rent it from him. Since he had no other use for it, Noah had agreed. Ever since Jenny had moved in with Neil, the two of them basically acted like the trailer was just another part of Noah's house, rarely even bothering to knock before walking through the front door.

Coming from their own homes inside Kirtland, Marco, Renée and Gary didn't arrive for another half-hour, but the seven of them settled easily into a comfortable camaraderie. It would be Gary's first time out in the field, but he was already confident that he could trust these people with his life.

"First off," Noah said, "Allison wants us to get moving as soon as we can, and we probably should handle most of our preparations while we are on the plane. I just want to go over a few things with you now, before we head out."

"I'm definitely ready," Neil said. "Mr. Jefferson, he was, well, he was quite a guy."

"He was one of the best," Gary said. There was a nostalgic look on his face as he spoke.

"That he was," Noah said. "And someone has taken him away from us. Donald Jefferson wasn't a part of our team, but he was a part of our family, in a sense. In Team Camelot, we never leave anyone behind. We may not be able to bring him back, but we can certainly get him some kind of justice."

"So, what's the stuff you wanted to talk about before we go?" Marco asked.

"There is an assassin out there, Caleb Dawson. He's working for an international criminal known only as Spear. No one knows who Spear is, so it's our job to track him down and eliminate him. The plan is for us to begin by finding Mr. Dawson and getting close to him."

As a team, they spent the next few hours thinking up and detailing ideas and contingency plans. Noah watched them all closely as they worked, as always taking in the details of their personalities, their gestures and movements, even the way they spoke to each other. Every bit of interaction between them was filed away in his memory, giving him substantially more background data for the times when he needed to adjust his own public persona. Having no emotions, he found it necessary to emulate others in order to keep people from realizing that he was different. Studying those around him gave him many different personality traits he could draw from to create whatever persona he needed for the moment.

The information he got from the process was invaluable. He had watched most of these people long enough to know which gestures or facial expressions might be the most important on their mission. He could even recognize which gestures indicated undue stress or exhaustion, which ones demonstrated a level of seriousness, or a cry for help. All of these things helped to make him the team leader that he was, even though they were simply things he had learned to do without even thinking about it.

He had long ago become accustomed to the way they appeared to balance each other, how a comment started by one would be picked up by another. He saw the way they checked their strengths and weaknesses against each other, holding nothing back, ensuring they would know where they might need to fill in the possible cracks between their skills, attempting to ensure no mistakes might cause the mission to fail. They had worked together, all but Gary, for a little over two and a half years, now. Renée was the newest member of the team, but she seemed to fit in as if she had always been there.

Noah made other, less technical observations as well, filing away some of the information in a less conscious manner. Neil had a wide, honest grin and very serious eyes. Jenny moved like a dancer and had a quiet laugh, even though she was one of the most deadly killers Noah had ever known. Marco's mildly noticeable Cajun accent was coming out, while Gary's softer, yet no less distinctive Mid-Atlantic accent did not stand out the way it might.

He stood in the doorway, watching his team interact. He thought that Jefferson would have been quite proud that it was they who would be setting out to avenge his death.

Noah closed his eyes as his thoughts wandered back to Donald. Already Donald's funeral was beginning to feel like it had happened a year ago, but the determination it provoked in him was even stronger than usual. He was going to get Dawson, and he was going to get Spear, as well. Failure was simply not an option.

"What about equipment?" Neil asked. "I'll need a few things to help pull this off."

"I had Wally put together everything he could think of," Noah replied. "If you have things to add, call him now. He'll make sure it's all waiting for us at the airport. Meanwhile, I want you to all get some rest. We fly out tomorrow morning at four a.m."

The others all agreed quickly and got ready to go home. A few minutes later, Noah and Sarah were alone together.

"I'm going to go crazy the whole time you're gone," Sarah

said. "I know you're not supposed to call home when you're on a mission, but try when you get a chance, please?"

"I will, babe." Noah took her hand and led her to the bedroom, and held her through the night. She woke at six the next morning, saw that his side of the bed was empty and lay down to go back to sleep. The tears made it difficult, but finally she drifted off an hour later.

————

CALEB DAWSON HAD COME up through several stages in his life, from the military to working for criminal organizations, starting out as just another bit of muscle who enforced the rules that came down from on high. He had become widely known and feared, so that merely the mention of sending him to visit someone would produce a lot of cooperation in a hurry.

As the old saying goes, anyone who can properly handle a small task will be given a bigger one. It wasn't long before he was elevated to enforcer, charged with ensuring that other members of the organization would know better than to try to skim off the profits, or be too loose with information that should be kept confidential. He was "the guy," the one who would leave you alive, but make sure you never, ever wanted him to visit you again. A single visit from him was enough to ensure obedience and cooperation for the rest of a man's natural life.

But then he had come across one who wasn't that easy to scare, one who felt he was strong enough and tough enough to take on even the bosses of the organization. Dawson couldn't let anyone get that sort of attitude, because it could come back to haunt him. That's why, despite the fact that the man had more than two dozen of his own soldiers ready to protect him, Dawson had managed to eliminate all of them and dragged the man in front of Spear.

The boss had asked a few questions, then told Dawson to kill the fellow. Without hesitating even for a second, Dawson had grabbed the man by his head and twisted hard, snapping his neck. The spinal cord was broken, and it was only a matter of seconds before the lack of oxygen to the brain put an end to the pained, frightened expression on his face.

From that moment on, he had been the boss's right hand man. Only Spear could give him orders, and that was exactly the way Dawson wanted it. He didn't have to work often, and that was fine by him. He was rich and he was good looking. It left him plenty of time to indulge himself in all the things he actually enjoyed.

Of course, there was always more work coming. That was why he was currently in Paris. There was an assignment coming for him, and he would need to handle it quickly and efficiently.

———

THE GULFSTREAM WAS WAITING at the Kirtland Airfield when they arrived at four, and the team relaxed for the flight. They got some sleep, but most of the time was spent talking about what they expected to find when they arrived. Arrangements had been made in advance for vehicles and accommodations, so they were on station less than an hour after the plane landed.

Rather than putting them up in a hotel, Molly had arranged a house. The keys were hidden near the front door, and Noah retrieved them and unlocked it. They walked in to find that it was luxuriously appointed, and certainly big enough for their purposes.

"Do we know which rooms we're set up in?" Marco asked.

Gary dropped his bags near the coffee table and turned to look at Noah.

"There are three bedrooms in the house." Noah stepped forward as he spoke. "Gary and I will be using the first one at the top of the stairs. Neil and Jenny can take the next room, you and

Renée in the third." He looked at Neil, who nodded in confirmation.

Noah nodded. "All right," he said. "The minute I know what Dawson's doing, I will alert all of you by subcom. Let's get some rest."

The team quickly complied and withdrew to their individual spaces. They would be starting work the following morning, and as always, Noah wanted them rested and ready.

———

ONE OF THE things Wally had given them was a box containing what looked like simple jewelry, four men's wristwatches and and two ladies' style watches. A card stuck in the box explained that they were portable Wi-Fi hotspots, each powered by one of the newly developed diamond batteries that were good for years on a single charge. By keeping one on them at all times, their subcoms could communicate over virtually unlimited distance through the Internet.

"But that's not all," Wally had said. "I got to thinking about extended capabilities, so I talked to this young lady," he said, nodding toward a petite, dark-haired technician. "She came up with an absolutely brilliant idea. Did you know that you can make phone calls through the Internet?"

Noah raised one eyebrow and looked at him. "Yes," he said simply.

"Well, yeah, so did I," Wally said with a grimace, "but it hadn't occurred to me that the subcoms could do it. Janelle thought of that, and set up a routing server right here in our building. All you have to do is say 'subcom phone call' and your subcom immediately connects to that server. Each of them has its own serial number, so the server will recognize it and allow you to make calls either by naming your contacts, or by speaking the number you want to call. It will also allow calls to be placed to you through the subcom, but that's something that should be used only sparingly."

Noah nodded. "That's definitely a nice addition," he said. He looked at the technician. "Any other special features I should know about?"

"Yes," she said. "You can also set the server to record everything that comes through the subcom. That way, you or someone else can go through the recording at a later date in order to make sure that all the information is properly documented. It could be very useful, if there's any question about how you performed your mission."

"Thank you," Noah said. "I think that's an excellent idea." The girl blushed, and Noah turned back to Wally.

"Did you get everything else I asked for?" he asked.

"And then some," Wally said. "I understand you may be having to set up bait for the killer, so I'm sending Geraldo with you. Geraldo is a surrogate victim, a slightly animatronic mannequin. He can make a lot of natural seeming movements, but he doesn't have any real intelligence, unlike Esmeralda. He's designed so that you can make him taller or shorter, fatter or thinner, lengthen or shorten his arms and legs, and I'm sending a realistic looking silicon mask of each of your faces. Set him upright, and your killer would have to be within a few feet to realize he wasn't alive."

Once again, Noah nodded. "He might come in very handy."

It was early the next morning when the team assembled in the main room, the one they all called the conference room, and Noah thought of privately as the *command center*. It felt appropriate. War was what he was planning for, if it came to it. He hoped the others were ready.

On the wall-mounted wide screen, Neil called up the footage of Caleb Dawson, then paced slowly around the room while he prepared to explain the details of their next move.

"Late yesterday, we got word Dawson has been seen regularly near the Eiffel Tower. We don't know who his target is, but we need to get as close to him as we can, and as quickly as we can. He's supposed to be leaving Paris within a week, so we don't have a lot of time."

"Which means if he's going to kill someone here, he has to do it within that time frame." Gary, sitting on the couch farthest from Noah, picked up on the detail Noah was hoping they'd all notice. This was their window of opportunity.

Standing behind Gary, Marco leaned against the back of the couch and asked, "And we have no idea who his target is?"

"Not yet," Noah answered. "Apparently, he is waiting for someone to approach him with that information. Unfortunately, we have no idea who it will be or how they are supposed to identify themselves. And if he doesn't get the word soon, he's going to be heading toward London again."

"He's not going to make this easy," Jenny commented. "From everything I've read, he's a sneaky bastard."

Noah agreed. Dawson may appear to be boxing himself in by such a short timeframe, but he hadn't become so elusive by not being flexible.

Neil echoed the concern. "Dawson has stayed alive by *not* making things easy. In all the assassinations he's been linked to, he's never killed twice in a row in the same fashion."

"Yes," Noah acknowledged. "From the hallucinogenic drug he gave Donald Jefferson to a sniper's rifle. He always chooses something different. And the problem is he seems to wait till the last possible moment to choose."

"Random choice, that's the key," Gary said, and Noah could see that his mind was already jumping ahead in the plan.

"There's a certain logic to that," Marco added. "If I don't know what I'm going to do, then neither does anybody else." He met Noah's eyes and Noah could see that the plan was starting to come together for him as well.

"And that's why we have to get as close to him as we possibly can, right under his skin. We have to know what he's going to do at the same time he knows it himself. The problem is that we may not be able to do so while in Paris, so we are probably going to make our move in London. Neil?"

Neil moved over to the computer console, starting to type while saying, "Well, I've been in contact with our gal in London, and she's going to loan us the extra men we'll need when we get there."

"Does that include the electronics technician you wanted?" asked Noah, knowing that Neil had been speaking on the phone about it since the crack of dawn.

"That's right," Neil confirmed. He then keyed a picture onto the screen and started to explain, "We're looking at the kind of hotel Dawson seems to favor, small but classy. He selects these at random also. In this case, we're going to make his random selection for him. This will be the one he chooses, absolutely under our control. All previous identification has been removed. Right now, it's a total blank." He looked up at the others, then nodded to let Noah know that he was finished.

Noah looked over his team. They were ready, he knew, ready to avenge Donald Jefferson. "All right," he said to the team. "We can't afford any mistakes. If we lose Dawson, we'll lose our chance to identify his boss, Spear."

"Noah, we're not going to let that happen."

"We know what this one means," added Jenny. "To all of us." Neil and Marco nodded with her, meeting Noah's gaze with assurance and fortitude. Noah wasn't sure what he should say, what he could say. He'd taken on personal missions before, but he had always avoided asking others to put themselves at risk. Even the times when he had gone to rescue Sarah from one terrible situation or another, he had planned to go alone until the rest of them insisted on going along to help.

He remembered a particular mission, one not even remotely sanctioned, or even known about, by Allison. It had meant breaking a lot of laws, but it was the only way to save Sarah, and Allison herself, before it was over.

Marco had sat patiently through his short speech, his face expressionless, then asked, "Are you done?"

"Yes," Noah said.

"Good," Marco had said in his typically dry way. "Noah, not often, but every now and then, you just plain talk too much."

Neil and Gary reinforced the statement with wry nods of agreement.

Noah had learned from them and knew now not to discount what it had meant for his team to help a friend. He lifted his chin in appreciation, acknowledging their unified front. Perhaps they did know exactly what this one meant to him. He was fully aware that it meant just as much to them.

The week passed, and there was no sign of Dawson's handler showing up. Time ran out, and then they got the word that Dawson was preparing to go back to London. Noah had Neil make all the arrangements for them to travel, and they prepared to make their move when they got back to merry old England.

FOUR

Noah had the team stagger their arrivals in England, for no other reason than the convenience of setting them to different tasks in different locations before they came together again late Thursday afternoon. They knew that things could go terribly wrong on a job like this, but Noah seemed confident that they were ready for Dawson. When Dawson failed to arrive before the following Monday morning, however, the feeling of readiness was overshadowed by a looming sense of potential disaster.

Noah called one last meeting with Catherine Potts, his old friend in the London office, just to cover all their bases. He wanted to make certain that they'd have resources and support beyond what they'd already asked, should the need arise. Dawson was one of the most dangerous men in the world, possibly even the equal of Noah himself; it wouldn't pay to fail to be cautious enough.

The accommodating Catherine shifted several agents into Noah's periphery, where they would stay awaiting his orders. Noah felt that he now had enough extra personnel to fill cracks in the plan, if any opened up.

By the time he finally caught a cab back to Neil's blank hotel, traffic in that direction had frozen like ice. Ahead, Noah could just make out a double-decker bus laying on its side and what was left of the lorry it had collided with. The delay could make him late for Dawson's arrival, scheduled for just before noon, but it was just at that moment when Marco called to say that Dawson's plane was going to be delayed, as well.

If anything could go wrong, apparently it would. As he sat behind the disabled lorry and bus, waiting for whatever emergency crew was coming, Neil subcommed him to say that they were hastily rewiring surveillance equipment they had installed in the hotel. Someone had plugged them into the hotel's power without using a step down adapter and fried several of the transformers. They were working as fast as they could, but it was going to take time.

Crane trucks were brought in and the wreckage was moved out of the way. Noah arrived at the hotel at 11:30, well in advance of Dawson's scheduled arrival. Now that his flight was running late, they would have some extra time to ensure that their preparations were complete.

"The outside camera is fully operational, and this one will be ready in a minute." Noah knew the voice wasn't Neil's and the accent told him that it belonged to one of the MI6 agents already assigned to help them.

"Good."

That voice, however, he knew well; even with just the one short word, he could recognize Jenny's voice easily. Both Jenny and the unfamiliar agent looked at him when he opened the door and entered. "Anything new on Dawson's plane?" he asked.

"It's running over an hour late." Jenny shrugged. With a small gesture, she indicated the man she was with. "Noah, this is Albert Corey from MI6. He's here to help Neil with some of our electronics work."

And helping with the camera wiring, as well, I see, Noah

thought. He stepped forward to shake Albert Corey's hand, saying honestly, "Glad to have you aboard, Albert."

"Thank you, sir. It's an honor to work with you." It was a sincere response. "I was new on the job when you saved the Queen, and I've wanted to shake your hand ever since."

Noah let go of his hand and turned back to Jenny. "An hour late," he said. "I wonder how that happened."

"Is it likely to cause a problem?" she asked, walking with him through the ornate but uncomplicated lobby, carrying the toolbox Albert had been using to fix the camera.

Noah led her behind the front desk as he answered. "It could. If he has to make his phone call at a pre-arranged time, if he has to make the call before he checks in to his," Noah gestured at the nameless, marquee-less room, "hotel." They were already cutting the schedule close. If the plane was any later, Dawson could drop out of character to choose a hotel closer to the airport. That would mean that all their preparations were for nothing. "I want everybody to keep subcoms on," he said. "We use radios only with those who are out of subcom range."

Noah pushed on the rows of small shelves lining the back wall behind the desk. The entire section swung inward, revealing the secret room behind. This room actually *did* look like a command center. Cemented and unfinished walls framed the E & E equipment they'd brought in. Gary's makeup supplies and his and Marco's clothing changes were sitting in one corner, and Neil's electronics were scattered throughout the rest of it.

Noah weaved toward where Neil sat at a makeshift desk, staring into a computer monitor. "Anything new, Neil?" he asked, sliding out of his trench jacket.

The skinny kid looked up from the screen. "Dawson's plane will touch down in just about three minutes."

"Good," Noah said, feeling a sudden sense of déjà vu. Somehow, he had the feeling that he and Neil Blessing had done this exact thing sometime before.

Neil saw Noah pause to stare at him while folding his jacket over his forearm. He wondered, not for the first time, what Noah saw when he looked at him. Was he just the computer geek? Or was there more to their friendship than that?

Neil turned his attention back to the computer. "Twenty-five minutes," he said to Noah. "That's all I'll need once he hits his cab."

Noah dropped his jacket onto one of the tables as Neil turned up the volume on the scanner to his right. The squawking voice from the box clarified why Neil had suddenly turned it up. They were listening for the movements of the taxi cabs going to and from the airport. The dispatcher was in the employ of MI6. As requested, she was sending a majority of the drivers away from the airport, giving Dawson limited choices on the ones he could take.

———

MARCO TURIN LEANED CASUALLY against the door of his appropriated taxi, looking menacing and in desperate need of a fare all at once. He maintained the casual pose effortlessly while marking every face that emerged from the airport's main doors.

He growled at anyone who approached him for a lift; they'd have to find other ways to get where they were going. He was saving his ride for Caleb Dawson.

Marco had liked Donald Jefferson. For Marco, catching the man's killer made this personal enough on its own, but there was also the fact that Jefferson had been like a father figure to most of them. Marco had never been one to take defeat or loss easily, particularly when it involved someone he cared about. He wasn't one to let things like that go, not if there was something he could do about it.

When he saw the assassin finally emerge from the airport, he had to consciously force the contempt off his face.

He watched Dawson stroll to a telephone booth, ignoring

Marco as he carelessly tore a page from the chained down telephone book. When Dawson dropped his head, Marco allowed himself one last vindictive smile in his direction. "You're ours, Dawson," he whispered, but by the time Dawson looked up from folding his torn phone page, all he saw was a muscled cabbie, desperate for a fare.

Sure enough, Dawson walked toward him. Marco abandoned his casual lean, stepping out toward Dawson and then to the back door of his car. He yanked it open with a jaunty, "Cab, sir?"

Dawson looked at him, giving Marco the impression of a spider staring down a fly. "No, thanks," he answered. With a cold smile, he shifted directions, fluidly moving to the next cabbie down the line.

"Hey!" Marco shouted, his Liverpool accent impeccable. "I'm the first cab in the bloody line. Yer got to ride with me!"

Dawson gave him the spidery look again, peering at Marco as though he was not worth the spider's effort, then turned away. Marco watched as Dawson stepped up to the window of the second cab. Though now some distance away, he distinctly heard him ask the driver, "Say, do you know where the St. Aloysius is?"

Marco smiled sardonically as Gary popped his head up at Dawson's question, the glasses on his nose, the pencil in his mouth, and the papers in his lap giving him the absolute appearance of distracted and aloof. "The St. Aloysius?" Gary said, taking the pencil out of his mouth and reaching for the ripped paper Dawson handed him, blinking his eyes as though trying to place where he'd heard the name before.

Despite the morning's unexpected disasters, Marco felt confident in their plan. A smile appeared on his face. Gary was good. Gary was *very* good.

"*Oh*, the St. Aloysius Hotel in Kensington." Gary nodded with a self-deprecating shrug, acting as though he should have recognized the name right off. He stepped out of the car with an easy smile. "Sure, mate, I know where it is." Gary moved around the front of his own car. "As a matter of fact, I took this nice lady there last week."

Marco slipped around his car and into his cab's driver's seat, continuing to watch Gary and Dawson with a slight smirk on his face. It was going right according to plan.

Dawson was already opening the back door. "Spare me the details. I'm in a hurry."

Gary stepped quickly in front of him, cutting off Dawson's access to the door handle, opening it for him instead. "Ah, please," he protested. "Let me get that for you, sir. Can I take your bags?"

"I can manage," Dawson intoned, annoyed and sounding like a man who annoyed easily. An attitude like that might make their job a little easier.

"The St. Aloysius it is," Gary said loudly, ensuring that Neil would pick up the transmission from his hidden radio. He shut the door for Dawson, and as he crossed back to the driver's side, he threw Marco a small smile.

Welcome to our parlor, said the spiders to the fly, Marco thought, grinning. *Make no mistake, Dawson,* we *are the real spiders here.*

———

"ALL RIGHT, you heard it, the St. Aloysius," said Noah.

Neil's fingers flashed across the keyboard as Noah walked to look over his shoulder. In seconds, the information they wanted was splayed out before them. "The St. Aloysius Hotel," read Neil, "226 Kensington Way." He looked up at Jenny's questioning glance. "S-T-A-L-O-Y-S-I-U-S," he spelled.

Jenny immediately set to work, applying the adhesive lettering she would need for the hotel's sign and front desk.

From Neil's computer, they heard Dawson ask Gary, "How long will it take to get to the hotel?"

"Depends on traffic," Gary answered smoothly, epitomizing

the voice of a tired cabbie who dealt with traffic all too often. "Twenty, maybe twenty-five minutes."

"The GPS says fifteen," snarked Dawson. "Now, if you can't do it in that, I've got to find a cabbie who can."

"Hey," Gary protested indignantly, "if any cabbie can get you there in fifteen minutes, *I* can." The car's motor jumped as Gary started it and pulled into traffic. He knew Marco would already be pushing ahead of him, preparing to stall in any way he could.

"Fifteen minutes, Noah," lamented Neil, standing up from his desk and pulling his jacket from the back of his chair in one smooth movement. "It's just not enough time." He moved hastily to the door.

"We don't have a choice." Noah gestured, Neil's concern echoing in his own voice. "We have to make it work."

———

WHILE GARY MADE his way toward the hotel with an irritated Dawson in the back seat, Neil was busy hanging Jenny's hastily made *St. Aloysius Hotel* sign above the front door. Marco was breaking speed limits and changing into a cop's uniform while he drove. Albert Corey was tracking Gary's progress on the large computerized map linked to Neil's main computer, and Noah was completing the replacement names for the streets outside. All of them were doing what they could to ensure that they'd be ready in time.

When Neil finished hanging the hotel sign, he checked Jenny's progress in the lobby, then moved back into the command center to check on Noah. As he entered, the bleeping spot on his computerized map confirmed what he had suspected. "We'll never be ready at the pace he's going," he told Noah. It wasn't a complaint, just the truth.

Noah glanced back at the map. "Marco will do what he can, but Dawson's insistence he be here in fifteen minutes probably means he has to make the phone call to get his assignment. If we slow him down too much, it could be a problem."

Neil accepted Noah's statement as truth also. They'd just have to do the best they could and hope that Dawson didn't get spooked by the glitches in their matrix.

Noah handed him the completed street signs. Neil took them carefully, double checking for errors while nearly running to put them in place. From the corner of his eye, he saw Albert Corey open the glass burner, pulling out an elegant goblet with an elaborate "SA" now cresting its side.

In all, it took Neil less than five minutes to get outside, set up the step ladder, and place the new street signs. When he got back inside, Jenny had finished much of the lobby and had moved on to Dawson's bedroom, apparently having to reset the bugs, only just realizing that they had also been affected by the morning's blown wires.

Noah wasn't going to think about backup plans just yet. He had great confidence in this team. If it could be done, they would do it, and maybe even make it with time to spare.

————

JENNY MOVED RAPIDLY around the room they'd selected for Dawson. She set new towels in the bathroom, arranging the newly embroidered *SA* monograms ornately on the towel racks, adding other finishing touches as she slipped from area to area, her mind all business. She was almost finished when she realized that morning's camera problems had included the hidden scope in the bedroom mirror. Alerting the others to the problem, she quickly set to work.

Abandoning her current decorating endeavors, she retrieved a repaired camera from Corey and set about placing it behind the two-way mirror. Tilting it to face her, she spoke aloud to test the audio. "All set, Noah."

She stepped back, waiting.

"Jenny, give me a level." Noah's voice came through the subcom behind her ear.

She smiled in relief as she stared into the mirror, picturing Noah's serious face looking back at her. She felt unable to resist. "Magic Mirror on the wall," she teasingly misquoted.

"All right, you'd better finish up in there," Noah instructed.

She could hear in his voice that he had caught the humor, even if it was lost on him. "Just another minute," she said, completely back to business.

———

NOAH WATCHED Jenny a moment longer to ensure the video and audio feed were indeed working. When both were confirmed and seemed unlikely to blow out on them again, he turned back to the map, checking Gary and Dawson's progress. They were getting much too close; the team still needed more time.

He wasn't concerned yet, however. Marco was still out there, ready to get in Gary's way.

Noah turned up the audio on the communication speaker and sat down to hear how Marco and Gary handled themselves. He believed that both could cope with the situation, but couldn't quite extinguish the thought that his friends would be in close proximity to a killer they'd be purposely annoying, a killer who was known best for his unpredictable actions and his fondness for violence.

———

GARY DROVE FAST, going just enough over the speed limit to convince Dawson that he'd picked the right cabbie for a hasty trip. So far, Dawson seemed relatively content, which was good, but Gary was gritting his teeth because he knew he wasn't giving his teammates the time they needed for Dawson's arrival.

Where are you, Marco? Not for the first time, Gary wished he had been given one of the subcoms that allowed the rest of the team to be in constant communication with one another.

As he rounded the next corner, his question was answered. Marco had made it to the exact spot where he was supposed to meet them. Gary felt a wave of gratitude. Once confirming that it really was Marco he saw, he punched his gas pedal a little harder, zooming the cab past the cars building themselves into a traffic jam on the other side of the street.

A siren sprang to life behind him. He glanced into the rearview mirror, watching Dawson's annoyed realization that the siren was meant for them. Gary dropped his foot off the pedal, turning his eyes to Dawson with a repentant shrug. "Oh, bloody now what?" he said aloud, making himself sound as antsy and anxious as Dawson looked. "I guess I put me foot in it a bit," he apologized, working his London accent overtime. It was one of his favorites. "But don't worry, I'll bluff me way out of it."

Dawson said nothing.

Gary pulled the car to the side of the road and stopped, watching in his rearview mirror as Marco slowly stepped off his commandeered police motorcycle. In the patrolman's uniform he wore, complete with helmet and dark glasses, he looked nothing like the taxi driver Dawson had dismissed earlier.

He swaggered unhurriedly to the cab window, slowly pulling off his gloves. Gary almost couldn't hold back his grin, because Marco was actually doing pretty good. The agent had to have really hurried in order to get changed and get in place, but he was managing to look like the poster boy of habitually slow, unhurried traffic cops.

"Might I see your license, sir?" he asked, sounding bored.

"O' course, mate," answered Gary, digging in his wallet for the appropriate document. "Did I do something wrong?"

Marco leaned down in the window. "You were going more than twenty over the speed limit."

"Twenty?" Gary blurted indignantly. "Why, I never..."

Marco responded with a slow nod.

Glancing again at Dawson in the rearview mirror, Gary pretended to change his tactics. He slumped closer to the window and spoke to Marco in a soft, supplicating voice. "Listen, mate, this fare of mine is in a bit of a hurry. You see, I picked him up at Heathrow—"

"Could I just see your license, please, sir?" Marco cut him off flatly.

"Would you have a heart, mate?" Gary returned, exasperated.

"Just get it over with," ordered Dawson from the back. "I'll pay you what the ticket costs."

Gary nodded, defeated, pulling out his license and handing it to Marco with a bitter shrug. "Lousy coppers," he muttered, unaware that back in the command center, Albert Corey was trying not to smile at their antics. "I mean, 'ow's a bloke supposed to make a living these days?"

Marco took the license and then looked at him closely, as if comparing his face to the photo on the document. "Thank you, sir," Marco stated.

Gary gave him a *yeah, whatever* look in return.

As Marco ambled back to his bike with the license and clipboard, at an achingly slow pace, Gary shrugged helplessly at Dawson. The assassin glared at him, but said nothing.

———

IN THE COMMAND CENTER, Noah waited for Marco to report in with his take on the situation.

"Dawson looks nervous," reported Marco over his radio. "I'll hold him as long as I can." Noah glanced at his watch and then up at Neil, who, aided by Corey, was busy making *St. Aloysius* labels for the lobby's desktop magazines and reference books.

Sensing Noah's gaze, Neil looked up from what he was doing and focused on the speaker to hear what was going on with his fellow agents.

"I know you're in a hurry," Gary was saying to Dawson. "I'm sorry about this."

"Yeah, keep it going, Gary," Neil encouraged aloud, as though Gary could hear him. "We need the minutes, buddy." Noah nodded at Neil's words, still listening to the speaker intently, hoping Neil's encouragement, as well as his own, was somehow carried through.

"What's the holdup?" they heard Dawson complain. "Why is he taking so long?"

FIVE

GARY GRIMACED. HE WAS STARTING TO GET A BIT nervous. They could only push this for so long before they lost the bird they were trying to cage. He hoped Noah was picking up on it. "I don't know," he said in response to Dawson's irritated query. "Your guess is as good as mine, mate."

"I'm going to find myself another cab," Dawson stated.

Gary cringed. *Hurry, Marco, hurry*. Aloud, he begged, "Would you have a heart, guv? I need the fare." He implored Dawson with his eyes, hoping the books stacked on the front passenger seat had successfully given him the look of a struggling night student. Not that he expected a man like Dawson to have actual sympathy for anyone.

After a moment, Dawson sat back with a forced nod, but Gary had a feeling his consent had more to do with the lack of other cabs on the street than from any sympathy he might feel for his own supposed need of money.

———

NOAH NODDED when he didn't hear Dawson getting out of the car. Mentally, he applauded Gary for his skills.

"The room is set, Noah," called Jenny, coming down the back stairway on the far side of the command center.

"Good job, Jenny," he acknowledged.

Over the speaker, he heard Dawson say, "I'm not going to wait much longer, you know."

Noah knew it was true. He spoke, knowing Marco would hear him via subcom. "Better move, Marco."

"Right," came the instant reply. He could imagine Marco just waiting for permission to bail Gary out of the tense situation. He had a sudden mental image of Marco as a barely controlled attack dog, waiting only for the word to lunge.

Pushing the visual from his mind, Noah refocused on the activity in the cab.

———

GARY SIGHED in relief when Marco started back toward him. His face was grim as Marco handed him the clipboard with a silent nod. "You think you'd be out catching criminals, 'stead of bothering honest working people," Gary complained as Marco pointed to where Gary's signature was needed.

He ripped the fake ticket free and handed it through the window. Gary seized it crossly out of his hands.

"Drive a bit more carefully next time, sir," Marco advised in a droll voice.

Gary simply nodded, reaching out for the return of his license as Marco started to walk away. After three steps, Marco turned and handed the license back to him. "Sorry, sir," he said. "Almost forgot."

Gary snatched it out of his hands briskly, starting the car with a frustrated fervor that didn't feel entirely pretend.

As the car bolted away, Marco walked back to the motorcycle, muttering to Noah, "I tried to hold him as long as I could."

"We need more time, Marco," Noah confirmed, "seven

minutes." Groaning, Marco swung onto the motorcycle and shot off toward the next stopping point.

"All the cameras are set, and the microphone is under the front desk," reported Neil from the doorway.

"Gary is doing what he can. Let's just hope Marco can get to the next point before they do." Neil nodded.

Corey stepped up to pass Neil the new sign-in book for their hotel guests. "Only the best for the St. Aloysius," he quipped.

"Talk about how to impress," bantered Neil, carrying the book promptly out front.

Marco pushed the police bike as fast as it could go, feeling adrenaline feed his system as he swerved in and out of traffic. He cut through two side streets and rode the sidewalk down another before finally pulling into an underground parking garage. There was no way Gary would beat him to the next point, he was sure of it. Even so, he yanked the sunglasses off his face and ran all out for his waiting truck.

Jenny pulled open Neil's laser engraver. It was the same machine they'd used to print the front desk book covers. She pulled several dark wood *St. Aloysius* labeled key chains out of it carefully. Clipping room keys to the wood as fast as possible, she checked Gary's progress on the map anxiously. He was almost to the second point.

"Noah," she called, pulling him back from the front desk, knowing he'd want to monitor what was happening in the cab.

Gary was driving fast, but not as fast as he'd been driving before. He almost hit another traffic jam, but cut across a side street, telling Dawson he knew a shortcut while complaining that traffic was getting worse all over the city. In the back seat, Dawson said nothing, simply sat looking both snide and petulant.

Turning down another side street, Gary hoped again that Marco had made it to position in time. Sure enough, just in front of them, a large truck backed across the street, cutting off their exit. Gary pulled the cab up to the truck just in time to hear

Marco choke out the engine. "Looks like they've stalled," he commented.

Dawson said nothing, but the frustrated look he gave Gary evidenced his murderous nature.

"Oh, come on, come on!" Gary groaned aloud. He leaned out the window, shouting, "Come on, would you move it!" He could barely see Marco's silhouette in the truck's cab. "Move the bloody thing, will yer?" he shouted again.

Marco made an angry gesture with his hand out the window and gunned the engine a bit, making the gears grind.

"I told you I was on a tight schedule," iced Dawson from the back.

"Give me a break," Gary complained in response. "What would you have me do, guv? You want me to drive through it?"

"Look, I've got to get to a phone, so either back up or I'm going to get out here."

Gary looked in the mirror and grinned. "A phone? Is that all you need?" He took a cell phone out of his pocket and tried to pass it through the window to the passenger compartment.

Dawson stared at him coldly. "I need a real phone," he said. "One that doesn't broadcast openly through the air."

Gary let the grin fade, then shifted into reverse. Right on cue, two of their British associates pulled a large blue garbage truck into the street behind them, boxing them in. Gary stopped short his reverse, turning around to look dumbfounded at the truck, as though he couldn't understand how his luck had turned so bad. "Blast! What's this, now?" he moaned.

Dawson's look was growing icier by the second. Gary decided to attempt the misery-loves-company approach. "Can you believe this?" he asked. He knew before he finished that Dawson wasn't going for it.

"This is ridiculous. I'm getting out."

"No, no, no. Hey!" cried Gary as Dawson reached for the door. "I told you I'd get you there." Dawson sat back as Gary pulled the wheel to the right, guiding the car onto the sidewalk and around the back of Marco's truck, mentally apologizing to Noah for not being able to stall for more time.

Marco stepped out of his truck, watched from the corner of the building as Gary pulled away, then ran back into the parking garage while pushing the button on his radio. "Noah, I couldn't hold them any longer, we almost lost him." He swung back onto the motorbike, gunning the engine.

He waved to the London agents as he rode out of the parking garage and sped back toward the hotel.

Having listened to the exchange over the speaker, Noah knew both Gary and Marco had done the best they could. "No more time," he said aloud, crossing over to the coat rack so he could slip into his freshly embroidered blazer.

"Are we ready?" asked Renée as she and Jenny hurried to finish off their current projects.

"We're about to find out," said Noah.

Together, the three moved out of the command center. Noah took his place standing behind the front desk while Jenny and Renée ran upstairs.

Through the opaque glass-front window, Noah watched Gary pull up outside.

———

"I'm sorry it took a little longer than fifteen minutes," Gary said, stopping the car in front of the hotel.

A London agent, acting as doorman, stepped up to the car to open the door for Dawson.

"Ah, forget it," Dawson sneered fiercely, stepping out of the car and yanking his bags with him. "You know, you ought to do yourself a favor and keep your big mouth shut!" he added through the window, throwing his fare in at Gary, then stalking away without another word.

Ouch, thought Gary merrily as he pocketed the money with a smile. *I guess he didn't like me trying to talk my way out of Marco's ticket.* He watched Dawson enter and hoped the others were ready for him.

Noah Wolf gave the illusion of being busy by fiddling with the hotel room keys and the boxes they belonged to, making himself appear completely oblivious to the arriving guest.

"Good morning," Dawson clipped precisely, calling the deskman's attention.

Noah spun toward him as though he hadn't heard him come in. "Oh, sorry! Good morning, sir," he greeted in a subdued, but jaunty British accent.

"I'd like to have a room, please," said Dawson.

"A room, yes, we have one of our very best available, room twelve," he answered, moving back to the room boxes to pull out the key.

"I'd like to pick my own," Dawson stopped him pointedly.

"I beg your pardon?" Noah glanced back at him, the oddness of the request showing in his face. Inwardly, he was pleased, knowing his team was ready for this. Pleased even more so that Dawson, for all his unpredictable behavior, was still, in fact, predictable. Jenny and Neil were waiting and listening, ready to put whatever number on the door Dawson requested.

"I'd like to pick my own," Dawson repeated. Noah watched him glance around, eyes settling on one of the tour brochures Jenny had placed in the front rack. On one of them, a large number seven was printed across the top. "Let me have room seven, will you?" Dawson requested.

"Room seven?" Noah clarified, returning the room twelve key to its box and moving to the one that said seven. They were all the same to him, every key would open Dawson's door. "Yes, I do believe you're in luck," he said, pulling the identical card out of the box. "Room seven is available." He picked up a hotel registration sheet and handed it to Dawson. It would give Jenny and Neil the short time they needed to change the numbers on the doors. "If you'll just fill out the guest registration."

Dawson took the sheet without comment and started filling in the blanks.

As Noah watched, he caught sight of Marco, now dressed as a bellman, stepping into the lobby. He had tucked some false teeth into his mouth, a simple change that was enough to make him look entirely different.

Anyone else who had known Donald Jefferson would not have been able to maintain composure the way Noah could. He stood there, waiting for the "guest" to finish completing the form, a polite half grin on his face even as he contemplated just how he would kill the man in front of him. If Noah had felt the emotion that the rest of them were feeling, the rage at having lost their friend and patriarch, Dawson would clearly have recognized the expression he would have been wearing. It was why Noah chose to put himself on the desk, rather than anyone else.

Recognizing the necessity of keeping a neutral expression, the assassin held his little grin and rang the bell on the counter to his left. The loud sound cut through the thoughts of violence in his mind, refocusing him on his task.

Dawson looked up questioningly when he heard the bell.

Noah dismissed the curiosity with a tight smile, gesturing to Marco as he stepped toward them in his bellhop disguise. "If you would just show this gentlemen to room seven, please," said Noah in a clipped British accent as he held the key out to Marco.

"Sah," Marco said, taking the key. Then turning to Dawson, he added, "If ye'd like to follow me, sah?" while picking up his bags.

"Do enjoy your stay, sir," said Noah as Dawson strolled after Marco.

"Yeah, thanks," Dawson muttered, as though bothered with the subtleties of polite interaction.

Noah watched him until he was out of view, still keeping his expression blank and neutral. When Dawson was gone, he turned and pushed open the hidden door once again and slipped into his command center. He closed it quickly behind him and realized that he was feeling a sense of relief at not having to look at Caleb Dawson any longer.

"Are you all right?"

Noah turned his head, expecting to see Neil behind him, but the keen eyes regarding him were blue, rather than brown. It was Gary, and Noah hadn't even realized that he had made it back inside the hotel yet. The actor, now in his first role as a field agent, had made good time getting rid of the taxi cab and slipping through the back door.

Noah nodded and walked toward Neil's desk. He could feel Gary's eyes following him as he went, and then sat down in the chair beside the desk.

"I wanted to kill him," he confessed. "I wanted to reach across the counter and grab him by the throat, drag him across it and beat him to a pulp."

"He killed your friend, Noah." Gary didn't blink or fidget with pity when he said it. His voice was blunt, as open and raw as Noah's confession. "No one's going to fault you for feeling that way."

Noah nodded, but his thoughts were complex. On his last mission, he had lost his unemotional edge, reverting back to the emotions of his childhood self for a time. He wasn't used to feeling anything at all, and it had been made clear that if he lost that edge for good, he might not be capable of continuing as Camelot.

Neither of them spoke, and a moment later, they heard Marco's voice coming from the hallway camera monitor. "Here we are, sah." The two agents looked down at the video feed to see Marco letting Dawson into his room. Noah pushed a button, switching their view to the bedroom camera as soon as the two of them had entered. "All set," Marco was saying. "Hope you enjoy your stay."

"All right," said Noah, watching Dawson. He realized that he wasn't feeling any actual emotion, despite the fact that he still wanted to kill Dawson at the earliest opportunity. "The trap's been set. Let's spring it."

SIX

Still in the command center, Gary moved over to the voice recorder Neil had set up for him and popped in the disc Noah gave him. They were working so smoothly together, almost as if Gary had been part of the team for years. For his own part when he thought about his teammates, Gary didn't feel the slightest hesitation to trust any of them.

He pressed play on the machine in front of him and listened. It was a recording of Dawson's brief conversation with Noah at the front desk. He picked one sentence from the recording and set it to loop. While in the cab, he'd already heard Dawson's voice quite a lot. It wouldn't take him long to perfect it.

"*I'd like to pick my own room,*" the disc repeated twice.

Gary paused the player and repeated the sentence aloud, copying only the cadence of the voice at first, adding more of Dawson's intonation when he spoke it again. He was aware, somewhere in his mind, that Noah was behind him, checking his progress, perhaps checking how well he'd really be able to do this, wanting to see if he was as good as Wally Lawson believed him to be.

"Sounds good," he heard Noah say confidently, shifting from observing Gary and back to monitoring Dawson.

"No," Gary said. "I need to put a little more tenor into it."

———

"I hope you're comfortable," Marco-the-bellhop could be heard saying to Dawson.

With one ear still monitoring Gary's progress, Noah took a position standing between Neil and Jenny, whose eyes hadn't left the monitor since they returned to the command center. Neil turned the screen slightly, allowing Noah a better view.

"If there's anything else you need, sah, please don't hesitate to give us a ring." Marco handed Dawson his room key.

"Thank you," Dawson replied, sounding bored. He dropped a generous tip into Marco's outstretched hand.

"Thank *you*, sah," Marco said, smiling and leaving quickly.

This is it, thought Noah. Dawson would make his call now and they'd have him. He could feel his anticipation rise as Dawson walked to the phone on the nightstand and picked it up. From the corner of his eye, he saw Neil check the status of their planted wire, noting that it activated automatically when Dawson picked up the phone.

"Come on," Neil muttered when the assassin visibly hesitated. "Damn." He slapped the tabletop when Dawson put the phone down again.

Noah and Jenny exchanged looks for a second, then turned back to the monitor.

"He's leaving the room," Noah said as he began moving toward his position at the front desk.

"As long as he doesn't go for the phone in the lobby, we're all good," Gary said over his shoulder. With all the trouble they had had that morning, the lobby phone had not gotten a bug planted in it.

Noah nodded his acknowledgment, moving quickly in order to beat Dawson to the desk. He shut the secret door on the others, picked up a prop stack of mail and feigned boredom as he flipped slowly through the envelopes. He was just in time to hear Dawson's soft-soled shoes as he came down the stairs.

As they had expected, with Noah standing there at the desk, Dawson gave the lobby telephone a pass, barely glancing at it before walking outside. Noah kept a cautious eye on him, hoping he wouldn't go too far. The minute the front door closed behind him, Noah whispered softly, "Marco, do you have him?"

"I do," Marco sent back. The subcutaneous communication system that was implanted against the bone just behind their ears made it possible for them to communicate with each other without anyone else being aware. After leaving Dawson at his room, Marco had quickly switched into his disguise as a window washer at a building across the street, and now watched Dawson walk lightly down the hotel's front steps and head directly to the phone booth at the corner, one of the few that remained in this part of London. Marco moved the digital shotgun microphone out from under his arm, aiming it covertly. "Right on target, Noah," he answered.

Noah moved back into the hidden command center just in time to hear the phone being dialed through the amplifier as Neil turned up the volume. Noah slipped casually between Jenny and Neil, resting a hand on the back of each of their chairs as they all leaned in to hear what Dawson was saying.

Neil had already shifted their monitor's view to the outside camera and though the angle was irregular, they could clearly make out Dawson standing in the phone booth. Neil zoomed in tight and adjusted focus on the keypad. As Dawson dialed, Neil quickly wrote down the numbers he was punching in.

The plan was working. They were still ahead in this game. Even with the glitches, everything was coming together just the way it needed to.

"Hello?" a woman's sultry voice asked, and the sensitive shotgun microphone picked it up and transmitted it to the command center.

"This is Jonathan," Dawson said, his voice loud through the speakers. "I thought I would give you a call, since I'm in the city."

"You're late," huffed the voice, some of the sultriness replaced with annoyance. "I was just about to give up on you."

"Then you're too impatient," snapped Dawson. "London traffic is always a problem, you should have made allowances for that. Do you have the package I'm looking for?"

"Yes," she said, slightly subdued. "I have it."

"Very good," Dawson said. "Now, where are we supposed to meet up?"

"At the landing, by the river," she answered. "There is a bistro called Alejandro's." Neil nodded at Noah's questioning glance, indicating he'd already begun locating the address.

"Be there at one thirty," Dawson ordered. "And have the package with you."

"How will I recognize you?"

Dawson's eyes followed a bus as it drove by, noticing the flower printed across its side. "Wear a pink carnation, and I'll find you," he said, and then hung up the phone.

Noah checked his watch while Gary quickly grabbed the phone. "That's only a little more than an hour," Noah said. "This could throw a monkey wrench into the plan."

"Let's see if I can still catch her," Gary said, already dialing the number.

Noah waited, leaning onto the back of his chair as Gary waited for an answer to his call.

"Hello?" answered the same sultry voice, edged with a touch of confusion.

"It's me again, Jonathan," Gary said. Noah nodded, because the voice was a perfect match for Dawson's own. Noah knew that Gary was very good at voice impersonation, and he'd even taught Noah some tricks for a couple of missions. According to Wally, there were very few people who could imitate a voice as neatly and quickly as Gary just had.

"What now?" the woman asked, annoyance back in her voice. "Want to make it a daisy instead of a carnation?"

"No," clipped Gary with Dawson's voice. "I decided I don't want to wait that long. The sooner I deal with this job and get it over with, the sooner I can get out of London."

Noah could hear the woman's confusion in the brief silence that followed. "Look, that's the way I work," Gary said, tinging his voice with a touch of menace. He met Noah's eyes as if to reassure him that he wouldn't mess it up. The look seemed to say that he knew just how far he could push her.

"Where do you want me to go, then?" the woman asked.

"Just come to my hotel, the St. Aloysius. Do you know where it is?" Gary asked, hoping she didn't.

"No."

"It's at the corner of Lansdowne Street and Marbury Road," Gary said, rattling off their actual address smoothly. "I'm in room eight."

"I can find you."

"Be here in thirty minutes. And don't bother with the carnation," he finished snidely, cutting the connection.

Noah tapped Gary's shoulder in appreciation. "Let's go," he said unnecessarily. The rest of the team was already up and moving, and Noah collected the extra MI6 agents as they all got into position.

———

NEIL STEPPED out the back door and down to the street corner. He snapped the ladder he carried with him into place and smoothly removed the fake signs they'd used to manipulate Dawson. Hopefully, when Dawson left, he wouldn't feel the need to double check his location.

Back in the command center, Noah watched as Neil called up the recording they'd taken of the woman's voice. It was a bit grainy, having come from the amplifier, but it would suffice. He set one sentence to loop just as Gary had done with Dawson's voice, then looked up to check on Gary's progress, knowing that Renée might need his help before she'd be ready.

A dressing screen had been set up in the back of the room, and Gary emerged from behind it. He was wearing a suit similar to the one Dawson had worn, with the jacket over one arm as he quickly adjusted his tie.

Noah waved him over, helping him slip into the suit jacket while Neil played the recording, letting it loop twice. Renée held up a hand to tell him to stop the loop and repeated the sentence aloud, imitating the voice as well as she could. "What now? Want to make it a daisy instead of a carnation?"

"I think the resonance should be a little higher," Gary advised. He sat down beside her and explained what he meant. Noah watched and listened for a moment, but then, satisfied that Renée would be able to pull it off, he moved back to watch Dawson on the monitor.

Dawson was calmly practicing his golf putt across the hotel room floor, tapping golf balls into a water glass.

"For a guy who makes his living by killing people," Neil commented, "he's certainly relaxed."

"That's what makes him so good at what he does," Noah remarked, nodding his head. "He has to keep himself that way, ready for anything that might happen." Dawson leaned his golf club against the wall and checked his watch, then picked up his briefcase and started for the door.

"He's leaving early?" Neil asked.

"He's a careful man," Noah answered. "He probably wants to get a good look at the bistro before he goes in." He adjusted his own tie and started back toward his front desk position.

"Noah?" Still staring at the monitor, the view now flipped to the outside camera, Neil cutting Noah's exit short. "If I'm not mistaken, here comes Dawson's lady." She'd clearly been a lot closer to their location than they thought she was.

Gary, busy helping Renée pin a carnation onto the dress suit she'd changed into, popped his head up. He looked first at Noah, then craned his neck around to Neil, trying to see if he was serious, then glanced back again at Noah.

"It's time," Noah said. "It's now or never."

"This is going to be close." Gary gripped Renée's shoulders in a quick, encouraging gesture before bolting up the back stairs toward room eight.

Noah slipped swiftly into the lobby and Renée, still fiddling with the flower, moved over to watch the action on the monitor with Neil and Jenny.

———

Noah made it into position just in time to see a tall, stylish blonde walk through the front door.

Albert Corey, now dressed as a bellhop, stepped up swiftly to greet her. "Excuse me," she asked him. "Could you tell me where room eight is, please?"

"Certainly, madam," Albert answered cordially. "If you only turn right at the top of the first flight of stairs, you'll find it right there."

"Thank you." The woman started up the stairs just as Dawson was starting down. Watching, Jenny and Neil held their breaths as the two of them passed each other, sighing in relief when no recognition passed between them.

At the top of the back stairs, down the hallway from room eight, Gary waited until Dawson was out of sight before hastily slipping into his room. The last thing they needed was for Dawson to get a glimpse of someone dressed exactly like himself hanging around his hotel room.

Less than a minute after Gary shut the door, there was a knock. He closed his eyes, taking a second to focus, forcing a Dawson-like expression onto his face. The best way to not be discovered as a fake was to be as close to the real thing as possible, and Gary was a consummate actor. He drew a deep breath and a bored sneer appeared on his lips as he cracked the door open.

The blonde woman outside his doorway smiled when she saw him. Gary opened the door wider.

"Jonathan," said the woman. "It's good to finally put a face to the name."

"Did you bring it?" Gary asked, his tone anything but friendly.

She blinked, looked down, and took a large envelope from her bag. "It's all in there," she said, and turned to leave.

"Hold on," Gary stopped her. "Who pays off when I finish the job?"

"I do," she answered, her own voice now clipped and professional. "As I said, it's all in there. Let me know when it's done."

She turned to walk away and Gary stepped out into the hall behind her. "There's one more thing," he said, and she stopped to look back at him. When she did so, doors on either side of her opened and four men and a woman suddenly surrounded her. Her eyes went wide as she looked at them, then turned back to Gary.

"I'm afraid you're going to be a guest of the British government for a while," Gary said. "Do enjoy your stay."

———

NOAH OPENED the envelope Gary had handed to him, sliding the contents carefully into his hand. A newspaper clipping appeared with a paperclipped, hand written note attached to the back. He turned the clipping right side up, holding it out so the agents gathered around him could see it. The picture accompanying the article showed them a very tall young man wearing horn-rimmed glasses.

"Apparently this is the target," Noah said, catching Neil's eye with a meaningful and slightly regretful look.

"Looks like I'm elected," Neil said, his lanky height making him the most logical double for the man on Spear's hit list.

Noah read the note accompanying the article. It read, *"Leonard Hapgood, Vice President of Lending for Commerce Bank of New York, will be at the Teagarden Hotel, room 221. He'll be in his room from 2:30 to 5:00 pm today working on a speech, and he'll be alone."*

"At least we know when and where he's supposed to make the hit," Gary said.

"As well as who he's supposed to kill," said Noah with another glance at Neil.

"Okay, I'm personally hoping we can avoid letting it actually come to that," Neil said with a nervous grin.

Neil stripped off the windbreaker he'd been wearing and replaced it with a dark blue suit jacket. Gary picked up a modified digital camera and flipped the desk light toward the large map on the back wall while Neil buttoned the top buttons of his shirt and clipped on a necktie, then added a pair of glasses.

Noah fed the article they'd received into the printer, checking to make certain the camera was already connected. He looked up, indicating to Gary that he was set, and said, "Okay, we're good."

Neil posed in front of the map layout as the picture was snapped and automatically transferred to a copy of the newspaper article, overlaying the image of the real Leonard Hapgood. Noah picked it up as it slid from the machine. Briefly checking it for flaws, he then slid it and the written note back into the brown envelope Renée held open for him.

"You're on," he said to her.

The look she threw back flashed confidence. She couldn't mimic voices quite as well as Gary, but she could improvise just fine.

———

THE TAXI DRIVER let Dawson off in front of the bistro, leaving him at the area farthest from the adjacent river. Grateful for the lack of speeding tickets and truck blockades, Dawson gave the driver a healthy tip.

As he walked away, any thought of the cab and its driver vanished from his mind. He didn't notice that the driver kept watching him as he carefully evaluated his contact's chosen setting, nor did he notice him lift his microphone and say, "He's all yours, *Cajun*," with a heavy British accent.

"An' he be mine for shore, I guar-on-tee, *Brit*," Marco replied, emphasizing his natural accent in response to the MI6 agent's subtle barb, but he grinned, and said sincerely, "Without you guys, this job would be a lot worse. We do appreciate it."

"You're most welcome," said the cab driver.

SEVEN

Marco had changed clothes again. This time, he'd selected a tourist-style shirt and no hat, blending in easily as he followed his quarry's path toward the bistro, hanging back enough to avoid notice, but staying close enough to keep track of him.

The day was warm, and there were a lot of people on the street to blend in with. Marco usually tried to avoid crowds, but this time, he was glad to see the area packed and busy. A lot of the people were dressed just like him. Not once did Dawson even glance in his direction.

Nearly thirty minutes later, just after one, Dawson started a gradual stroll back down the walk to the river. Marco followed carefully, knowing he'd be easier to spot on the less crowded trail. He didn't want to tip his hand, but he wanted to stay close enough to ensure Renée had backup if she needed it.

He saw her before Dawson did, wearing her pink carnation with a dazzlingly smart looking dress. As much as Marco knew Renée wouldn't appreciate it, he couldn't help feeling protective when he saw her; their relationship was pretty solid, and they were seriously considering marriage. Easing himself down on a nearby park bench, just up the hill from where she stood, he prepared to keep careful watch for the slightest hint of danger.

Dawson spotted her, eyes lingering on the carnation and Renée's sleek form. He walked slowly down the steps leading to the river, keeping his eyes pinned on hers, ignoring the boats bobbing in the river just yards away. "That's a lovely flower," he said.

"Thank you," she answered. "I'm wearing it for a friend." Marco innately evaluated her voice as he watched, deciding that her impersonation of the woman on the phone was pretty close.

"A friend named Jonathan?" Dawson asked, still sounding bored.

"Yes, actually," Renée said in the same casual manner. She handed him the envelope, eyeing him appraisingly. "So you're the famous man," she said.

Dawson's eyes flickered, but he didn't seem interested in pursuing her praise. "And you're Spear's messenger," he replied.

Renée smiled, tilting her head brazenly. "For the moment," she said.

Dawson looked her up and down. "Well, I can say you're the prettiest one I've seen so far." A couple strolling along blocked Marco's view when they stopped. He stood, shifting casually to another bench just a few yards down the walk. Dawson didn't seem to notice the movement and Marco decided his view of the two had actually improved with the switch, but he'd missed part of the conversation in doing so.

Dawson now held the envelope Renée had brought. It was already open and he was looking down at Neil's picture with a slightly confused look on his face.

For a moment, Marco thought they must have messed up somehow, but quickly, he realized Dawson wasn't thinking about the clipping at all. Dawson pinned Renée with a stern look and said, "You called me the famous man. Why is that?"

"Your last job attracted a lot of attention," she said. "And I do mean a lot."

Dawson frowned.

"That doesn't please you?" Renée asked.

"Of course not," he said. "Remember, I work in one of the few businesses where fame is not something one hopes for."

Renée nodded, blatantly unsympathetic.

"Now, the hotel where this guy's staying, how far is it from here?" Dawson moved back to business.

"Just under a mile," she answered and even Marco could hear her fake British accent slip.

"And when I'm done, who pays?" asked Dawson, cocking an eyebrow in her direction.

"Call me. I'll be there." The accent was back in place. Marco wondered if Dawson had even noticed. "You know, if you think about it, being famous could have its advantages." Renée held out a slip of paper with a phone number.

Dawson caught it out of her hand, crinkling it as he said, "You're not the girl I talked to on the phone. You're an American, right?" He leaned in toward her.

Damn, thought Marco, he *had* noticed. He tensed, ready to take action if Dawson pushed, ready to do whatever was necessary to keep Reneé safe.

He shouldn't have worried. Renée smiled slyly, unfazed by the assassin's discovery, and dropped the accent entirely. "Should I take that as a compliment? I'm sorry, I've been pretending to be a local for so long it's become a habit. I'm actually from Florida."

Dawson watched her face closely and smiled back as the tension left his shoulders. Marco felt his own shoulders ease as well. For the moment, the serious and calm Caleb Dawson looked embarrassed by his suspicious mind.

"Take it any way you like," he answered her. "I was planning to leave tonight, but maybe I'll stay."

Hook, line, and sinker! Good girl, Marco cheered silently.

Dawson lifted his briefcase and left, walking past Marco without so much as a hint of recognition. Marco stood to follow, throwing Renée a brief, impressed smile.

NOAH PICKED up the phone and dialed. "Catherine? It's Noah. We need control of the Teagarden Hotel within the next two hours."

Catherine Potts, E & E's liaison with MI6, was silent for only a couple of seconds. "Well, and you don't want much, do you? Stay on the line for a few minutes, and I'll do what I can." Hold music began to play and Noah looked over at Gary and Neil.

"I'm on hold," he said. "Gary, you'll need to be on the desk. Do something about your appearance, because we can't risk Dawson recognizing you."

"Yes, sir," Gary said. He sat down at a table at the back of the hidden room and opened his makeup case. A quickly applied wig of gray hair was followed by a realistic looking mask that made his nose look longer and added several lines to his face. He might have looked like his own father, but he didn't look like himself.

The line came to life again and Noah turned his attention back to it. "All right, it's done. I have four of my agents headed there right now, to secure everything until you arrive. What's going on, Noah?"

"We are setting up the bait for Dawson," Noah replied. "That's where he's supposed to make his next hit, and we need to get control of the environment as quickly as we can. Tell your people that we will be there within the next thirty minutes."

"Will do, love," Catherine said. "Be sure to stop in and say hello before you leave, will you?"

"If we have time," Noah said. "Your people have the messenger who brought the instructions. Be sure to let me know if you manage to get any usable intelligence out of her."

"We certainly shall," Catherine said. "Good luck, Noah."

"Thanks," Noah said, and then he ended the call. He stepped out into the lobby and motioned for Albert Corey to come closer.

"Yes, sir?" Albert said.

"We'll be leaving shortly," Noah said. "You're going to have to take care of this place by yourself until we get back."

"Not a problem, sir," Albert said. "I shall simply say that you had to step out for a bit, and left me to man the lobby."

"That's perfect," Noah said.

Ten minutes later, Noah, Gary, Neil and Jenny were in a rental car and heading toward the Teagarden. It was only a fifteen minute drive, so they made it in the allotted time Noah had given to Catherine. The MI6 agents were in place, and quickly made it clear that their orders were to support Noah and his team in any way he needed. He assigned each of them a position, cautioning them not to make any move without a direct order from himself or Jenny.

Jenny was sent up to room two twenty-one, to explain to the real Leonard Hapgood what was about to take place. The rest of them then got busy checking out the hotel, to make sure they knew exactly where they would need to be to carry out the plan and keep Neil completely safe.

"Noah?"

Noah blinked and looked away from the drawer he was checking as he realized Gary was speaking to him again. He walked over to see what Gary was looking at. The young actor's eyes met his as he pulled back a panel in the wall. "There's a crawl space back there, but I think it only leads next door."

"Is it shown in the hotel's building plans?"

"Not directly. They turned the large suites on this floor into split rooms a few years ago, I think. The crawlspace developed from the construction of a new wall that had to be built around the plumbing."

"I'd assume that if we didn't know about it, neither will Dawson, but just to be safe, let's find something to block any hidden access before we have Neil sitting in his room alone."

"The hotel safe," Gary said after looking around for a second.

Noah nodded in agreement. He walked over to the large metal

safe under the desk. It took both of them to shift it in front of the access panel. Gary fiddled with it a bit while Noah went back to sweeping the desk. His mind was going over the plan, trying to look for any place where he could go wrong.

"I think we're secure," Gary commented, breaking into Noah's thoughts again. "Dawson's not going to have very many choices on how he gets up there."

"Let's hope we've thought of all of them," said Noah.

Jenny walked into the hotel office with a grim smile just as Gary went to check the vantage points from the window. Noah fought the urge to watch Gary in motion, fighting the urge to look for traces of Donald. Donald had been the one to recruit him, and the two of them had spent a lot of time together. The young actor had picked up an awful lot of Donald Jefferson's mannerisms, and occasionally they shone through.

"How's Hapgood?" Noah asked Jenny, peeling his eyes away from Gary while setting a picture frame back onto the desk, now certain that it was free of bugs.

"He's upset," she answered easily, lifting her eyebrows. "It's not every day you find out a professional assassin is out to kill you."

"Will he cooperate?" asked Gary from the window.

"He's not happy about it." She shrugged in his direction. "But he's agreed to stay out of it till this is all over. I stashed him in an empty room on the sixth floor, with a couple of Catherine's people to keep him company."

"All right," Noah accepted. "Now the question is, how will Dawson try to kill him?"

"There's a few rooftops out here," Gary said. "They'd be high enough to give him a clear shot."

"If that's how he's going to make his move, I'll make it easy for him," answered Neil, turning to point at Geraldo, who had become a surprisingly realistic facsimile of himself. "The joints are motorized, and I've programmed the controller to make random movements. This guy can scratch his ear, look around and even sneeze, so unless Dawson is right on top of him, he's going to look alive."

"That may be too easy," Noah commented, staring down at the animatronic mannequin. "We have to remember, this man is unpredictable. There's no telling where he may come from." He had a feeling that Gary and Neil could hear his concerns in his voice; despite his lack of emotion, Neil was important to him. He did not want the young man to be killed, not even as part of the mission.

"I'm going to be a couple of doors down the hall," Gary said, accurately reading Noah's tone. They'd need someone close by to give Neil backup. He moved out the door at Noah's nod, carefully checking the hallway for any possible access as he went.

"I'll be close by, as well," Jenny said. "I'm not letting my Pooh-bear out of my sight." Neil rolled his eyes as he moved the dummy to the chair behind the desk, thinking about how to anchor it.

Noah paused, catching Neil's eye and giving him a mean-ingful look. Neil smiled back, trying to look like he wasn't nearly as scared as he really was.

From the look on Noah's face, he wasn't pulling it off very well.

———

MARCO WAS ONLY a little surprised that Dawson chose to walk to Hapgood's hotel. It made following him both easy and hard. When the crowds thinned out, Marco had to stay farther back, trying to avoid letting Dawson realize he was there.

He moved closer as they approached the hotel, jogging up the stairs behind Dawson, hoping to get into a decent observation point before he crossed the street to the hotel lobby.

Dawson was smart, however, and once he reached the top of the stairs leading up from the river walk, his casual stroll turned into a brisk jog. He disappeared behind a tall red double-decker bus parked at the curb. By the time Marco bolted across the street after him, he was gone.

All Marco knew for certain was that he couldn't have gone into the hotel just yet, at least not by the front doors. He'd had those in sight the whole time. He ran down the sidewalk to the corner, but didn't find any trace of Dawson that way either.

He suddenly found himself worried, a feeling that he wasn't familiar with. He didn't want to let Noah down, and he didn't want to lose Donald Jefferson's killer. He wanted to see this man understand the pain he'd caused through his ruthless career. But mostly, the worry emerged from the growing, slightly irrational fear that his failure to keep Dawson in sight would result in Neil's death, or Gary's, or Noah's or Renée's or Jenny's. The very thought that one of them might be hurt or killed because he lost track of Dawson bothered Marco terribly.

He clenched his left fist, digging his fingernails into the palm of his hand. With a deep sigh, he consciously pulled himself back into control and released his fist, shook off the abrupt worry, and forced his mind to think rationally.

The team had known all along that trailing Dawson this way would be difficult. They'd known they might lose him and had planned for this contingency. He quickly focused his emotions. "Noah from Marco," he said softly into his subcom. "I lost Dawson."

———

UP IN HAPGOOD'S ROOM, Neil had just finished setting Geraldo up behind the desk when Noah came back in from his final sweep of the hallway. He'd looked grim ever since Marco's announcement, but Neil knew it couldn't change the plan. They'd known all along that tracking an elusive and deadly killer would be difficult, even with the deck stacked in their favor.

Marco had done the best he could. Neil knew that the big lug had his back; he always did. Now they would simply have to adapt, which was what they were best at. Roll with the punches and figure out how to make the plan come off, no matter what went wrong.

Neil stood up straight to see Noah looking steady and confident as ever, and it occurred to him suddenly that there was probably no other man in the world he respected and trusted as much.

"All right," Noah addressed him. "We are as ready as we're going to be." Neil fought to keep himself from smiling as he met Noah's eyes. He couldn't let any sign of nervousness, real or imagined, creep onto his face. He couldn't give Noah Wolf any reason to take him out of the game.

"Neil, we can call this off."

"Not a chance, Noah," Neil answered quickly, resolutely, meeting Noah Wolf's eyes dead on. He knew that Sarah considered Neil the little brother she had never had, and Noah was likely to feel a burden to keep him safe. The truth, however, was that Neil was finally becoming a genuine E & E agent, and he wasn't about to let himself be pushed to the background anymore.

"There's no telling where or how he's going to make the hit," Noah pressed, moving toward him. "This is a big hotel, we can't cover it all."

Neil matched his gaze. "I always d-did like surprises," he quipped, realizing too late that he'd been stuttering while he said it.

Noah's frown deepened. The look he gave Neil made it clear that Noah would not be pleased should he allow himself to be harmed in any way.

Neil knew more smiling was the absolute wrong response to Noah's increased sternness, but the smirk was already there, widening without conscious thought. What he hoped Noah saw behind it was the seriousness in his eyes. He had finally accepted his job, was happy to do it, could do it, and had *always* done it well. Ever since he and Jenny had gotten together, he knew he would be happy doing nothing else, and wouldn't feel right about backing down, no matter how much sense it might make.

Noah finally nodded, his stern expression easing slightly. He laid a hand on Neil's shoulder a bit too firmly, then slipped back into the hallway without another word.

EIGHT

Noah walked out the hotel's front doors, still shaking his head at the exchange with Neil in Hapgood's room. When it came to stubbornness and determination, Neil was just as bad as Marco, but he was also a part of Team Camelot. Neil would play his part in this plan, and it was up to Noah and the others to make sure he stayed safe.

However, intelligent or not, if the skinny kid took any unnecessary chances, Noah would introduce him to a new level of pain and suffering. There was no way he'd let them lose Neil, or any of the others, on this mission. Not now. Not ever. And definitely *not* to the man who'd killed Donald Jefferson.

From down the street, Marco jogged quickly up to Noah's side. "Sorry I lost him," he said.

Noah nodded. "I know," he answered simply. "Still no sign of him?" Marco said nothing, knowing that Noah already knew the answer and didn't expect it to magically change. Instead, he said, "I'll go and cover the back," before quickly walking away.

———

CALEB DAWSON HAD ENJOYED the walk from the bistro and thought he'd like to come back sometime when he could enjoy the atmosphere better. He'd had the feeling that he was being watched, but so far he hadn't seen anything that could confirm the suspicion. Like many professional assassins, he was prone toward paranoia when he was on a job, but he also believed that the paranoia was a big part of what made him so good at what he did.

When he neared his target's hotel, he changed his pace, trying to see if anyone behind him did the same. He saw no one, but the paranoid feeling remained. Spontaneously, he jumped onto the double-decker bus that was just pulling out, riding it a block before jumping down when it slowed at a stop sign.

Again, he saw no evidence that he was being followed, but decided to make his way to the hotel's back entrance anyway. He still had time. As long as he was gone quickly after the job was done, he could take his time getting there.

As he walked toward the back of the hotel, scanning the sidewalk crowd for anything unusual, he passed a "service entry only" sign and changed his mind again. If he was lucky, a service elevator would send him where he wanted to go, and no one in the hotel would see him at all.

Inside, Dawson found several laundry carts full of clean linen, ready to be moved onto the service elevators behind them. Of course, that meant that staff would be coming to load them onto the elevators, and he didn't want to run into them. He quickly changed his mind once again, stepping into the service stairs and quietly closing the door behind him.

He ran into no one on the way up and no one ran into him. When he knocked on the door of the hotel room just below Hapgood's and found it empty, he set his final course of action in motion and got to work.

With the handkerchief in his briefcase, he picked up the phone and used a pencil to dial the front desk. "Room 221, please," he requested when a woman with a nasal accent asked how she could help him.

———

Neil was staying out of sight, against the outer wall and in a position where he couldn't be seen from the hallway unless the door was actually open. His doppelgänger was still sitting at the desk, waiting for whatever attack was coming, but Neil didn't really believe Dawson would go for a sniper shot. He wasn't willing to guess what approach the assassin would use, but he was fairly certain that it wouldn't be a rifle from a distance.

Unfortunately, most other approaches required Dawson to come into physical contact with his victim. The dummy looked good from as close as ten feet, but any nearer and it would be obvious that it was a mannequin.

When the room phone rang, he got a burst of adrenaline. The game was undoubtedly about to begin, and this would probably be the opening gambit. "Got a call," he whispered to Noah through the subcom. "Listen closely."

He stayed low at his side and moved closer to the desk, then reached up and picked up the receiver, bringing it down below the desk and putting it to his ear. "Hello?"

"Hello, Mr. Hapgood?" The caller had a shrill voice and a strong British accent.

"Yes?"

"My name is Gerald Anderson. I'm with one of the local trade unions. I was wondering if I might be able to come up and see you for a few moments?"

"What union did you say?" Neil asked, stalling.

"I'm the secretary of the London Construction Union. It'd be a big help to us, Mr. Hapgood."

"Okay," he answered in a controlled voice. "What time did you want to come up?"

"Fifteen minutes?"

"Fine," Neil said, checking his watch. "I'll be here."

"Thank you, Mr. Hapgood."

"You heard it, fifteen minutes," Neil said quietly to Noah via subcom.

"He can't be far," Noah answered. "That means he probably got into the building without us seeing him."

"Yeah," Neil said. "The only question now is what he has in mind. If he's coming here, Noah, my stunt double isn't going to be any good."

———

ONE FLOOR DOWN, Dawson was proceeding as quickly as possible. He wanted to finish the job quickly and enjoy the rest of the day, maybe spend some time learning more about the flirtatious redhead Spear had used to contact him. She might actually make this trip more than just business.

"Yes, *thank you*, Mr. Hapgood," he sneered aloud and got to work pulling tools from his briefcase. He stood on a chair and cut a hole in the ceiling with one of his own specially designed tools. The hole opened up the empty space remaining between his floor and the next. One blast would take out the whole room, above and below.

The fake golf balls came out of his bag next. He removed them from their plastic wrapping and crushed them together until they formed a clay-like mass.

Down in front of the hotel, Marco was getting antsy. At least one of them should have caught a glimpse of Dawson by now. "Gary, you see anything?" he asked via subcom.

"No, nothing yet," Gary said. "We are watching, but there's no sign of activity at the moment." He extended a snake camera under the door to the room he was hiding in and looked out into the hallway, feeling more and more like Neil was a sitting duck. If Dawson was already in the building, even being just two doors away was too far.

The entire floor of the hotel felt quiet. Gary moved the camera around to see if there was an additional angle he was missing, even though he'd already checked half a dozen times.

Slowly, the fifteen minutes were ticking by.

Marco ducked when he saw Dawson emerge from the service entry. "Noah," he said, and Noah could sense the anxiety in his transmission. "Dawson's just come out of the back of the hotel."

"I don't like that," said Noah. "He likes to set up the job and be gone." He stood there, thinking about how he might approach such an assassination, and suddenly his eyes went wide. "Neil! Get out of there! Get out now!" he ordered.

Neil wasted no time complying. Doing his job well was one thing, but being stupid was something else entirely, and something he didn't want to be accused of. He leapt to his feet and ran for the door, snatching it open and throwing himself out into the hallway as Jenny and Gary came bursting out of their own rooms.

He'd barely gotten out of the room when he felt the explosion swell behind him. Time seemed to slow down and speed up all at once, sound catching up with him somewhere in the middle. The door behind him slammed and flew off its hinges, thrown like a brick by the blast. It caught him as he tried to turn toward Jenny and slammed him into the opposite wall. He landed in a crumpled heap at its base.

He managed not to lose consciousness, but he was disoriented, unable to figure out which way was up or down. Despite the ringing in his ears, he heard Gary pounding toward him, heard the shout of his own name cut through the fuzzy haze.

"*Neil!*" Jenny screamed, and then she had slid to the floor beside him. Neil felt both of them grab his arms and tried unsuccessfully to answer.

"*Neil!*" Jenny repeated, with such force and worry that Neil felt he ought to be flattered. He tried to pull himself together, tried to get his mouth to work, his brain to function. On an innate level, he realized the team needed to know he was okay. More pointedly, he needed *Noah* to know he was okay. Noah might not have genuine emotions, but he was quite capable of blaming himself when one of the team was injured.

He struggled to pull himself upright, but Gary's forceful hands wouldn't let go. He had thrown off the shattered door and was attempting to look into Neil's eyes.

Neil blinked carefully and shifted. Gary didn't move, holding him tight. "*Neil*, are you okay?"

Neil coughed, working his throat. "I'm all right!" he croaked, trying again to move himself up or, at the least, shift away from the piece of wood digging into his back. He tested the other sensations in his body as he did so, hoping to find that what he was telling Gary was really true.

"Are you *sure*?" Jenny didn't sound convinced and Gary's grip didn't lessen in the slightest.

"I'm okay!" Neil insisted again. Either the annoyance in his voice finally prompted Gary to let go or he'd actually been convincing in his insistence, because Gary's strong hands were suddenly gone.

"Neil," Noah's voice said in his ear, "are you sure? Don't move if you're not certain."

As he assured Noah that he was all right, a steadying hand returned to his arm. A careful grip, just above his elbow. As insistent as Neil had felt only moments before that he was fine, he was grateful for the firm hold. The anchoring touch reduced the ringing in his ears and the tingling spinning out from the back of his head.

He realized it was Jenny holding onto him as he checked the rest of his body, discovering, thankfully, that nothing felt acutely painful. He started to believe he really was fine. He released a rough lungful of air and felt the tightness in his chest level out.

Already, the smoke was clearing and the air he drew in to himself felt fresher and cleaner than he'd expected. He relaxed, leaned back against the wall, and closed his eyes to whisper a short prayer of thanks. He heard Gary sigh, sounding relieved.

"*Good,*" Neil heard Noah say, and then he listened to the

conversation going on inside his head as Marco and Noah began discussing the next step. They were still in the game and way ahead of Spear, even if it didn't feel like it.

"All right, we are still on track," Noah said next. "We are one step away from Spear. Let's get back to our own hotel. MI6 can handle the cleanup and police activity here."

Marco heard through the subcoms that Neil seemed okay, but the smoke streaming from the windows above had fed the worry in his gut. The callous, too casual stance of Dawson as he exited the hotel and moved to the river walk further fed his anger. "Noah, I think Dawson is heading back to the bistro. Do you want me to stay on him? Or do you need my help back here?"

Marco felt torn. He didn't want to chance losing Dawson again, but he knew that if Neil was injured, the other agents would need his help. He also wanted to visibly see that Neil was okay.

"You'd better stay on him," answered Noah. "Gary and Jenny and I can handle things here," Noah further assured. "I already asked Catherine to get the taxis away from that area. We don't want Dawson to somehow end up at the real St. Aloysius, so all the cabs you see are hers. They know where to take him."

"You got it. I'm on it, Noah," he said, but then Noah heard, "I'm just..."

"Neil does seem to be okay." Noah cut his question short, making it seem as if he was reading his mind. "You heard what he said. We figured it out in time and he got out of there."

Marco heard, and was grateful for, the hidden subtext in Noah's statement. Things hadn't gone according to plan, but they'd pulled together as a team.

Neil was okay. Neil was okay. They'd made it work and Marco could bear no blame.

"Thanks, Noah," he finished simply.

"Marco?"

"Yeah?"

"You'd better give Renée a head's up. She could be back at the hotel by now, and we might be late. She might be worried."

"On it, Noah." Renée was wearing her hotspot and Noah could have reached her himself, but Marco appreciated the gesture of letting him do it. "Marco to Renée," he said, and she acknowledged almost instantly. "I'm staying on Dawson for the moment, but the rest of them should be back shortly. You okay?"

"I heard," she said. "And I'm fine, honey. I will admit, though, I was pretty scared when he called me out on being a fake."

Marco chuckled. "You were? Couldn't tell it from where I was standing."

"Hey, I knew you had my back. You think I did okay?"

"*Cher*," Marco said, "you were great."

———

By the time Noah made it to the fifth floor, Gary was having a hard time keeping Neil stationary and sirens were blaring in the distance. The hotel personnel had already called the police. Both were reasons Noah wanted to get them out of there as soon as possible.

After speaking with Marco, he'd called Albert Corey at their base of operations, asking the London agent to come deal with the local authorities. Albert confirmed that he was already on his way, ready and willing to do whatever they needed.

The third reason they needed to leave quickly was Renée. If Dawson went straight back to the hotel, even if returning via the bistro, there was a strong likelihood that he'd beat them back to their St. Aloysius. Renée was critical to their plans, but Noah didn't want her to expose herself to Dawson until they were all in place for backup.

As he made his way down the hall, he could hear tones of disagreement going on between his team members, their voices arguing in hushed tones. He couldn't hear all of what was being said, but he could imagine, and he hoped Neil was as okay as he was insisting. Gary and Jenny seemed to be having a hard time getting him to sit still.

"Is he all right?" Noah asked them as he drew close.

Neil was sitting with his back to the wall, his low voice making an intent case to the other agents. He looked pale, and a little shaky.

"He seems to be," Gary answered, releasing Neil's shoulder and rising from his crouch. He took an added step back to allow Noah room, looking relieved at his presence.

"*He* is fine," Neil carefully enunciated, throwing a glare at Gary before starting to get up again. To his obvious annoyance, Noah clamped a hand on his shoulder, keeping him floor-bound while taking over Gary's previous position of squatting in front of him.

Neil met his eyes immediately. The pupils were even and his eyes full of clarity. Noah looked up at Gary for anything else he might need to know.

"Just banged up with a few scratches, I think," Gary answered, "but he's bruised his back pretty close to the kidney."

"But that's *all* it is," Neil cut in. "A bruise. I'll let you know if anything else seems wrong."

Noah, again, peered intently into Neil's eyes, then nodded. "I think you'll make it," he said. He hooked a hand under Neil's shoulder and helped him get to his feet. "What about Geraldo? Is it salvageable?"

"He'll be fine," Neil said. "He might need some new clothes, and we won't be able to use my face again most likely, but he's made of steel and ceramic. Not much chance the explosion could have damaged him more than I can fix. Let's go, if we don't get back to our hotel soon, we won't be there to back up Renée."

NINE

Marco followed Dawson vigilantly as he strolled the river walk, looking like any overworked businessman anxious to enjoy some fresh air at the close of a hectic workday. As they got closer to the bistro, Marco spotted the taxis waiting in a line, relieved that Catherine Potts had already taken care of switching them out for agents of her own. When the river walk ended, that precaution paid off. Dawson stepped into the third cab in the line and told the driver to take him to the St. Aloysius Hotel.

Marco relaxed, watching him go, the anxiety that had been eating his stomach fading into memory. Of course, he still had one reason to worry; they'd set Renée up in a position where Dawson would most likely decide to kill her before it was over. He hoped her performance that night would be as good as it had been that afternoon.

———

By the time they exited the hotel's grand lobby, Neil had convinced the others that his injuries were minimal. The four of them hurried to their car and rushed back to the phony St. Aloysius, arriving just as dusk was seizing the city. They found Renée waiting for them in the command center.

"How'd it go?" she asked.

"Smooth as butter," Neil lied, shooting Gary a warning look.

Jenny scowled. "Not so much," he said. "Neil was almost killed by a bomb blast. Dawson decided to blow up a big part of the hotel, rather than get too close."

During the ride back from the Teagarden, Neil had very carefully tried to maneuver Noah and Gary and Jenny into letting it go, but obviously Jenny wasn't having any. Gary rolled his eyes, but Marco's voice suddenly came through the subcoms.

"Dawson's on his way," Marco told them. "He'll be there in less than five."

"Are we all set?" Noah looked at Renée, then back to Neil. They both nodded.

"Yes," Renée said. "Catherine's people have briefed me on everything they got out of the real messenger, so I can play the part. She's never met Spear, she's always worked through a contact person; the odds are good that Spear doesn't know anything about her at all."

"All right," Noah said. "You'd better head on up."

With a deep breath and a confident smile, she started up the stairs.

"And you'd better get some ice on your back if you don't want to wake up too stiff to move tomorrow," Noah chided Neil, who was already back to work on his computer.

"There's an ice pack in the brown supply box," Gary said as he moved up the stairs after Renée.

"I know," Neil said sarcastically, now completely annoyed with the unnecessary fussing. "I packed it."

———

THE SUN WAS GETTING low in the sky by the time Dawson made it back to his hotel room. He was still feeling the rush he often felt after successful jobs, and this time he was allowing himself to enjoy the feeling just a little more. All that remained was arranging the funds transfer. After that, he could be gone, if he wanted to be.

That was something else to consider, however. The payment arrangement would give him a chance to see Spear's redhead again. Maybe, if things went well, he really would contemplate staying a few more days. He'd certainly earned it this time.

A new clerk was manning the front desk when he walked in and he figured it must be time for the night shift. The man barely seemed to notice him as he passed. Dawson was fine with that. Hotel night staffers were never as observant as the day personnel.

The stairs and hallway were well lit and as he opened the lock on his hotel room door, he had to let his eyes adjust to the darkness. He shut the door behind him and felt around the wall for the light switch. He found it easily, flipping on the entryway light before moving farther into the room, preparing to relax a bit before he decided whether or not to leave.

He reached out to flip on the main light at the edge of the entry hall and was pleasantly surprised by the sight that greeted him.

"Welcome home." Spear's redhead was standing on the far side of his room, looking sly and inviting.

"Well, well, well," he said, setting his briefcase on the floor and letting a smile spread over his face. "I was looking forward to seeing you again, but I didn't expect to find you waiting for me."

She shrugged demurely. "I wanted to see you again, as well," she said. "It isn't often that a lowly messenger gets to meet a man of your caliber."

Dawson chuckled at her pun. "Caliber? That's an interesting choice of words. Aren't you concerned about my reputation?"

Renée shrugged again. "You're talking about the fact that you try to never let anyone see your face and live? If that's what you have in mind, I've already seen enough to sign my death warrant, haven't I? On the other hand, are you sure you would want to anger our employer? He does use me a lot, you know."

"Messengers are expendable, my dear," Dawson said. "However, I have made exceptions to that rule in the past. If Spear trusts you, then perhaps I can as well. I suppose a lot of it depends on what other benefits you might bring to the relationship."

"Well, the main benefit I bring," Renée said, "is your payday." She picked up a small USB drive that was laying on the bed and held it out to him. "This is the confirmation of payment, just as you required."

Dawson took the drive and walked over to the table in the room, where a laptop was sitting. He opened it up and turned it on, then plugged the thumb drive into the USB port and tapped a sequence on the keyboard. A window opened up and he checked the information that was displayed, then turned back to her with a smile.

"Perfect, of course," he said. "Now, the question on my mind is why you decided to be here when I returned."

She smiled. "I would think that would be obvious," she said. "I have been playing messenger for Spear and his people for more than a year, now. Obviously I'm not afraid of what's going on, so I thought perhaps it might be time to try to move up in the organization. My contacts don't want to allow that; I thought perhaps you and I might come to an arrangement that would benefit both of us."

Back in the command center, Noah and Neil looked at one another. This was the point where things could get dicey. While it wasn't a common practice, all E & E operatives were aware that there were no limits to what they might have to do in service of the mission, and that included sexual activities. Both Marco and Renée had been fully briefed on the plan to get close to Spear, and that it could conceivably involve Renée engaging in a sexual relationship with Dawson. Neither was thrilled about the idea, but both of them understood the importance of the mission. As Neil had put it, people in their line of work couldn't afford jealousies.

Marco had agreed, and assured Renée that he would not hold against her whatever she had to do.

Dawson looked her over, and admitted silently to himself that he had been hoping for just such an eventuality. This woman was quite attractive, and exuded a sensuality that had caught his attention the first time he laid eyes on her at the bistro.

"And what would be my part of this arrangement?" he asked.

Renée moved toward him, her slow, sensual walk causing him to look her over again.

"That's pretty simple," she said. "I want to go with you when you leave. If the people you deal with become aware that you trust me, then I might get a shot at more important responsibilities. I'm a girl who likes the material things in life, Jonathan. Being a messenger doesn't pay well enough to keep me in the style to which I hope to become accustomed."

Dawson grinned as she raised her arms and put them around his neck. "Oh, I think we can definitely be of benefit to one another."

Their lips met, and Renée forced herself not to consider the fact that the entire team was going to be able to hear what would happen next. She had every intention of convincing Dawson that he was the most exciting lover she had ever known, and she only hoped that Marco would understand that it was an act. In reality, kissing this man was the most disgusting, vile thing she felt she had ever done.

Dawson let go and stepped back, looking her in the eye. "You know, it occurs to me that I don't even know your name."

She smiled. "It's Abigail, Abigail Willis. My friends call me Abby, so you can, too."

———

Two hours later, Dawson and Renée left the hotel. The intelligence they had on the assassin indicated that he was due to return to his employer after this last hit, and Noah had devised a plan that would keep a trackable asset on Dawson.

That asset was Renée. Now posing as Dawson's lover, Renée would be able to keep them apprised of his location, and sometimes his plans. With her wristwatch hotspot, she was rarely going to be out of contact for more than a short time.

That was about the only comfort Marco was getting from the deal. He was the one assigned to follow them when they left, although they already knew that Dawson was taking Renée straight to Heathrow. He hadn't told her yet where they were going, but there was little doubt that he would plan on meeting Spear within the next few days.

The next thirty minutes saw the E & E agents furiously preparing to leave England. A lot of their equipment would be taken care of by the MI6 agents and, where necessary, sent to them later. They would take only what they could, the essentials.

"Neil, don't lift that, it's too heavy."

"I can carry my own computer, Gary, I brought it in here."

"We just don't want you straining your back," Jenny said, taking the computer out of his hands before he had time to protest. He watched her carry the computer outside, and when he looked back, Gary was laughing.

"Uh huh," Neil said. "Better laugh it up now, because someday soon, you're going to get kicked in the shin and I'll convince everyone on the team that your leg is broken."

Gary laughed more.

"*I'm* actually part of this team, remember?" Neil complained. "I mean, did everyone forget that Gary is just a loaner?"

Gary's smile abruptly died. The look he threw Neil spoke volumes. He wasn't part of the team. He'd been brought in for one mission, and one mission only. The rest of them pointedly ignored the silent exchange.

The illusion of the alternative was enticing. The ability to think as if he really was part of the team had come about so easily that it already felt real. And because it was so easy to think about, it was easy to joke about also.

Neil stopped and returned the look, but Marco interrupted the silence over the subcoms.

"You might not believe this, Noah," Marco said, "but Dawson just bought two tickets to Atlanta."

"Interesting news," Noah agreed. "What about us?"

"Our plane is waiting on the runway now. I spoke to the pilot and crew, and the flight plan is being filed now. All you have to do is get here."

"You heard the man," Noah said. "Let's go."

With a last look at Neil, Gary nodded quickly. He picked up his own equipment and headed out.

The final item in the room was the E & E printer, already folded into its case and ready to move. Neil reached for the handle, but Noah beat him to it. The younger agent exhaled, exasperated, but it didn't seem to bother Noah.

He set a gentle hand on Neil's shoulder. "Neil," he said, giving his shoulder a squeeze. "Sometimes you've got to learn to take some help from your friends." Then, looking around the empty room with a satisfied nod, he gave Neil's shoulder one last squeeze and followed Gary out the back door.

———

"WHAT?" Gary tore his gaze from the scenery outside the car window, meeting Neil's eyes.

"I asked if you were okay, man. You looked a little out of it."

"Tired, I guess," he answered, his mood still dark. "It's been a long couple days, for everyone."

"Yeah." Neil seemed to accept the answer. "We've got a long flight ahead of us. Hopefully you can sleep on the plane. You didn't really look rested when you showed up at Noah's the other night."

"I don't always sleep well on planes," he hedged, shrugging, then considered Neil with a critical eye. "You look kind of tired yourself."

"Like you said," Neil said, "it's been a long few days for all of us."

Gary nodded his head toward the front seat of the car they rode in. Cut off from their conversation by the taxi partition, they could still see Noah at the wheel and Jenny looking tired in the passenger seat. "For Noah most of all; I'm not sure he's really slept at all."

"He never does on a mission. It's just the way he is."

"He needs to rest," Gary said. "We are the ones who are all dependent on him. He's got to be able to think clearly, or we could all end up dead."

Neil flashed a half-smile, nodding in return. "Don't worry about Noah," he said. "He's always on top of his game. That's why he's the best."

"I know that," Gary said, "but anybody can become exhausted, right?"

"I guess so," Neil said, offering a grin. He looked out his window a moment later to see that they'd arrived at the airport. Marco was waiting for them at the foot of the ramp leading into the Gulfstream.

"Now, if you can just manage not to get blown up again," Gary threw at him suddenly, "everything might be okay, but just remember that your kidneys can only take so much abuse."

Neil shot him a dirty look, but Gary only grinned. On the other side of the car, Marco leaned in through Neil's open door. He'd apparently overheard, because he laid a hand on Neil's shoulder and asked seriously, "Are you all right?"

"He bruised his back in the explosion," Jenny explained as she got out of the car. "He tried to catch a door that got blown off its hinges."

Noah popped the trunk and Gary started unloading the things they were taking with them.

"Neil, are you okay?" Marco asked.

"As long as he doesn't strain himself, he should be," Noah cut in. Gary looked out at the co-pilot, who was jogging across the tarmac to join them, and kept his gaze pinned to the approaching figure, eyes averted from Neil's, pretending to be completely focused on other things.

Neil scowled deeper, glaring at Gary over the car's roof. "Will you all just drop it already?" Gary chuckled as he picked up a couple of bags and headed toward the airplane.

TEN

The Gulfstream G550 carried them all the way to Atlanta. It was a long flight, and though Noah had encouraged his team to rest, he knew none of them got much sleep. He himself managed to doze less than an hour in all. He called Sarah and spent a half hour assuring her that everyone was okay, then checked in with Allison to give her a progress update. The rest of the time, he simply sat there and considered what could go wrong with the rest of his plans.

One of the advantages to using the Gulfstream was that it was not necessary to make connecting flights. Dawson and Renée were flying Delta, which required them to make a connection in New York City's LaGuardia, while the rest of the team flew nonstop to Hartsfield-Jackson airport in Atlanta.

"Noah," Neil said, touching Noah's shoulder to get his attention. "The pilot says we'll be touching down in about twenty minutes."

Noah blinked, looking up into his face. "How far behind us is Dawson's plane?" he asked, sitting up straight and buckling his seat belt.

"Over eight hours," Marco answered from the seat adjacent. "Renée says they have a six hour layover at New York, and they just touched down an hour ago. By the time they board their connecting flight and get here, you can add another three hours to that, so we've got about eight hours to get ready."

Noah nodded. "That should be plenty. Now, all we have to do is make them count."

———

BY THE TIME Dawson's plane touched down that evening, the team was more than ready to effectively follow his movements, tracking him and Renée as he hailed a cab from the airport. Although this one wasn't driven by an agent, Neil tapped into the dispatcher's feed and, using two different cars, they were able to follow the yellow taxi easily.

Noah drove one of the cars with Gary as a passenger, while Jenny and Neil took the other. Marco was on a motorcycle once again, keeping the taxi in view while staying back as far as he could. Whenever he lost them for a moment, he would message Renée. She would make a comment about a landmark or something as a way to direct him back onto their trail.

Thirty minutes later, the taxi pulled up at the Alpine Air Hotel, a luxury hotel in one of the ritzier areas of the city. Noah and Jenny drove on past while Marco turned his motorcycle in to the gas station lot across the street.

Marco climbed off the bike and began pumping gas into its tank while he reported to Noah. "Okay, they just took their bags and went inside," he said. "Their taxi is driving away now."

"Good," Noah said. "That means things are in place. Marco, you and Gary will be staying in the hotel with them. Neil, Jenny and I will go to the Marriott down the street. Meet us there, so that you and Gary can get into character."

"You got it, boss," Marco said. He topped off the gas tank and replaced the nozzle on the pump, tore off the receipt for the gas and climbed back onto the bike. Five minutes later, he had pulled into the Marriott parking lot beside Noah's car.

It took less than an hour for Gary to get him and Marco made up and ready to make a move. Marco, a Louisiana Cajun of Italian descent, looked absolutely nothing like himself with blond hair and beard, with startling blue eyes behind stylish glasses. Gary had added two inches of height and ten inches of girth, then applied a mask and hairpiece to age him thirty years. The cover identities Molly had created for this phase of the operation made Gary a reclusive, eccentric billionaire who was known for his rudeness, while Marco was a combination of private nurse and bodyguard.

"I think we are ready," Gary said, and then he crinkled his face into a glare. "Unless you young people have something else you want to complain about," he said sarcastically. "I can't understand young folks these days, doing nothing but griping and complaining all the time, that's all they do."

Neil chuckled, but Noah simply raised an eyebrow. "You sound like Robert De Niro," he said. "Is that intentional?"

Gary blinked. "Well, yeah," he said in his own voice. "You ever heard anybody who can do cranky like De Niro?"

"I suppose not." Noah turned to Marco. "Remember, stay as close as you safely can to Renée, but without making it obvious. Dawson may feel possessive toward her, and you can't afford to put yourself on his radar."

"Don't worry about me," Marco said. "What happens on a mission stays on a mission, right? Any jealousy I might feel won't be a problem. I'll just make sure to be listening closely, in case she needs to be pulled out."

"That's fine, but don't pull her out unless she asks for it. This is the best shot we have at getting to Spear. I don't want to delay it any longer than absolutely necessary."

Marco nodded, and then he and Gary left. An hour later, he contacted Noah to report that they were checked in to their hotel room, on the same floor as Dawson and Renée.

Renée did not get any privacy, so she wasn't able to report directly as often as Noah would have liked. On the other hand, she was quite adept at steering whatever conversation she was having into a direction that would allow Noah, Marco and the others to figure out what was happening. She was obviously going to great lengths to keep Dawson entertained with her, and she was enjoying rather significant success.

It was the following morning before the two of them made an appearance outside the room, going to the breakfast room off the hotel lobby. Unlike cheaper hotels that offered a continental breakfast, the Alpine Air had a breakfast chef on duty from five a.m. until eleven, and breakfast made to order was included with the room.

Gary and Marco, given a heads-up by Renée as she asked Dawson about where they were going to have breakfast, were already in the breakfast room when the two of them arrived. Marco had told Renée where they were, but she carefully avoided looking at them as she entered with her new escort.

Ironically, Dawson chose the table directly beside the two of them, and then turned and nodded amicably at Gary.

"Morning, sir," he said politely. "Nice day, isn't it?"

Gary glared at him. "It'll be a nice day when I finally get old enough to not have to put up with this asshole," he said, pointing at Marco. Marco rolled his eyes in a long-suffering gesture, and Dawson stifled a grin.

"Oh? Is he mean to you?" Renée asked.

Gary looked at her, and his eyes softened a bit as he remained in character. "You wouldn't believe it," he said. "He won't even let me have my cigar. My doctor says I can have one a day, but this young punk refuses to let me have it."

"Because we're in a non-smoking hotel, Mr. Constantine," Marco said. "If you wait until after breakfast, we can go out into the courtyard, where you can smoke." His Cajun accent was gone, and he sounded surprisingly effeminate.

Gary made a point of turning his attention away from the couple at the next table, so they did likewise. The two men were able to listen to the simple conversation between Dawson and Renée, but there was nothing in it to suggest when they might be going to meet with Dawson's employer. The only thing they overheard was something about Dawson taking Renée out shopping for the morning.

"Okay," Marco said softly to his subcom, transmitting to the others, "they just left the breakfast room. They're going shopping, but I'm sure you already caught that."

"We did," Noah said. "I've already got Jenny out there to follow. She's the only one Dawson hasn't seen up close at least once, but she's wearing a wig and sunglasses anyway. You need to see if you can get into their room, try to find anything that might give you some clue as to who Spear might be."

"I'm on it," Marco said. He and Gary were finished with breakfast anyway, so he got up and pushed Gary's wheelchair back toward the elevator.

Unfortunately, the search turned up nothing. Marco was careful to make sure everything was put back exactly where he had found it when he entered the room, but he almost took too long doing so. Luckily, Renée managed to switch on her subcom and comment that they were back at the hotel much sooner than she expected, which gave them time to get out before she and Dawson made it up the elevator.

The rest of the day passed slowly, as Dawson and Renée remained in the room, except for mealtimes. For lunch, they went to a small café down the street, while they took dinner in the hotel's own four-star restaurant, the Matterhorn. To outward appearances, they could have been an average couple, and Renée only tried once to bring up the idea of going to meet Spear.

"We'll go when it's time to go," Dawson said. "Don't push it, sweetheart. The last thing you want is to become annoying, right?"

She smiled, but the implied threat in his words came through crystal clear.

The following morning, Renée was still sleeping when she felt something move on the bed. Her mind instantly recalled where she was and what was happening as she waited for Dawson to speak. "Are you going to sleep all day?"

Renée opened her eyes and looked up into Dawson's own. He was sitting on the edge of the bed, smiling down at her.

"It doesn't sound like that bad an idea," she said. "Is there a reason to get up?"

"We have a meeting," Dawson said. "Spear has requested my presence, so we had better be there."

She sat up on the bed and stretched. "What kind of meeting? Are we finally going to see him?"

"I don't actually know if he will be there or not. He heads up the organization, but he isn't always handling everything himself. We're supposed to go to the office and check in, probably to receive another assignment. There will at least be someone there who can let him know that you are with me, wanting to meet him."

She grinned at him, leaning back and propping herself on her hands. "I hope so," she said. "On the other hand, if I have to go with you on an assignment for a while, that would be a good consolation prize."

Dawson chuckled. "I'm not sure I can handle you on a long-term basis," he said. "A man in my line of work has to get some rest now and then."

She reached over quickly and grabbed the front of his shirt, pulling him toward her. "You can rest later," she said. "I have something else in mind at the moment."

A half-hour later, after a quick shower together, they dressed and left their hotel. A car was waiting for them out in front of the building, and the driver held the door open as they slid into the back seat.

When the door closed, Renée realized that the windows were completely blacked out. A light came on in the passenger compartment and she saw that there was a bar and a selection of edibles. Dawson reached over and picked up a bottle, then held it out to her.

"A good year," he said. "Will you join me?"

"Of course," Renée said. Dawson cracked the bottle open and poured the wine, passing the glass to her and then picking up his own.

Renée held her glass out for a toast. "To the wonderful time we've had together," she said. "May it happen again sometime soon."

"Maybe sooner than you think," Dawson said. "You haven't gotten rid of me yet, you know. Spear may not be interested in talking to you. You might just need to stay with me for a while."

Renée cocked her head and batted her eyes at him. "Now, just a little while ago you said you didn't think you could handle me any longer."

"Yes, well, that was a line. A man has to keep a girl flattered, doesn't he?"

She giggled. "It certainly doesn't hurt."

Dawson looked at her for a moment, his own smile broad. "You're an amazing woman, Abby. I think you are the only woman I've ever known who was aware of what I do and wasn't terrified of me."

She shrugged. "I'm just too logical for that, I guess. If you decided you wanted me dead, I would probably have been dead before I knew it. No point in worrying about something I can't control, is there?"

He chuckled. "I don't think that's all there is to it," he said. "There are some women who like to associate with violent men, they get some kind of thrill out of it. I suspect you might be one of those. Am I right?"

She leaned close to him and whispered in his ear. "I suppose you could say I have been known to hang out with killers before," she said. "They are certainly powerful men, and everyone likes a powerful man."

The ride in the blacked out car lasted about forty minutes, and then they came to a stop. The door opened once again and the driver stood there, holding it open and looking straight ahead as they stepped out onto the gravel under their feet. There was a house in front of them, a large Southern- looking mansion with four large columns holding up part of the roof over the front porch.

"Gone with the Wind," Renée said. "Reminds me of that house in the movie."

Dawson looked at the house for a moment, then turned back to her. "I suppose it does, now that you mention it. I hadn't really thought about it before."

He started walking toward the house and she fell in behind. "This is where the organization meets?"

"Not really. It would probably be more accurate to say that the organization was born here, and has already been through several different versions of itself. There are offices deep in the city, but this is where we tend to meet most of the time. Very few people have any idea where this place is. Even I don't know, which is why I have to rely on the chauffeurs."

He took her hand and led her toward the house, walking her up the steps onto the grand porch. He never got a chance to ring the doorbell, because the door opened and a distinguished-looking gentleman stood there.

ELEVEN

"It's good to see you again, Mr. Lancaster," the man said. He waited until they entered, then closed the door and turned toward them again. "I hope you will understand that we have some construction going on, and ignore the less than aesthetic look of the place. The Director believes there must be a spy in the organization, probably one of the American federal agents. One of the presidential candidates who claims to have knowledge of it has been talking about an organization like ours, and the Director is making some changes to the place in the hope that he might be able to ferret out the intruder, if there is one. Please follow me."

He led them deeper into the house and into a large room that was set up like an office, but with a round table to one side. When the door shut behind them, the genial attitude lessened slightly. He motioned for the two of them to each take a chair as he rounded the desk and sat behind it. When he had done so, he looked at Renée as if seeing her for the first time.

"Young lady, my name is Joshua. To be honest, I wasn't expecting Mr. Lancaster to be bringing a guest. May I know who you are?"

"I'm Abby Willis," Renée said. "I've been running messages for you now and then."

Joshua looked at her for a moment, then turned to Dawson again. "Really, Mr. Lancaster? You've been consorting with peripherals?"

Dawson grinned. "You can relax, Joshua," he said. "There's a lot more to Ms. Willis than meets the eye."

"As with any of us," Joshua said. "However, it's the parts we can't see that have the most potential to bring damage into our lives. I'm sure you have done your due diligence, to ensure that she is not some sort of agent?"

Renée burst out laughing. "Me? Oh, you've got to be kidding."

Dawson glanced at her and she caught the scowl on his face, so she got herself quickly under control. "Sorry about that," she said. "It just never occurred to me anyone could possibly think such a thing."

"Well, that's the one thing that we all know far too well," Joshua said. "The people most likely to be the ones you cannot trust are the ones who seem the most trustworthy."

"I'm confident that we are safe at the moment," Dawson said. "Why don't you just tell us why we're here?"

Joshua looked at him for a second, then picked up some papers from his desk. "I'm afraid the Director has a new task for you," he said. "This time, you will be going to Sydney."

Dawson nodded. "And the target?" he asked.

"Patrick McNealy," Joshua said. "He is the Australian Banking Association's deputy director. The Director has been grooming someone to take his place, should anything happen to him. Those plans are now in place, and it's time for the sad event to come about."

Dawson took the file that Joshua passed to him and glanced through it, taking a good look at the photographs of Mr. McNealy.

"This guy is a banker? He looks more like a fry cook at a fast food joint."

"Yes, well, appearances can be deceiving," Joshua said. "Mr. McNealy is in control of a great deal of the transactional policies of the Australian bankers. Having someone of his own in that position will be of great advantage to the Director."

"No doubt," Dawson said. "That would put him in a position to make sure his money gets properly laundered." He looked up at Joshua again. "Payment through the usual routes?"

"Of course," Joshua said. "Deposited to your account, the same as always."

Dawson nodded, then turned to look at Renée once again. When he turned back to Joshua, he was grinning.

"Ms. Willis is interested in meeting the Director," he said. "She has been working for him off and on for some time now, and is hoping to work her way into some greater responsibilities. Do you think you can arrange such a meeting?"

"Certainly I could," Joshua said. "The question is, why should I? As I pointed out before, Mr. Lancaster, we don't really know who this is sitting beside you."

"Oh, come on," Renée said. "How hard is it to go back to your records and see how long I've been working for you guys?"

"Now, you see, Ms. Willis, therein lies the problem. While other organizations might keep records of employees, even short-term employees such as yourself, we do not. I'm afraid any record of your assistance to us is only in the memory of the person who recruited you each time you were needed. Since we insist on strict secrecy, I'm confident that you probably don't even know who that was. Would I be correct in that assumption?"

Renée made a face and stuck her tongue out at him. "That doesn't help," she said. "No, I didn't know his name. He just called me up when he needed something, and he always paid half up front. For the kind of money he was paying, I'll do pretty much whatever I'm asked to do."

Joshua gave her a sarcastic grin. "I have no doubt that this is true," he said. "After all, you seem to have attached yourself to Mr. Lancaster. And I must say, that truly does surprise me. Mr. Lancaster is not one who normally allows such familiar association."

"Maybe I just got tired of being alone," Dawson said. "That does happen to some of us, you know."

Joshua shot him a look, but said nothing. A moment later, he turned back to Renée.

"Unfortunately, young lady, I will not be able to help you to achieve your desires. First, I would be reluctant to do so in any case, but then there remains the fact that the Director is not in the country at this moment." He turned to Dawson. "In fact, he will be waiting for you in Sydney."

Dawson nodded as if he was not surprised. He turned toward Renée and smiled. "I guess you're stuck with me a little while longer," he said.

Renée blew him a kiss. "You say that like it's a bad thing."

"I am not, however," Joshua said, "without some other news. There is a reception this evening, and you, Mr. Lancaster, are expected to attend. You may bring your friend along if you wish, but a few of the council members would like to speak with you about your most recent assignment."

Dawson looked at him. "In what regard?"

"It seems that you may have inadvertently caused an issue," Joshua said. "The death of Mr. Hapgood, while perfectly in accordance with your assignment, was so obviously contrived that the man the Director had intended to replace him has fallen under suspicion. As a result, the post has been given to someone else." Joshua almost seemed happy. "I do believe I have warned you before about some of your more spectacular techniques. The Council is not pleased, Mr. Lancaster."

"Fine, I'll go talk to them," Dawson said. "When and where?"

Joshua let out a sigh and passed him a slip of paper. "The address is there. A reception three nights hence at the Royal Crown, seven p.m. Be sure to be there."

"No problem," Dawson said. He took the paper and got to his feet, and Renée followed him out the door.

"Don't let Joshua get to you," he said as the chauffeur held the door open for them to climb back inside. "He's just an old grouch."

She grinned at him, but his cell phone chimed at that moment and he took it out and looked at the screen. She couldn't see it, but it seemed that there was something on it that troubled him.

"Something wrong?" she asked, but he put the phone away quickly and smiled at her.

"Nothing at all," he said, and then he turned to her. "I think it's time I treated you to some of the finer things in life. When we get back to the hotel, go ahead and pack up."

"We're going somewhere?" she asked.

"Yes," he said. "A much nicer hotel that I like to frequent now and then. You're going to love it."

She smiled, and told herself that she would let the others know as soon as she got a moment to herself and could activate her subcom. The only problem with that was Dawson's habit of staying right beside her all the time. The bastard wouldn't even let her go to the bathroom alone, but she'd find a way. There was no other choice.

———

"SOMETHING IS WRONG," Noah said two mornings later. "It's been too long since we've heard from Renée."

Marco looked from Noah to the clock in the room and then turned back to his boss. "Almost thirty-nine hours," he said. "We haven't heard a thing since before they went to bed two nights ago. Noah, you don't think Dawson caught her out?"

"We don't know much of anything at the moment," Noah said. "I've already notified Allison that she's gone silent, and she's calling in favors from other agencies to see if anyone has a lead on her. We need to get some kind of idea what's going on with her, and quickly."

"I should've planted a bug while I was searching the room," Marco said. "Then at least we'd know if they were still in there. The way it is right now, we don't know squat. He could have killed her and taken off."

"No," Neil said, sitting at his computer. "I've just gotten into the hotel's security video feed, and they left together about midnight the night before last. I was able to track them out of the room, down the hall, down the elevator and out the front lobby doors. They got into a taxi, but that was the last I saw. Unfortunately, I couldn't get the car number from the camera angle on the outside."

Marco let out a sigh. "But she didn't say anything to anyone? Why would she leave without saying something to one of us?"

"Her subcom was off," Neil said. "I don't know why, but she hadn't turned it on before they left, and the server says it's off now. For whatever reason, she must not have wanted any of us to hear what was going on."

Noah turned to him. "What about the taxi? Can't you find out what cars were here last night, see where they went?"

"You know I can, and I'm already on it," Neil said. "Unfortunately, it's going to take a little time. Most taxi cab companies don't bother to keep their records online, so I'm having to do things the old-fashioned way. I've got a liaison request in through our guy in Atlanta, to have the FBI contact all of the taxi companies and get us their dispatch schedules and tracking reports. They can probably zip that stuff up and email it, but it still isn't going to be here in the next ten minutes. We're talking hours, maybe even a day or more before I find out what car that was."

"Maybe something's wrong with her subcom," Marco said. "I mean, it's a gadget, right? Could be something was wrong with it. She might be trying to reach us and even more worried than we are when she can't get a response."

"No." It was Neil who spoke. "Ever since they set up the telephone interface, our subcoms log on to the server as soon as they come online. I checked the server logs and she was on it twice during the night. I don't know why she's gone silent, but it's not because of equipment malfunction."

Marco scowled. "I can't imagine any other reason she would do this," he said. "Unless Dawson isn't letting her out of his sight, and she's being careful to keep it turned off whenever he's close by. Still, you'd think she would find some chance to at least send a message, let us know where she is and if she's okay or not."

Jenny leaned forward. "I've kinda felt she shouldn't have been on this assignment. I should have gone in, not her. Renée doesn't have the field experience for something like this."

"No," Noah said. "What she does have is the build and general appearance that we know appeals to Dawson. She has also had all the training, and has been judged a capable field agent. I'm confident she can do her job; I just don't know why she's gone radio silent on us."

It was a complicated mission, but its end goal was one that they all believed in. They were out to identify and eliminate the international crime lord known as Spear; partly as revenge for the loss of their friend Donald Jefferson, but mostly because Donald's assassination had given them the first real lead they'd ever had. Spear had been on the international radar for quite some time, but no one had ever gotten close to finding out who he was.

"She was keeping fairly close contact," Noah said, "until she suddenly stopped. Now all we know is that she left the hotel with Dawson. Allison, as you can imagine, is quite concerned."

"We need to find her and pull her out, then?" Marco asked.

Noah looked him in the eye. "You're assuming she's even receptive to coming back."

Marco stared back, trying not to accept the subtlety of his meaning. Neil, Gary and Jenny looked at one another, then turned their own attention to Noah.

"We have to accept the possibility that she might not be," Noah said. "The fact that she left with Dawson and didn't bother to check in with any of us could mean that she doesn't intend to come in. They could even mean that she's already told him what's going on, about all of us."

"I can't believe that," Marco said. "She'd never do something like that of her own free will. Could Dawson be drugging her?"

Noah looked at Neil, who shrugged. "She seemed perfectly lucid on the security video as they were leaving," he said. "I saw no sign that she was coerced, drugged or under any other kind of duress."

"Maybe that's a signal in itself," Marco said. "Maybe she was hoping you'd see that, realize that she was being forced to keep up an act to survive."

"We're not going to write her off just yet, Marco," Noah said. "The trouble is, we have to get this settled relatively soon. Unfortunately..." He trailed off without finishing his sentence.

"What, Noah?" Marco asked, staring at him. "What is it that you're not saying?"

"According to Doctor Parker, when one of our people suddenly becomes noncommunicative, it generally means they've turned traitor. It's quite possible that Renée is actively working against us even now."

"What?" Marco's eyes narrowed, and he shook his head vigorously. "Oh, no," he said, his Cajun accent raging to the forefront again. "I *gar-on-tee* she not gonna do nutting along dem lines!"

"Marco, we believe you," Neil said. "The only problem is that even Allison has to report to people, the oversight committees and such. If they get the idea that one of our people has gone rogue..."

Noah looked at his team, at their silent but grave faces. They all knew what that meant. If Renée was thought to be a traitor, it would be Team Camelot who would be ordered to either capture or eliminate her.

"I know her better than any of you," Marco said, "and I'm telling you, she would never do such a thing. It ain't even a possibility, Noah."

"No," Neil stated, quietly but firmly. "I agree with Marco. She is completely trustworthy."

Noah looked at him for a moment. "We've been given a week to prove Renée is not a turncoat. But it cannot interfere with our current mission. We still need all the information Dawson can give us, anything that can help us to identify and eliminate Spear."

"What do you suggest, Noah?" Neil asked.

"Marco," Noah said, "when we do find her, you'll need to be the one to go and find out what's going on. We'll cover you, but Renée is more likely to talk to you than any of us." Noah looked at the window for a moment. It looked like it might rain. "We have to find out what's going on before this gets out of our control."

"Noah," Gary said, "do you really think that's wise? Dawson has seen Marco several times, albeit in different disguises."

Noah nodded. "I'm afraid it's necessary," he said. "Gary, you need to work your magic with him. It will need to look as different as possible from any of the disguises he used before."

Gary clicked his teeth and looked nervous. "I'll do what I can," he said.

"We'll do fine," Marco said. "How soon do you want me to go looking for her?"

"There is no point in looking until we get a lead on where she might be," Noah said. He then added, "I can't emphasize enough how dangerous this is, Marco." He hesitated. "If we find out that Renée has gone rogue on us..."

"Noah," Marco began, but he couldn't seem to find the words to complete whatever he was trying to say.

"You need to understand something, Marco." He spoke firmly, actually addressing them all. "We all need to get this right in our heads. As unlikely as it is, if it turns out to be true, we will have no choice but to eliminate the problem."

"Noah, are you saying we would have to kill her?" Marco asked.

"Yes." Noah looked from Marco to Gary to Neil and then to

Jenny. "If Renée does prove to be a traitor, Marco, we will have to kill her."

Marco stared at him. "Noah, there has to be an explanation. There's no way I could..."

"You won't have to," Noah said. "It's my responsibility, if it comes to that. All I want you to do is try to find out what's going on with her. If there's any hope of bringing her back, it's probably going to be because of you."

Marco looked at him for a few seconds longer, then shook his head and lowered his eyes to the floor. He and Renée had become very close over the past few months, and it was understood that they were intending to be married. Everyone knew it, and the whole team had accepted her as if she were family.

But now, she was being accused of treachery and treason. When they found her, he was expected to go in, understand the situation, and if Renée really had somehow turned traitor— which he did not believe for even a moment—he was to report that fact back to Noah, which would mean he would be signing her death warrant. He simply couldn't imagine what life would be like without her, and he certainly couldn't believe he would ever be the one to cause her death.

His eyes closed. The very thought of betraying her that way was more than he could handle.

Another day passed, and then another. As each one went by without any further leads, Marco felt his hopes weakening, and nothing the others could say was making him feel any better.

TWELVE

Noah's phone rang and he saw that it was Allison calling. It was the fourth time he had spoken to her that day.

"Camelot," he said as he answered.

"Camelot, report." Allison's voice was as clipped as ever.

"We are trying to ascertain what might have happened to Renée," Noah said. "Everything started off according to plan, but the second day into her mission, she stopped communicating with us. She has now been missing for more than four days, and we're doing everything we can to try to track down where she and Dawson may have gone. At this point, I'm not willing to believe that she's gone rogue; I suspect she may have needed some time to convince Dawson he could trust her. Until we know differently, I'm not going to assume that she's a security risk."

"Noah, I understand your reluctance," Allison said, "but I can't afford to lose your entire team."

"I'm aware of that," Noah said. "I'm just trying to be certain of what I'm dealing with before I make an official report. Marco, as soon as we locate her, is going to try to make contact. That should give us a concrete idea of whether she's salvageable or not."

"And if you determine that she cannot be salvaged?"

"I will then proceed accordingly," Noah said. "I understand the protocol, and if necessary, I will terminate her with extreme prejudice."

"Very good," Allison said. "In the meantime, I have another situation that I need to discuss with you. I'm transmitting some pictures to your phone, can you see them?"

Noah put her on speaker and called up the pictures that had come in by SMS. "I see them," he said.

"Dr. Harold Simpson. According to our intel, he's an extremely wealthy orthopedic surgeon who lives in Melbourne, Australia, but he also has a practice here in the United States. The NSA has asked us to arrange for him to have an accident. They believe that he may be deeply involved with Spear, to the point that a lot of his money might be supporting what Spear and his organization are doing. Trying to put a stop to him through conventional channels has been failing for more than a year, because his lawyers seem to intimidate everyone, including judges on both sides of the ocean. He's considered a very serious threat, and he arrived in Atlanta two days ago."

"Do you have his location?" Noah asked.

"You know as much about him as I do, at the moment. Hell, maybe more. The main reason they want us to eliminate him is because there is a lot of concern that he could actually displace Spear and become even more of a problem. While we can't prove it to the satisfaction of a court of law, there is an awful lot of evidence that he has been involved in a number of high-profile assassinations."

"Assassinations? And the NSA is certain about that?"

"That's what they tell me, yes," Allison said. "The problem is that they have a couple of witnesses who claim he's arranging an assassination right now, that this is what he's doing in the States at the moment."

"Who?" Noah asked. "Any idea?"

"The target? One of three, according to chatter: John Stansberry, head of the truckers union; Albert Linden from Liondale

Pharmaceutical Company; or, and this is the one that we are most afraid of, Congressman Barton Sneed, who sits on the House Ways and Means committee. All of them are involved in some important negotiations with countries in the East, and will probably be helpful in getting the treaties we want. Somebody else wants to make sure those treaties don't happen, so they've approached Doctor Simpson about making sure they don't." She paused and said, "Ironically, Simpson and all three of the potential victims are going to be at a reception tonight, right there in Atlanta. Caleb Dawson is also on the guest list."

"What time is the reception?" Noah asked, his eyes opening wide. "And where?"

"It's set for seven p.m. at the Royal Crown Convention Center. I already arranged your invitations, under your mission identities, and they are waiting for you at the front desk of your hotel." She paused for a couple of seconds, then went on. "This might give you the chance to confirm whether Renée has turned on us as well. If she's sticking close to Dawson, she'll probably be with him tonight."

"I had the same thought," Noah said. "If nothing else, it might create an opportunity for Marco to get close to her and get her to talk."

"That would be great if you can pull it off," Allison said. "But remember, your primary mission is to eliminate Simpson. With him gone, his companies will go into a tailspin, and most of the criminal community will be scrambling to try to salvage whatever position they can. It could give us a breather while we work on taking out Spear."

"Once we find Renée, I'm going to make sure we stay on top of her. I'm not going to risk letting her get away again. I would say the odds are good that she and Dawson can still lead us to Spear, and he is our primary target. Eliminating Dawson, and Renée if necessary, can wait until after we've taken him down."

"I'm in agreement with you on that," Allison said. "And,

Noah? If there's any way to save her, do it. Even if it means we have to lock her up back here for a while, I'd rather have her alive."

"I'll do what I can," Noah said, and then the line went dead as it always did when Allison was done talking.

———

THE RECEPTION WAS A LAVISH AFFAIR, with music, dancing, food, attractive socialites and well-dressed men trying to impress them. Noah had encouraged Gary to do everything he could to disguise them, and the results had been surprisingly good.

Champagne glass in hand, wearing an uncomfortable tuxedo, a beard and a dental appliance that made his mouth look strange, Noah stood quietly near the back of the room and kept his eyes on the crowd. He had not yet seen Dawson or Renée, but with over five hundred guests wandering through the place, it was difficult to focus his attention completely. Noah had shaken dozens of hands and forced himself to laugh at some very stupid jokes.

Even with all the distractions, he was keeping his eyes open for Doctor Simpson. When the man arrived, he was prepared to do whatever was necessary to calmly take him out, preferably without drawing excessive attention to himself or his team.

Not drawing attention was made easier by the fact that Noah now looked like a man nearly 30 years older than he truly was. His hair was long and gray, and the beard he was wearing, though neatly trimmed, had the slightly scraggly look that gray whiskers always seem to take on. Combined with the false teeth, it was highly doubtful that anyone he knew would recognize him, including possibly his own wife.

Neil, in disguise after his picture was on the newspaper clipping Dawson had seen, was a short distance across the room from him with Jenny, looking like the young entrepreneur couple they were supposed to be. Neil's cover was that he was a Silicon Valley tech billionaire, with Jenny as his wife. They were mingling with the other guests, and Noah suspected they were fending off a number of requests for investment into various ventures.

Gary and Marco had resumed their earlier disguises, with Gary back in his wheelchair, looking like he was already knocking on death's door. Noah couldn't help admiring the way Gary would cough and pick up his oxygen mask from time to time, maintaining the illusion that he was an elderly man with breathing problems. Marco was dressed as his caretaker once again, pulling off the same effeminate persona he had used before. The illusion that the old man in the wheelchair was someone wealthy and powerful would account for why they would be at such a reception.

"Marco to Noah," Noah heard in his subcom. "Gary and I are in position where we can watch the main entrance. I'll give you a heads-up if I see them."

"Roger that," Noah replied softly. "Everybody else, keep your eyes peeled as well. We may only get one chance to talk to her, so be prepared to create a diversion to break her free from Dawson for a few seconds. Jenny, you might be our best bet for that. Dawson hasn't seen you, yet, so there is less chance of you being recognized than any of us."

"Understood," Jenny said. "Should I spill a drink on him?"

"I don't know that that would do it. We need to find something that will engage his attention completely for at least a minute or so. That's going to be critical."

Noah glanced over toward where Neil and Jenny were standing, and that was when he saw Renée, making her entrance with Dawson right beside her.

Noah watched as the hostess greeted Renée with a smile, even giving Dawson a gentle kiss on the cheek. Renée was lovely as usual, dressed in a stunning green gown, her red hair pulled back away from her face into a sophisticated coiffure. A brilliant diamond necklace adorned her throat, matched by the earrings that dangled from her lobes. Noah looked for signs of nervousness, perhaps even an indication of mental or physical abuse, and although Renée seemed like she might be feeling a little uncomfortable, she did not appear to be under duress.

"They're here," Noah said. "Came in the side entrance, apparently. They seem to be talking with the hostess, so see what you can do, Jenny. Marco, you're on."

"No problem," Marco said. He began wheeling Gary toward where Renée and Dawson were standing.

Jenny put down her drink and leaned over to Neil for a second, whispering, "Be ready on my signal." He barely nodded as she turned and walked away, headed directly for Caleb Dawson.

Renée spotted her first, and her eyes met hers for only a second, then looked away pointedly as Jenny headed straight toward the man standing next to her.

"You," Jenny said loudly. "I know you, don't I? Aren't you the son of a bitch that cut me off when I was pulling into the parking lot a little while ago?"

Dawson's eyebrows rose as he looked at the short blonde who was bearing down on him. "I'm sorry," he said. "I have absolutely no idea what you're talking about."

"About twenty minutes ago," Jenny said angrily. "You were driving the flashy red Ferrari, right? I was just about to turn in when you cut across in front of me. I had to slam on the brakes and the car behind me couldn't stop in time, so I got hit. I hope you've got good insurance, you jerk, because I plan to file a claim based on your reckless driving."

Dawson tried a smile as if he was hoping to defuse the situation and draw less attention to himself. "Now I know you're mistaken," he said. "I arrived by limousine, just a few moments ago. I don't even own an automobile, much less a Ferrari. Please, my dear lady, let me buy you a drink and we can all settle back down."

"Settle down?" Jenny asked, her eyes wide and her face angry. "You lying piece of filth, I'm not going to calm down! My husband and I could've been badly injured because of your stupidity, and you're going to pay for it. Don't tell *me* to settle down..."

A number of people were turning to watch the altercation, and a few of them moved closer, just in case they might get to actually watch some kind of a fight. Marco maneuvered Gary's wheelchair carefully, but the encroaching crowd made it easier for him to let it bump into Renée, causing her to turn and look at them.

"Oh, so sorry, dear," Gary said in a thick southern drawl. "I'm afraid my man is a bit on the clumsy side this evening."

Renée smiled down at him, but then she waved a hand in dismissal.

"Oh, it's no problem," she said. "No problem at all." She turned back toward Dawson, ignoring them once again.

Marco stared at her. Disguise or no disguise, he had no doubt she would recognize him this close. Something was wrong, but he had no idea what it could be.

"I just—wanted to be sure you're okay," he said haltingly. "I didn't mean to run the wheelchair into you like that."

"I'm fine," she said, glancing back at him, "no problem, really." She put a smile back on her face. "I think you just got caught in the crush of the crowd."

Marco looked her in the eye for a moment, then nodded once and pushed Gary on past. As he moved away, he whispered, "Did you catch that, Noah?"

"I couldn't hear her," Noah said. "Her subcom is obviously still off and your volume is too low. What did she have to say?"

"She didn't even recognize me, Noah. I mean, not at all. How in the hell could she not even recognize me after as long as we been together?"

Noah thought about it for a moment. "There are two possibilities I can think of," he said. "The first is that whatever the situation, she's afraid that acknowledging you even slightly might give her away. The other possibility..."

"Yeah? What's the other one?"

"I'm not sure yet. Let's observe for a bit, but remember to keep your eyes out for Doctor Simpson."

From the corner of her eye, Jenny saw Marco push the wheelchair away. "So you're serious?" she asked, letting a little of the anger slip out of her voice. "You honestly don't have a car?"

Dawson let his smile grow a little wider. "I promise you, dear lady, the only cars I own are a couple of scale models on the shelf in my home. And just for the record, neither of them is a Ferrari."

She looked him in the eye for a few seconds, then visibly relaxed. "All right," she said, "then I must apologize. I hope you'll forgive me, but you do look very much like whoever the fellow was driving the Ferrari. I was almost certain it was you, but apparently I was mistaken." She held a hand behind her back and wiggled her fingers to signal Neil to come closer.

THIRTEEN

Neil joined them a moment later and Jenny turned to him. "Honey, you were right," she said. "This wasn't the guy in the Ferrari."

Neil grinned at Dawson. "I tried to tell her," he said, "but she gets pretty stubborn sometimes." He held out a hand. "Jason Turner," he said. "I'm truly sorry that my wife accosted you this way."

Dawson shook his hand and smiled. "Harold Lancaster," he said. "It's all fine, I assure you."

Renée turned back toward them, and Neil let his eyes drift over to her.

Dawson saw where his attention was located and said, "Mr. Turner. May I introduce Ms. Willis?"

Neil smiled at Renée. "Ms. Willis, it's so good to see you again," he said. "We should apologize to you, as well. Caroline didn't really mean to make a scene, but it turns out it was simply a case of mistaken identity."

Renée only stared at him, her eyes wide and looking a little frightened. It lasted only a moment, but it was obvious that the whole situation had caught her off guard. Neil was surprised, but he kept his expression blank and friendly.

Dawson looked at Neil curiously. "You know each other?" he asked.

"Oh, yes," Neil said. "Not well, but Ms. Willis was my assistant in London for a short time. I don't recall the name of the temp agency you were working for, Ms. Willis, but I do remember that you were the most efficient assistant they ever sent me." He smiled broadly at her. "And now that I think of it, you owe me a dance."

"I—I do?" Renée asked.

"Why, yes. You remember, you accompanied me to the unveiling of our new computer system at Whitehall, and we were so busy with all of the questions we never got to participate in the festivities. You promised me a dance the next time we had the opportunity, and here we are." He waved his hands to indicate the dance floor, where an orchestra was playing while couples danced, then held out his arm. "Shall we?" He looked around at Jenny for just a second and she smiled, and then he turned back to Renée.

Renée glanced at Dawson, who looked slightly annoyed, but nodded, and then slipped her hand into the crook of Neil's elbow. She let him lead her onto the dance floor as the orchestra began to play a waltz.

"Now, don't expect too much," Neil said. "I'm afraid I'm still not that good a dancer."

"Oh, I'm sure it'll be fine," Renée said. "And I need you to forgive me, but I really don't remember working with you. How long ago was it?"

"Oh, a couple of years," Neil replied. "I suppose I should be offended, but I'm not really all that surprised. I suppose I'm just not really all that memorable."

Renée smiled and did not object when he held her a little closer. He had his face over her right shoulder, and it took him a moment to realize that something was troubling him. He looked at her out of the corner of his eye, taking in her hair and ear, and that's when it hit him.

Each member of Team Camelot had a subcom inserted

against the bone of the skull just behind the right ear. Each of them had the scar, a two centimeter incision that had been repaired with surgical adhesive rather than stitches. It made the scar small and almost invisible, but not quite.

This woman had no scar. He looked more closely at her hairline, and it dawned on him that she was wearing a mask. It was excellent, the skin tone and texture perfect, but it was still a mask. As he stared at the line, he realized that her hair was also dyed; blonde roots were just barely beginning to show.

The woman he was dancing with and embracing was not Renée. This was an imposter.

He didn't say anything, simply continued to dance and make small talk until the music ended, then walked her back to where Dawson was waiting.

"I must thank you, sir," he said. "That was a dance that was long overdue." He leaned forward conspiratorially. "Of course, it would've been nice if she at least remembered me."

Dawson smiled. "I think we all run into that from time to time," he said. "Each of us hopes to be memorable, don't you think? That way, we'll never be forgotten."

"Of course," Neil said. He turned to Jenny. "We should go, darling." He turned back to Dawson for a moment. "We seem to be popular among those who are seeking financing, and Caroline doesn't know how to say no as well as I can. I need to keep a close eye on her." He extended a hand and Dawson shook with him, and then he turned to Renée. "Ms. Willis, it was delightful to see you again." With that, the two of them turned and walked away.

Noah had been watching the entire encounter, and he stayed focused as Dawson turned toward Renée. The man said something Noah could not overhear, and Renée looked startled. She recovered quickly, however, and the two of them walked into the crowd as if nothing had happened.

"Neil, how did she seem to you?" Noah asked.

"At first, I was a little puzzled," Neil said. "She seemed scared for a moment there, as if she was afraid we were going to give her away, somehow. I thought maybe if I got her away from Dawson, she'd let me know what was going on, but I'm afraid it's worse than that."

"I think I know what you're going to say," Noah said. "That isn't Renée at all, is it?" He paused for a moment. "You got any kind of bug you can tag her with? Something they wouldn't detect, that would let us keep track of her location?"

"Not with me. If she would turn on a cell phone, I could possibly hack into it and track its GPS. That way, we could keep pretty close tabs on her."

His mind racing with possibilities, Noah looked over at Dawson and the woman who was impersonating Renée, or Abigail Willis, to be more precise. They were talking with another man, and Noah suddenly realized that it was in fact Doctor Simpson, who had finally arrived. The conversation appeared pleasant, if perhaps a bit formal. Simpson actually seemed to be impatient to talk with Dawson alone.

Noah thought it was interesting that his two targets were suddenly deep in conversation. The fake Renée was sent to fetch drinks or something, and the two men had moved to the side to try to get a moment of privacy.

"Marco to Noah," Noah heard. "You see them?"

"I'm watching," Noah said. "I wish I could hear them."

"I can," Marco said. "I have the little shotgun microphone up my sleeve, and it's plugged into an earbud. Let me turn it on and you can listen in."

There was a rustling noise, and then suddenly Noah could hear Dawson's voice, somewhat distorted through Marco's subcom. When Marco had put the earbud into his ear, it allowed the subcom to pick up the sounds coming from it when he aimed his wrist toward Dawson.

"... I got the job done, didn't I? Nobody gave me any instructions about making it look like an accident."

"We employ you, Mr. Lancaster," said a voice that had to be Simpson, "because you are supposed to be one of the best. It would seem to me that gaining that reputation would have required you to make reasonable decisions about some of your contracts. Why is it that you seem incapable of making such decisions when you're working for us?"

"I don't get that many complaints," Dawson said. "If you would prefer that I not work for you anymore, I would not necessarily find that objectionable. I wonder, though, how the Director would feel about it? I have been with him quite a bit longer than you, or the rest of the Council, for that matter."

Simpson glared at him. "I never said anything about letting you go," he said. "Don't think, however, that you are somehow indispensable. I have others who do the same kind of work you do, and while they may not be as creative as you are, they have yet to cause me any undue stress. The Director will probably discuss this with you when you see him, anyway. I just thought you might like to know that the Council is not pleased with your grandstanding."

"Duly noted," Dawson said. "Goodbye, Doctor Simpson. I shall give the Director your best wishes."

He turned and walked away, and Noah watched for a moment, then turned back and gave his attention to Simpson. As much as he preferred to take his targets more privately, Allison's orders were to eliminate Simpson at the earliest possible opportunity. It probably wasn't going to get much more convenient than this.

A lot of things were happening, and it would be up to Noah to try to figure it all out. And the worst of it was the fact that even Noah was troubled as he considered what might've happened to the real Renée.

Unfortunately, he did not have time to worry about that at the moment. He kept his eyes on Simpson and considered his next move carefully.

"Noah to Neil," he said. "I need a diversion. Keep your eyes on me and wait till I get close to Simpson, then make sure everyone is looking in your direction."

"Sure, boss," Neil said. "That's me, Mr. Diversion. What do you want me to do?"

"I'll handle it," Jenny cut in suddenly. "Go ahead, Noah, we got this under control."

"All right," Noah said as he pushed away from the wall and started toward Doctor Simpson. The man was talking to a young woman, and the expression on his face made it clear that he was definitely on the prowl. Noah continued toward them, then stopped just a couple of feet away from where Simpson stood.

"You son of a bitch!" he heard from behind him, and he recognized Jenny's voice. "How could you sleep with her? How could you do that to me?"

"But, baby, I..." That was Neil.

"I trusted you, you ass! I trusted you, and this is how you repay me!"

It was working. Everyone in the entire hall was looking toward the couple who seemed to be having some sort of massive argument in the middle of the floor. When Noah glanced at them for a split second, then turned back toward his objective, Jenny reached out and slapped Neil across the face. The crack of the slap was heard throughout the room, and most of the men there cringed or put a hand to their own cheeks in sympathy.

Noah stepped up behind Simpson, who was also staring toward the argument. Noah reached into his jacket pocket and pulled out a syringe that he had prepared before leaving the hotel.

In a split second, he stepped up behind Simpson and jabbed the needle into the back of his neck. The highly potent chemical inside went to work instantly, disabling all of the nerves in the neck and working its way into the spinal cord. Simpson barely had time to react before he lost all motor control and collapsed to the floor. Unconsciousness came only a few seconds later.

It was almost a minute before anyone realized that the man was down, and somebody started CPR on the assumption that he had suffered a heart attack.

———

THE ENTIRE TEAM had made it out before the police and ambulance arrived, and had returned to their hotel. They were gathered in Noah's room, trying to decide on a plan of action, but it was difficult to think of one.

"Are we just going to assume she's dead?" Marco asked, his expression dark as he adjusted the audio receiver sitting on the small breakfast area tabletop in their hotel room.

"What would be the point in keeping her alive?" Gary asked, although he appeared unhappy with his own questions. He sat on the bottom corner of Noah's bed, tension obvious in the way he was sitting. The actor seemed subdued, even though he had not known Renée nearly as long as the rest of them.

Noah sat across the table from Marco. He was leaning back in his chair, thinking very hard about what they had learned, and what it could possibly mean. "They don't know that much about Abigail Willis. That much is clear."

Neil nodded. "That could mean one of two things. They tried to get information out of her, but she died before they could, which doesn't make sense, not for such an elaborate charade..."

"Or?" Marco asked, clutching the drink he had made for himself and looking at the skinny young man.

Noah beat him to it. "Or Renée is alive and feeding them only enough information to make it possible for this woman to impersonate her." He hesitated for a moment, as if thinking about what he had just said. "She knows that if any one of us should get close to her replacement, as Neil did, the substitution would become obvious very quickly. She would also know that we would be able to spot a mask."

"Then they must be keeping her somewhere," Marco said, a

bit more animated. "Unfortunately, we have no idea where that might be, and this is a good sized city."

"This just isn't making any sense," Neil said, shaking his head. "If Dawson figured out that Renée is a federal agent, why wouldn't he simply get rid of her and try to pretend he had no idea who she was? Why would he go to the trouble of setting up a double for her and taking the double out in public?"

"That's an interesting question," Noah said. "And a very astute one. If they are keeping her alive, then I'd have to suspect the double is simply to try to keep the rest of us thinking everything is going according to plan, somehow. I'm sure she wouldn't mention the subcom, so they have no way of realizing that it was missing."

"I hate to bring this up," Marco said, "but what does this do to our mission? How are we supposed to figure out what Dawson has planned?"

"I don't know," Noah said, "but we need to figure out some way to stay on them. Any idea where they might be staying now?"

"Actually," Neil said, "I just happen to have gotten that information. See, after Simpson was discovered, the police were called. Dawson didn't get out fast enough, so he had to produce identification and let the police know where he is staying. I got into the computer at the Renaissance Days Hotel and verified that they are staying there, and I saw them on the hotel's security camera system. They're in room six forty-one."

Noah looked at him. "What do you think is the possibility they may have Renée there, as well?"

Neil bit his bottom lip. "I suppose it's possible," he said. "I saw the two of them walk out of the other hotel, but as far as I know, there are only two present at the Renaissance. If they have her there, they must be keeping her drugged or something."

Noah nodded. "I agree," he said. "But we won't know unless we go check. Neil, I want you and Gary to stay here and watch their hallway on the video. Marco, Jenny and I are headed over there to see if they have her. Let us know, once we are in place, when it's safe to go in."

"I'll have the van waiting," Marco said, and hurried out of the room.

Neil nodded at the other team members and smiled nervously. After all, their next move was predicated on the assumption that Renée was the enemy's prisoner and not a dead woman.

FOURTEEN

"Spectacular," Noah murmured. He was only talking to himself, overwhelmed by the architectural beauty about him. The Renaissance Days Hotel was actually more than a hundred years old, and the original construction had been preserved and restored. At one time, it had been one of the biggest hotels in the city of Atlanta. It was still one of the most impressive.

"Okay, they just left the room," Neil said. "Stay out of sight and I'll let you know if they leave the building or not."

"All right," Noah said. He motioned for Marco and Jenny to follow, and they slipped into the gift shop that was just off the lobby. It was packed with a lot of merchandise, and it was easy to hide behind the shelves and racks. A moment later, they spotted Dawson and Renée's double crossing the lobby and walking out the door.

"Okay, they're gone," Neil said. "They just got into a taxi and it's pulled away. You should have at least an hour."

"Roger that," Noah said. He collected the other two by eye and they left the gift shop and headed toward the elevator.

Marco made short work of the lock, using a device made for picking card-based security locks. He slipped a card into the slot, then turned on the keypad he held in his hand. A series of numbers lit up across the top, and he punched them in. The lock clicked, the light went green, and they hurried inside.

Renée was on one of the beds, lying on her side and apparently sleeping peacefully. She was pale and seemed a little too thin, Noah thought, but at least she was alive.

Jenny climbed onto the bed beside her and began to shake her, trying to wake her up while Marco climbed up on the other side. "Renée? Renée, come on, honey, it's Jenny."

"Jenny," Renée whispered. She barely got her eyes open and found Marco leaning over her, then managed a ghost of a smile. "I knew you would come," she said. "I knew it." Her eyes closed again and she slipped back into an obviously drug-induced sleep.

"Let's go, let's get her out of here," Noah said. "Marco, you take her down the service stairs. Jenny and I will go ahead and run interference."

Marco scooped her up and held her as if she was nothing while Noah and Jenny opened the door and Jenny peeked outside. She motioned for them to follow and hurried out into the hallway, then headed toward the elevators and the stairwell door.

Noah went down first, followed by Marco carrying Renée, with Jenny bringing up the rear. It took them a couple of minutes to get all the way down the six flights, and then they stepped out the service entrance of the building. Marco had parked the van they were using only a short distance away, and he ran briskly toward it.

Marco and Renée were inside by the time Noah and Jenny got to the vehicle. Noah climbed behind the wheel and started it up, and they were on the road only a moment later.

"Okay, you're all clear," Neil said. "I scrubbed the security video, so nobody will ever even know you were there."

"He'll know," Noah said. "The shape Renée is in, there's no way she got out alone. He'll know."

Renée gulped slightly as her eyes fluttered open. At first, she could not believe what she was seeing. "Noah?" she asked, her voice unbelieving. No, it wasn't possible, she thought, and nearly cried out at Dawson, telling him to stop tormenting her. "Marco..."

"Yes, it's me." He took her by the upper arms and helped her to sit upright. He smiled warmly at her disbelieving expression. His smile widened slightly as an uncertain hand lifted to touch his jaw and cheek, as if she too were searching for a mask, the fingers drawing a line up to his temple. "Are you all right?" he asked.

"Oh, Marco!" Renée threw herself into his arms, now fully recognizing her teammate and lover, grateful for his presence and so pleased that she had held on to her resolve. She had known they would come for her and—somehow—Renée also knew Marco would be the person she would see first upon awakening. "Oh, Marco, I..." she began, but he silenced her with a kiss.

Marco touched her hair, silently leaning forward to kiss her once again, and looked into Renée's exhausted eyes. He could not begin to guess what Dawson and his imposter had done to her, but it was obvious that she had been through some sort of ordeal. He would ask her about it later. At the moment, escape was paramount. "Can you move?" he asked her.

"Yes." With his help, she sat up and leaned against the side wall of the van. She teetered for a moment, feeling dizzy and spent, but his arm holding her steady gave her strength. "What are we going to do now?" she asked, still groggy.

———

"THIS WAS UNEXPECTED," the woman said, standing beside Dawson as they entered the now empty room. "I find it stunning, after all we did to her, that she managed an escape."

"Yes." Dawson stood behind her, placing his hands on her shoulders.

"Do you think her friends came and helped her?"

"Undoubtedly, although they obviously want us to think she did it on her own." It appeared as though Ms. Willis had simply awakened and managed to walk off while they were gone, but he was certain she was not capable of it. At least, she shouldn't have been, not after that last dosage, not to mention everything else she had been through; she couldn't possibly have had enough will to escape on her own. "It doesn't really matter how she got away, Michelle. The fact is that she's gone, so we need to make our own exit."

His hands touched Michelle's auburn hair and caressed her pale cheek. Pleased by his attention now that the redhead was gone, Michelle chuckled and allowed Dawson to turn her around to face him. She leaned forward for a kiss, and was not disappointed.

"Of course," he said afterward, "this does change a few things. Since we know they have her back, we certainly can't have two of her running around now, can we?"

"That's not a problem," Michelle said. "I'm sick of wearing that mask and wig, anyway."

"I'm sure, but that doesn't solve the entire problem. The fact that they have her means that they are aware that you were merely a doppelgänger. It's unlikely they will leave you alone; if you make an appearance anywhere around them, they are certain to do all they can to capture you. They'll want to break you, make you talk."

She looked at him and smiled, nervously. "You know I won't talk, right? Even if they were to get me, I won't say a word."

"I know," Dawson said. He leaned forward and kissed her again, and his hands closed around her throat as he did so.

She struggled. He liked it when they struggled, it made it more personal and intense for him.

Besides, everything was in place. He really didn't need her talents anymore.

———

THEY GOT BACK to the hotel at just before sunset and Renée assured them that, although she was fatigued, she felt well. Neil insisted, however, on checking her over personally. She had been drugged, as they had suspected, but it didn't look like it would have any lasting consequences.

After a good night's sleep, she would be up for breakfast and questioning.

Marco was the first person to suggest sending her back to Neverland, but Renée refused. After all, Renée reasoned, she was still an agent and since the mission was still in progress—and it did not seem she was compromised—she wanted to see it through.

"Besides," she said, settled into an arm chair and drinking a cup of tea before she turned in. "I have an idea."

Noah contacted Allison to let her know what had happened, and Allison reluctantly agreed to let her finish out the mission.

"Noah," she said privately to him, "just keep an eye on her. If anything seems off, you know what to do."

"Yes," he said. "Bring her back, alive, unless doing so would jeopardize the mission."

"Exactly. And if it does..."

"Then I will terminate her."

———

NEIL TOOK FIRST WATCH that night, and was relieved by Gary at two a.m. Gary was gone when breakfast was brought up by room service the following morning, and the rest of them all gathered in Noah's room to eat.

Renée ate ravenously: eggs, bacon, potatoes, cereal, orange juice and coffee. She was up an hour before the others and had forgotten how glorious it was to eat what she wanted when she wanted it. She winced at the thought of the scraped together doggy bags her abductors brought her to eat while she was held captive. No doubt it contained a narcotic of some kind, something to keep her quiet, but it was all they allowed her to eat, no matter how badly it was mushed together. The previous night, she had missed even that. Renée blinked and paused many times while she devoured her meal, thinking about what it had been like: the fear, anger and bewilderment. She had questioned her oppressors, but they never replied. Renée recalled being tied to a chair and questioned in rapid succession, giving them yes and no answers even as she tried not to.

Then, that woman had roughly covered her face with plaster for a mask mold. Renée had felt trapped under the heavy coating, trying to breathe, feeling closed off and frightened, but trying as hard as she could to hold onto her courage.

She had thought often of Marco when her thoughts would manage to become lucid for a moment. She actually wondered whether she would ever see him again.

"How are you feeling?" Noah asked.

She sat up straight, a bit startled, and looked over at him, then smiled. "Good morning." He brought the coffee pot over to their dining table and poured himself a cup. Marco, of course, was sitting beside her.

Renée had showered, changed clothes, and applied a little makeup. Her eyes seemed a bit vague, but brighter than the night before, he thought. She also seemed fragile in the same way as a patient often was while healing after a long illness. "Do you feel up to some questions?" he inquired, sitting in a chair at the closest corner to Renée. When she nodded, he asked, "When were you taken?"

"The day after we left this hotel. We went to that big one because he said he wanted to show me some of the finer things in life." She rolled her eyes. "We had gone that morning, to meet some guy who said Dawson was being sent to Sydney for a job, and it was on the way back when he said we were moving. I never got a chance to get alone and let you know, and then when we got to the new hotel, that woman was waiting. He said she was a friend, and she offered me a cup of tea. We sat down to drink some and I started feeling strange, and that's when he told me that Joshua had texted him in the car, telling him that I was an agent of the United States. I tried to laugh it off, but the woman, Michelle, held out her phone and showed a picture of me from back when I worked at the CIA." She shook her head. "I didn't even know there was such a picture. That was the last thing I remember until the next morning."

"Honey, why didn't you have your subcom on?" Marco asked. "At least we would've known what was happening, we could have come to you sooner."

Renée turned to look at him, biting her bottom lip for a second before she spoke. "He was spending a lot of time close to me," she said softly. "Like, really close. Sometimes he would lay close behind me and put his head right on top of me, right on my ear. I couldn't take the chance that one of you might say something and he could pick it up through conduction, because his ear was right against mine. I just thought it was a good idea to keep it off except when I needed it, and when I finally started to wake up, my watch was gone. I couldn't exactly search the room or call the desk for a Wi-Fi password, so I was basically screwed." She shrugged. "For what it's worth, I did turn it on a few times just to see if I might hear somebody, but there was never anything there."

"What were they doing to you?" Noah asked. He lifted the coffee cup to his mouth and looked over the brim.

Renée looked sideways at him. "Lots of questions and for the longest time, I ignored that picture and just stayed in character, told them only the script I was given. But honestly, with the drugs and everything, I have big gaps in my memory. I slept, woke and slept again. I can't really remember much during that time. Dawson told me once that I was a very strong woman, almost too strong to serve their purpose, but I could never get out of him what exactly that purpose was." She looked directly at Marco. "To be honest, I think Dawson and Michelle merely wanted me to give them as much information as I could about myself. The clues I gathered—with the limited information I had—make me think that Michelle, wearing a mask with my face, was going to kill someone and disappear. Then, when they let me go, *I* would be blamed for the murder. I know they were expecting me to be blamed for one, anyway." She shivered, her fingers clenching from where her hand lay on the tabletop. Renée felt Marco reach for her, his hand warm against her own as it rested on the table.

"I suppose that could make some kind of sense," Noah said, but he felt there had to be more to it. Something seemed out of place or unfinished but, like Renée, he could not quite put his finger on it.

"What about the job in Sydney? Do you have any idea what it was about, or who the target could be?"

Renée grimaced, deep in thought for a moment, but then shook her head. "I can't remember," she said. "I think I might have known, but now I can't remember any of the details."

The door to the dining room opened at that moment and Marco's fingers slipped away from hers.

Gary entered, engaged in an animated conversation with Neil and Jenny, who were right behind him. They greeted Renée warmly, pleased by how well she looked.

"We have an update," Neil said to Noah, cutting Gary off. "Dawson is gone. Gary followed him to the airport, and he got on a flight to Sydney."

"Sydney?" Renée asked.

"That's where they went," Gary replied. "Am I missing something?"

"Yes," Noah said. "That's where his next assignment is." He looked at Gary again. "What about his lady friend?"

"No sign of her," Gary said. "Just Dawson, all alone. I even looked over the rest of the people at the concourse who were waiting for the same flight, but there was no one there that could have been her."

"Then she's probably dead," Noah said. "He wouldn't want to take the chance she might be captured, she knows too much." He closed his eyes for a moment as if he were deep in thought, then shook his head and looked up again. "Renée? Was there anything particular about her that he might want to keep us from learning?"

Renée looked into his eyes for a few seconds, then shrugged her shoulders. "Noah, I really didn't have that much to do with her after she made the mask. I mean, I vaguely remember her being there talking to me sometimes, but it's in that gray area of my memory, because of the drugs. I couldn't really say if there was anything special about her at all."

Noah reported to Allison that Dawson had taken off for Australia, and they were ordered to follow. Fortunately, the Gulfstream was waiting at the airport and could be fueled and ready by the time they arrived. They quickly packed their bags and headed out, and all of them were able to sleep during the long flight.

Shortly before they landed, Noah received a call.

"Camelot," he answered.

"It's Allison," she said unnecessarily, fully aware that Noah's caller ID would tell him it was her. "We have a lead that may pay off for you. Somebody at the CIA picked up a little bit of information that indicates Dawson will be meeting Spear tonight in Sydney. The meeting is taking place at the U.S. Embassy there, and arrangements have already been made for you to attend. There is an embassy ball, and we have reason to believe that Dawson's target will also be present. Unfortunately, we don't know yet who it is."

"All right," Noah said. "We'll handle it. Of course, we'll have to be disguised once again. Dawson has seen all of us up close now, and more than once."

"Do what you have to do," Allison said. "This is your chance, Noah, to take Spear down once and for all. And don't miss Dawson, while you're at it. Donald deserves vengeance, as well."

"I won't," he said, but the line had already gone dead.

FIFTEEN

As Allison had promised, all the arrangements were made before they arrived. A car was waiting for them and took them to a hotel near the embassy, so they could rest for the remainder of the day and get freshened up. Clothes were also brought to them, suitable for attending a ball, and they spent a good part of the afternoon discussing just how they intended to approach the situation.

Gary was tasked with coming up with new disguises. Jenny became a brunette with an overbite and an acne problem, and even Noah admitted he wouldn't recognize her if he ran into her on the street. Neil, almost impossible to disguise because of his height, actually got stuffing put in his shoes to make him two inches taller. Some padding around his middle and some fake muscles added to chest and arms improved the disguise, but it was the addition of the beard and shoulder-length flowing brown hair that transformed him the rest of the way.

"I look like a biker that's been dressed up for a funeral or something," he joked.

"Don't knock it," Jenny said. "I think you actually look pretty good."

Marco and Gary, who were about the same height, both

became bald. With a pair of glasses and a little bit of stuffing inside their cheeks, they were completely unrecognizable.

Noah decided to forgo any disguise. As it happened, the only times Dawson had seen him, he had been wearing a wig and makeup or even more; he thought that perhaps the best disguise was to simply go as himself.

That left only Renée, who also refused a disguise.

"All I need is a decent gown," she said. "This face is exactly the one I need to wear into this fancy soirée."

Nobody was inclined to argue with her.

THE TIME ARRIVED, and they all got ready to go. Once Noah, Jenny and Marco had already entered, Renée walked with her two companions, Neil and Gary, into the ballroom.

Noah watched as the ballroom filled with elegant patrons, high-class patricians, and society devotees. Purses and pockets were checked for potential weapons, but no one fussed too much about the inconvenience. With such influential V.I.P.s out and about, how could they? Besides, it was an honor just being invited to such an event.

Two of the three potential targets had already arrived. The Saudi Prince was speaking directly to the United States Ambassador, a man named Hunter Jamison, as he glanced out of the corner of his eye at the sumptuous buffet being catered by the embassy's efficient kitchen staff. A man named Patrick McNealy, a high-ranking official in the Australian banking industry, was talking to a young woman at the other end of the buffet, and the third possible target, an American congressman named Levine, was flirting with one of the caterers while his muscular bodyguards stood by, giving suspicious and furtive glances at anyone who approached their charge. So far, no one associated with Dawson was visible.

An elegant middle-aged lady with a reddish tint to her upswept hair approached Noah, dressed in a pale blue beaded gown. She lifted a gloved hand to shake his own. "Mr. Rogers from the United States?" she asked. At his nod, she continued, "I am Dolores. Jorge Montoya, who assists Daniel Wentworth, is my husband."

"Very pleased to meet you, Mrs. Montoya." Daniel Wentworth was the technology attaché of the embassy, but he was also the E & E liaison in Sydney.

"Jorge tells me that Daniel will be here soon. A pouch needed to be delivered and apparently he was held up somewhere nearby. It shouldn't take him very long."

An impressive orchestra started gentle, graceful music just as Renée, Gary and Neil arrived. Noah watched her as she politely parted from her escorts and started to work the room. She introduced herself as Abigail Willis and immediately shook hands, graciously curtsied or allowed the men to kiss her fingers as she spoke kindly but fleetingly with them. Noah knew the woman well enough to see that she was getting a feel for the guests, obtaining information, checking to see if they seemed to recognize her as an associate of Dawson.

She was professional and infinitely approachable, he thought. Not just her manner, but she was quite stunning, possibly the loveliest woman in the room. Renée was the type of woman the men did not just lust after; most of them also wanted their photographs taken with her. He could just imagine the stories they told their friends back home, lies about the passionate nights spent with this gorgeous lady.

Ambassador Prakov arrived with his bride, Ivania, on his arm. He appeared as composed as ever, but he smiled ever so slightly when she whispered something into his ear. She led him onto the dance floor and they moved in close, swaying together, as did others.

Gary came up beside Noah. "Any sign of Dawson?"

"Not yet."

Suddenly, his attention was back on Renée. The man who

had pulled her onto the dance floor was tall, dark and imposing. His hands were moving in directions less than proper. His style, the way he held her, was too demanding and Noah could tell from her expression that she was not overly happy with his manners. He looked across the room and made eye contact with Marco, who had also been watching the scene. The backup man quickly made his presence known, cutting in on the aggressive Lothario. Marco's size was too intimidating to say no to, and soon he danced gracefully with a grateful Renée. At a loss, the man turned about and walked to a set of impressive stained glass double doors.

"I'm going to question him." Noah left Gary to track Renée's belligerent would-be suitor. He began to wonder if Dawson had fitted himself with a new mask and might have made demands. He was certain, if that was the case, that Renée would have sent signals to one of her team members; in fact, her subcom was definitely on. Yet, she had been through so much lately, it would not surprise Noah if the woman was off her game where Dawson was concerned.

He followed the man out onto the ballroom's long, wrap-around balcony and casually approached him, offering him a cigar; a moment later, Noah discovered the man was simply another jerk, like so many others. He had drunk too much before arriving at the party and, seeing a woman he liked, demanded what was not his. Noah was a little disappointed that he had no reason to treat the man with anything other than disdain, considering the liberties he had taken with one of his people. Still, it was a good sign as well. So far, there were no real threats.

When he returned to the ballroom, he saw Renée dancing with Daniel Wentworth. The man had finally arrived and, although Noah found it curious that he immediately decided to contact Renée rather than himself, he did not question the choice. Wentworth was likely just pleased she was well enough to attend the party.

Marco came up behind Noah in the jamb of the double-doors. "He cut in on me," he said, "and seemed to have something important to say to her. His assistant Montoya made it clear I should let him have her."

Noah watched as Renée looked up at Wentworth and nodded. Montoya was standing off to one side, also watching them. Noah listened closely to the low sounds coming through her subcom and nodded.

"I think he might be telling her that Dawson is here somewhere."

His eyes darted about the ballroom, searching, but there was no obvious sign of the assassin. "He's nowhere in sight," he said, "and if he *is* here, it doesn't look like he has made any move whatsoever to approach any of the potential targets."

"Mr. Rogers."

Noah had been so focused on looking for Dawson that he didn't realize that Wentworth and Renée had stepped away from the dance floor and now joined him, with Montoya shadowing. He shook Wentworth's hand and nodded at Renée, then shook hands with Montoya as well. "Glad you were able to make it," he said to Wentworth.

"Is everything secure?" Wentworth asked.

"Yes, so far. What do you think Dawson is waiting for?"

"No idea," the man replied. "I'm just a paper pusher, though, you're the one who has to deal with the likes of him."

"Noah," Marco whispered through the subcom. "I just heard from Neil. He has some reason to believe the Saudi is the target. We need to get him out of here."

Noah was quick. "Marco, go to the Saudi Prince, show him your credentials, and get him away from this ballroom. Use force if you have to."

"I'm going to move Mr. McNealy out onto the balcony," Renée said. "He's another possibility."

Jenny suddenly appeared at Noah's elbow. "I'll take the congressman," she said. "He likes blondes, anyway."

"Go," Noah said and watched as his people dispersed throughout the ballroom. He turned his attention away from them to speak with Wentworth, but saw that the man had moved across the room as well, to talk with Ambassador Jamison. He then watched as Marco moved the seemingly cooperative prince across the ballroom, followed by his guards, and out the double doors into the foyer.

Noah spoke softly into his subcom. "Neil, keep your eyes on Wentworth, make sure nothing happens to him."

"On it," the tall, young man replied, looking around for the liaison.

Renée, her arm entwined in McNealy's, gently pulled him along. The youthful woman who had been his date was peeved, but was being spoken with by his guards, who were left to appease her.

Everything seemed to be going well until Neil lost sight of Mr. Wentworth. He was no longer near the ambassador, and in fact, he did not appear to be in the room at all. Neil nearly made a move toward the foyer when, instinctively, his eyes focused on the open doors to the balcony. Something intuitive rumbled up from his gut and he moved to follow Renée and McNealy as Jenny appeared at the opposite side of the room with Congressman Levine. He stopped when he saw Renée, the bank official and Wentworth standing in a circle near a row of tall bushes, talking. There were others on the large outdoor balcony getting air, smoking, laughing and drinking. Nothing seemed amiss, but somehow Neil felt a tightening in the pit of his stomach, an awareness that kept him on alert. He moved closer to Renée, just in time to hear Wentworth say something that seemed a little odd.

"As you know, in Australia it's summer in the winter and winter during the summer, and never the twain shall meet." He then exited the balcony as Renée did exactly as she had been programmed to do.

Face impassive, the E & E agent pulled a gun from her purse, a firearm she had not had when she had entered the ballroom, and aimed it directly at Patrick McNealy's head. The man backed up, stunned and terrified.

"NO!" Neil shouted as he ran toward them, knowing already that he'd never make it in time. The gun fired, but not before a hand and body pressed its way through one of the tall bushes and pushed her arm upward, the bullet lodging into the ceiling above the balcony. Women screamed and glasses shattered as surprised guests got the fright of their lives. Renée, woozy and faint, collapsed into the arms of a fair-haired, tall and rugged man as McNealy stared in shock. For Neil, there had never been a more welcoming sight than that sudden appearance of Noah Wolf.

"All of you, Renée just tried to kill McNealy! Converge on us now!" Noah called, pulling the gun from Renée's hand.

Gary, who was still in the ballroom, headed toward the balcony and met Wentworth coming from that direction. He started to hurry past when he saw something out of the corner of his eye, then grabbed the liaison officer by the arm and dragged him aside. He was staring at him as Marco came hurrying in from the opposite direction and Jenny rushed toward the balcony.

"You're good," Gary said as he looked into the man's eyes. "Maybe even better than me."

"What are you talking about?" Ambassador Jamison asked, approaching them. He seemed confused by Gary's question and Wentworth's sudden expression of contempt.

"Grab him," Gary said to Marco, and Marco grabbed Wentworth by the arm. While Marco held him steady, Gary reached just inside the man's collar and pulled firmly at what looked like a flap of skin hanging loose. The mask he had spotted peeled off and underneath, arrogant and smirking, was Caleb Dawson. Gary was holding the mask out for the Ambassador to see when Mr. Montoya came in from the foyer, his eyes going wide when he saw what was happening.

Marco suddenly understood how Renée had gotten the gun. On the dance floor, it was slipped into her purse by Dawson. As Daniel Wentworth, he never would have been subjected to a search like a typical guest.

Jamison stood with his mouth open, sputtering, and that was

when Dawson made his move. His left hand whipped out and struck Marco in the face, causing him to lose his grip for a second. That second was all the man needed, as he kicked Gary in the groin and turned to run.

Marco had stumbled into Ambassador Jamison and the two of them almost went down together. By the time he recovered, Dawson made his way into the panicking crowd and vanished.

SIXTEEN

EMBASSY GUARDS BEGAN SEARCHING FOR THE REAL Wentworth, whose body was finally found stuffed into a trash container behind the embassy building. When they went back over his timeline for the day, it appeared that Dawson had killed him and replaced him at some point before lunch.

Patrick McNealy, after being quickly debriefed about what had happened, was immediately assigned special security by the Australian Secret Intelligence Service. He was spirited away less than half an hour after the attempt on his life, and ASIS agents would be protecting him for the foreseeable future.

It was quickly determined that Dawson had not returned to his hotel, and was currently in the wind. Despite every effort to locate him by facial recognition and every video source possible, there was no sign of the man anywhere.

Renée had been handed over to the embassy physician for examination, and he was able to confirm that she had trace amounts of numerous drugs in her system. Several of them were considered hypnotics, drugs that could cause someone to subconsciously obey commands.

"A posthypnotic suggestion?" Marco asked the doctor. "They honestly programmed her to commit a murder?"

"It's not the first time something like this has happened," Noah said. "It's been done before. When someone is under the influence of these drugs, the commands go directly to the subconscious mind, to surface when a particular phrase or event triggers it."

"But why?" Marco asked. "Why would they try to use her that way? She said they were planning to let the other woman commit a murder and try to pin it on her."

Noah shook his head. "This could have been a backup plan, maybe," he said. "Or perhaps this was the real plan all along and Renée was fed that story just in case we were to recover her. Knowing that Dawson was due to strike here, the odds were good that she would end up in a position to carry out her programming."

"Not that good," Neil said. "I would think it would be more likely she would have been shipped off for some kind of evaluation or treatment, after being kidnapped and tortured. If we had done that, if we'd sent her back to Neverland, what then?"

"Dawson was obviously ready to carry out the assassination himself. Finding Renée there was probably just a stroke of good luck for him, but one he had planned for. Disguised as Wentworth, he took advantage of the situation and this is the result."

"What I want to know," Marco growled, "is where he got off to. The man almost seemed to vanish into thin air."

"Others have said the same about us at times," Noah said. "Anyone in the assassination game learns to disappear in a crowd pretty quickly, or they don't last long. All he had to do was take off his jacket and drop it on the floor. In the press of the crowd like that, everyone was looking for the clothes he was wearing, especially since only a couple of us ever got a good look at his face at that moment."

Marco rubbed a hand over his face. "So, what now? Without Dawson, we don't have any leads on Spear."

"We have one," Noah said. "We know he was here at the reception. The ambassador is providing us with the entire guest list. Our quarry is somewhere on that list, and we are going to find him."

"But we still lost Dawson," Jenny said. "He's the one who actually killed Mr. Jefferson."

"He'll surface again," Noah said. "A man like him can't stop doing what he does." He looked around at the rest of them. "Neil, when the guest list gets to us, I want you to start going through it. Find out everything you can about everyone who was here tonight. Anything that looks the slightest bit off kilter, I want to know about it."

"You bet," Neil said.

Noah turned to Marco. "You need to stick with Renée. She's going to be pretty upset about all this, I imagine. You've got to keep reassuring her that we know it wasn't her fault, that she wasn't willingly participating in Dawson's scheme."

"I can handle that," Marco replied. He got up and left the small room they were using to go and sit in the embassy clinic with Renée. He wanted to be there when she came out of the sedation the doctor had given her.

"What about me?" Jenny asked. "What can I do, Noah?"

Noah looked her in the eye. "Keep your knives sharp," he said. "I suspect you're going to be doing some interrogation before long."

He left the room and walked outside the embassy, took out his cell phone and called Allison. It was nearly midnight in Sydney, making it just before eight a.m. back at Neverland.

Allison answered on the first ring. "Camelot, report."

"Renée was subjected to chemically enhanced psychological brainwashing," he said without preamble. "At the reception tonight, she attempted to murder Patrick McNealy. We were able to prevent it, and we had Dawson in our grasp for a few seconds, but he was able to escape. He had killed our liaison and replaced him, using a mask. It's what enabled him to get close enough to Renée to give her the trigger phrase that activated her programming."

"Dear God," Allison said. "How is she doing?"

"She's under sedation at the moment," Noah said. "I think it would be best to send her back as soon as possible, and I want Marco to go with her."

"I concur," Allison said. "Let's let Parker deal with her. What about Spear? Were you able to identify him?"

"Not yet," Noah said. "Going on the theory that he did show up at the reception as planned, I've assigned Neil to go through the guest list and look for anything out of the ordinary."

"And what about Dawson?"

"I don't know that we can locate him again right now," Noah said. "He'll surface again eventually, and I'll be happy to complete this mission when he does."

"Well, hell," Allison said bitterly. "This has turned into a disaster, Noah. Are you sure you're not still a little off your game?"

Noah was unfazed by the rancor in her voice. "I seem to be functioning normally," he said. "Normally for me, that is. There were variables thrown into the mix that were impossible to antici- pate, and we are all doing the best we can. I have no intention of letting Dawson get away with what he did to Mr. Jefferson, but as you have reminded me several times, Spear is the primary objec- tive. I would like to get as much assistance on trying to identify him as we can, and whatever help we can get in keeping him from leaving the country."

Allison was silent for a moment, then let out a sigh. "You're right, of course. I'll get CIA and NSA involved. They can watch the airports and seaports around Sydney, try to spot him if he makes a run for it. Have that guest list transmitted to me as soon as possible so that I can share it with them. Anyone on it who tries to leave the country will be considered suspect."

"That was my idea, as well. I'll have Neil send it to you as soon as we get it."

"See that you do," Allison said, and then the line was dead.

Noah walked back into the building and found Neil and Jenny standing in the hallway outside the clinic.

"I got the list," Neil said. "I just need to get back to my computer."

Noah nodded. "You two head on back to the hotel," he said. "I'll be there shortly. Oh, and Allison wants you to send her a copy of that list immediately." He turned and stepped into the clinic and headed toward the room where Renée was under the doctor's care.

Marco looked up as he entered. Renée was still sleeping, but Marco was holding her hand.

"Need me?" Marco asked.

"Not just yet," Noah said. "When she wakes up, I want you to take her directly to the airport. The two of you are getting on the Gulfstream and going back to Neverland."

Marco's eyes went wide. "Hey, come on," he said. "Boss man, you know I need to get my hands on that son of a bitch. After what he did to her, I want to rip him apart."

"I understand, but it's highly unlikely we're going to see Mr. Dawson again on this mission. You are emotional, Marco, and that's not going to help me. Neil, Jenny and I will concentrate on finding Spear; you concentrate on helping Renée get past this. Between you and Doctor Parker, I think it should go pretty well."

Marco stared at him for a second more, then his shoulders slumped in surrender. "Okay, okay," he said. "I get you, boss." His Cajun accent was strong, as it always was when he was stressed out.

"I think it's for the best, Marco," Noah said. "She needs the best care we can get her, and that's going to be back home."

Marco nodded. "Anything you want me to tell Sarah?"

"Just that I'm always thinking of her," Noah said. "I think she knows that, though, and I tend to call her at least once a day."

———

NOAH ARRIVED BACK at the hotel half an hour later to find Neil and Jenny in his room. Neil was drinking coffee and sitting at the table with his computer, but Jenny was sprawled on the bed, sound asleep.

"Hope you don't mind," Neil said. "She was dead tired, but she didn't want to leave me. Gary went on to his room and said he would see us in the morning."

"It's not a problem," Noah replied. "Are you finding anything?"

"I got three possibilities at the moment," Neil said. "One of them is Leonard Garfield, the Intelligence Liaison under Ambassador Jamison. He's actually CIA, of course, but there are some serious blank spots in his record and a couple of them correspond to when Dawson was completely off the radar. Could be they were meeting somewhere secret so that Garfield could give Dawson his orders."

"Wouldn't be the first time a CIA operative went rogue," Noah said. "On the other hand, those guys are under a lot of scrutiny. Who else you got?"

"Antonio Moretti. He's the commerce attaché for the Italian Embassy. Like Garfield, he's been out of sight more than once at times that correspond with Dawson also being in the wind. The fact that he made a beeline for the airport also looks a little suspicious, but he was scheduled to return to Italy for a couple of weeks."

"Forward that information to Allison," Noah said. "Who else?"

"The last one that looks a little strange to me is a guy named Julio Rodriguez. He's with the U.S. Embassy, just a low level clerk on the surface, but he does an awful lot of traveling. He's been out of the country eight times in the last five weeks. His most recent trip was to Atlanta, so he's a definite possibility."

"And is he still here in Sydney?"

"He's at the embassy right now. I gather he's actually staying to help the police with their investigation, but I'm not sure in what capacity."

"If he happened to be Spear, that could put him in the position to make sure suspicion doesn't fall on him. I think I might pay him a visit in the morning, try to get a feel for him." Noah looked over at Jenny. "I think maybe it's time we both get some sleep of our own," he said. "You can crash here with her, and I'll take the couch."

Neil shut down his computer, then nodded. "Sounds like a good idea." He got up and moved over to the bed, then laid down on it in his clothes beside Jenny.

Noah walked over to the couch that was on the opposite side of the table from the bed and sat down on it, then took out his phone. He hit a button and put it to his ear.

"Noah?" came Sarah's voice. "How's it going?"

"Not as well as I'd like," Noah said. "Marco and Renée are on the way home, you'll probably see them in the next day or so. Something went wrong and Renée is going to be seeing Doctor Parker for a while."

"Oh my goodness," Sarah said. "Was she hurt?"

"Not physically," Noah said. "I can't go into it over the phone, but her deep cover job blew up in our faces. Marco will fill you in when he sees you."

"And you're okay?"

"I'm fine," Noah said. "I just wanted to hear your voice."

"Me, too, baby," she said. "I was hoping you might call today. Is everything all right with your mission?"

"No, but we'll cope with it. I think we'll be able to pull it off before it's over."

They talked for a couple more minutes, and then Noah put the phone away and lay down on the couch. He was asleep only seconds later.

The very first rays of sunlight coming through the window brought Noah to full wakefulness in only seconds. He sat up on the couch and stretched, then made his way to the bathroom to take care of morning ablutions. He came out a moment later and gathered clean clothing, then went back in to get a shower.

By the time he came out again, Gary, Neil and Jenny were sitting up at the table. Neil had already made coffee in the little pot provided in the room, and Jenny poured a cup for Noah.

"Thanks," he said. "Neil? Anything new?"

"I got a message from Molly," Neil said. "Apparently, all three of my potential suspects have checked out and been cleared." He looked disgusted. "Back to square one, I guess."

"Don't get discouraged," Noah said. "We'll find him. Why don't you two go and get cleaned up, and then we'll head downstairs for breakfast. I want to go back to the embassy today and speak with the ambassador and Mr. Montoya. Maybe one of them could have a little insight into our problem."

Neil nodded and finished his own coffee, then Jenny followed him out the door.

Noah turned to Gary, who had not spoken a single word so far that morning. "Gary? Are you doing okay?"

Gary shrugged. "I feel like I should have figured out what was going to happen a lot sooner," he said. "We already knew, because of the doppelgänger they created for Renée, that Dawson was experienced with disguises and masks. I should've expected him to be posing as someone else, and it didn't occur to me until it was almost too late."

"At least you spotted him when it counted," Noah said. "I didn't get the chance to ask you, but what was it that tipped you off?"

Gary grinned sheepishly. "A stage actor like me is always looking for little details that could be used if I have to play a character, little things that make a character seem more real. When we met Mr. Wentworth yesterday, I happened to notice that he had an old tracheotomy scar at the base of his throat. It occurred to me that a scar like that would make almost any character more believable, because it would be difficult to imagine someone pretending to have had such a procedure. When I bumped into

Dawson disguised as Wentworth, my eyes automatically went to the scar—and it wasn't there."

Noah nodded. "So you knew it couldn't be Wentworth that quickly."

"Couldn't be," Gary said. "Scars don't go away, and there's no makeup that will cover them completely. Besides, Wentworth didn't seem embarrassed by it, so it would be illogical for him to have covered it up. I knew it had to be a mask, so when I grabbed one little spot that didn't stick properly, it came right off."

"And it's a good thing you saw it," Noah said. "At least we were able to confirm that Dawson was behind what happened."

SEVENTEEN

Jenny and Neil had gone back to their own room and showered, got dressed and returned within half an hour. When they knocked on the door, Noah and Gary simply stepped out and walked with them to the elevator.

The hotel had a breakfast bar as well as a restaurant, but Noah decided to go with the quicker route. The three of them gathered plates of eggs, bacon, mushrooms and hash browns, then took it all to a table that sat in the corner. Jenny set her plate down and fetched coffee for the four of them.

"Careful," she said. "It's very hot."

"Pretty strong, too," Neil said. "I've had strong coffee before, but this stuff could pick me up and carry me off."

Jenny grinned. "Don't worry, pookie, I'll protect you."

Neil gave her a mock glare for the nickname, then turned to Noah. "Do you honestly think the ambassador could have some idea who Spear might be?"

"Probably not directly," Noah said. "I'm just hoping he might know something about some of the other people who were present last night, something that might give us a lead. Same for Montoya; he might've observed something that will help us get back on track."

"That would be great," Jenny said. "I'm beginning to get an itch for interrogation." She shot the men an evil grin, and Gary shuddered.

"Sometimes, Jenny, you can be terrifying," Gary said.

"You might get your chance," Noah said to her. "Somebody like Spear probably has quite a few people working with him. At least some of them might be in the embassy, and if we can identify any strong possibilities, I'm inclined to let you take a shot at them." He leaned toward her, his gaze stern. "However, we won't resort to your more extreme techniques unless we are certain of who we're dealing with. The idea is to scare some information out of them, not cut it out."

Jenny stuck out her bottom lip. "Spoilsport," she grumbled, but then she looked at Gary from the corner of her eye. "Come on, Noah, you know I have to let my dark side out now and then. I haven't had the chance in a while, and it's starting to build up."

"Just keep it under control for now. With any luck, you'll have a target before long."

They talked about simple things while they finished eating, then went out to the car they were using and headed toward the embassy. Noah didn't bother to call ahead, but the security staff recognized him and passed the four of them through without any delays. They were ushered directly to the office of the ambassador, who was still wearing the same clothes he'd had on the night before.

"Mr. Rogers," Jamison said, shaking Noah's hand. "It's good to see you again."

Noah raised an eyebrow. "I doubt that," he said. "I wanted to check in and see if you might've come up with any new information."

"My security detail is working hard, but I'm afraid I don't have anything to report at the moment. To be honest, I was hoping you might have something to tell me."

"We're still working on the assumption that our quarry was

here last night," Noah said. "Are you aware of just who our target is?"

Jamison shook his head. "I'm afraid they don't let me have the details," he said. "Plausible deniability and all that. Mr. Wentworth was your man, and he kept things pretty close to the vest."

"I understand. The man we are looking for is essentially an international crime lord. He has arranged assassinations and even terror attacks in the past, and most of them are orchestrated in such a way as to get him some sort of power over governments and their agencies. Of all the people who were present last night, who would you suspect might be the biggest power players?"

It was Jamison's turn to raise an eyebrow. "Power players? My goodness, Mr. Rogers, that would be just about everyone. The biggest, however? I would probably say that you should look at Dermot Calloway. Well, perhaps him and Charles Olson. Calloway is a ranking member of the Australian intelligence community, but he's also one of the wealthiest men in the country, and maybe the world. I know he's got a lot of interests scattered throughout the global community. Olson is an American expatriate living here in Australia, but he's almost as big as Calloway in global business ventures. If any of the people I know could fit into the category of major power players, it would be those two."

Noah nodded. "And were either of them present here at the embassy last night?"

"They both were," Jamison said. "Believe me, you can't have any kind of diplomatic get together without those two showing up."

"Is there anyone in particular they tend to associate with here at the embassy?" Noah asked.

"Not in particular, I don't think. I mean, they know everybody here. I couldn't single someone out and say they spend more time talking to this one or that one."

Neil had his computer open on his lap and was typing, and he suddenly turned around to show the monitor to Ambassador

Jamison. There were two photos on the monitor. "Is this the pair you're talking about?"

Jamison leaned forward and squinted a bit, then nodded. "Yes, that's them."

Neil looked at Noah. "Olson is scheduled to fly out this morning, headed for Berlin. Calloway is supposed to be going to Melbourne for a business meeting this afternoon."

Noah looked at the ambassador.

"Well, Mr. Calloway has interests all over Australia, lots of businesses. I have to say that's not out of character for him. As for Olson, I really don't know a lot about how much he travels. I just know that he does. This could be something he's had planned for weeks, for all I know."

Noah said nothing and only looked him in the eye for a moment. The ambassador seemed uncomfortable under his gaze.

"Mr. Rogers, I'm not sure what it is you're looking for," he said. "Maybe if I knew more, I could..."

"Unfortunately, I can't tell you much more than I already have. The man who got away last night, Dawson, works for the man we were looking for. That's who gives him his orders and assigns his targets. Such a man would obviously be powerful, and that's why we think it could be one of the power players who were here last night."

Jamison looked uncomfortable. "I'm not sure I completely understand, but I probably don't want to. There might be a couple of other people here who could give you more information than I can. You can talk to my security chief, Captain Reynolds. Oh, and you might speak to Jorge Montoya. He was always in Wentworth's shadow, so if there was any connection to his office, Montoya might know something."

Noah nodded. "I was hoping to speak to Montoya. Where might I find him, and Captain Reynolds as well?"

Jamison touched a button on his phone and his receptionist stepped inside. "Janine, I want you to have Captain Reynolds and

Jorge Montoya brought to my conference room. Mr. Rogers and his staff need to speak with them."

The young woman smiled and nodded. "Right away, Mr. Ambassador," she said, and then she backed out of the door and pulled it closed behind her.

"They should be available within a few moments," Jamison said, turning back toward Noah. "Would any of you like some coffee or something?"

Neil looked up with a glint in his eye. "Would it happen to be American coffee?"

Jamison grinned. "Of course," he said. "Comes in a red can, unlike this rust remover they sell in the coffee shops down here."

All four of them accepted a cup and Jamison led them into the conference room. They sat down at a large oval table to wait for the men they were going to interrogate.

———

CAPTAIN WALTER REYNOLDS, U.S. Army special forces officer assigned to provide security to the ambassador, appeared a few moments later, carrying a cup of coffee of his own. Noah stood to shake hands with him and he took a seat directly across from where the three of them sat.

"Mr. Jamison tells me you are trying to identify someone who was here last night," he said. "How can I help you?"

"That's correct," Noah said. "I'm particularly interested in anything you can tell me about Dermot Calloway and Charles Olson. It's my understanding that both of them seem to be more powerful than would be expected under normal circumstances."

Reynolds leaned back in his chair and crossed one leg over the other, his entire posture relaxed and confident.

"Calloway is a local boy, grew up in the outback and became a self-made billionaire. He got his start by dealing in real estate, but now he's in just about every industry you can imagine. He made a few million buying up distressed properties and flipping them, then started making some very shrewd investments. Some people think he has a Midas touch, because anything he puts money into seems to succeed. There are probably a thousand companies around the world that wouldn't exist if he had not soaked a little money into them in the beginning."

"What kind of companies?" Neil asked. "Are we talking about particular industries?"

"Industries? You name it, he's in it. Everything from organic agriculture to high-tech companies, and probably everything in between. He owns farms and orchards, factories, chemical plants, drug companies, makes computer parts and weapons and just about anything else you can imagine."

"And all of it seems to be legitimate?" Noah asked.

"I didn't exactly say that," Reynolds said with a grin. "Calloway doesn't shy away from something just because it might not be legal. There's never been any provable evidence, but it's pretty much common knowledge that he owns some of the biggest cannabis fields in the world, and some of his weapons have been turning up in the middle of rebellions and other unsanctioned conflicts. He's probably one of the most diversified billionaires in the world."

"Makes you wonder how he keeps track of it all," Neil said. "A guy like that would have a team of people handling things, people who report to him." He looked at Noah. "He'd probably also have people who could fix problems before they got big enough to cause any interference in his operations."

"I agree," Noah said. "Captain Reynolds, in your opinion, would Mr. Calloway have any reason to want harm to come to Patrick McNealy?"

Reynolds bit his bottom lip and thought about it for a moment. "I couldn't point to any particular reason why he would," he said a few seconds later, "but McNealy is in a pretty powerful position in the banking industry here. He's the guy who runs any sort of financial investigations for the government. I can imagine that if Calloway had something he wanted to hide, something he wouldn't want the bank regulators to see, he might want to get rid of McNealy and hope for someone less thorough to take over."

Gary cleared his throat. "Or arrange for someone less thorough," he said. "Our target seems to be the kind of man who would not leave something like that to chance. He was almost certainly grooming someone for the position."

Noah nodded. "That's a good point. Neil, I want you to look at who would've taken his place if McNealy had been killed. See if you can find a connection to Calloway, or anyone else with that kind of power."

Neil set his computer on the table and opened it up. He began working quietly while the conversation went on.

"What about Olson?" Noah asked. "How does he compare to Calloway?"

"Probably just as rich," Reynolds said. "Not nearly as diversified, though. He made most of his money in medical technology. From what I understand, he actually invented a kind of prosthetic hand that works on spring action, with no power supply. That made him a small fortune and he was able to hire engineers to work on his more complicated ideas. His company, Olson Med, developed a chip that can go in the brain and relay instructions to artificial limbs that make it work like the real thing. I've seen a man who lost both legs just below the hip joint learn to tap dance with their technology. It's pretty damned impressive."

"And is he also involved in less legal activities?"

"Not as far as I know, but it's possible. As far as the Australian government is concerned, Olson coming here was one of the best things that ever happened to them. The taxes his company pays actually help the country out, and he's always running some sort of benefit or charity. I remember reading an article recently about how he gave away more than two billion dollars last year to various charities."

Jenny looked at Noah. "Could be camouflage," she said. "He

could be doing that just to make people think he's one of the good guys, when he's really one of the worst there is."

"I suppose that's possible," Noah said, "but one of the primary markers of a criminal organization is greed. They don't usually like to give up money or power, unless it's an exchange for something of greater value."

"I'm going to disagree with you on that, no," Gary said. "Al Capone was extremely well known for his generosity. He gave money to the church in Chicago, spent thousands of dollars every year buying Christmas presents for underprivileged kids, did all sorts of charitable works even though he was one of the most notorious crime bosses ever."

"Yes, but it was a power exchange," Noah said. "By doing so, he won the hearts of the people around him so that whenever the police tried to take action against him, their own citizens would try to interfere and protect him. The money he spent on those things was probably cheaper than any insurance he could have bought."

Gary looked at him for a second, then shrugged. "Okay, I guess I see your point."

"And Olson could be doing the same thing," Jenny said. "It's like I was saying, make himself look like some kind of miracle worker that everybody loves, and it would prove to be very difficult to bring any kind of prosecution against him."

Neil looked up. "Got something," he said. "The most likely man to replace McNealy if something happened to him would be Clarence Dartmouth. Dartmouth has been in charge of three different investigations into Calloway's operations, and all of them were closed with no findings of improper activities."

"Send a message back to Molly," Noah said. "Have Dartmouth picked up and questioned. I think there's a pretty good chance we have discovered the identity of our elusive Spear."

EIGHTEEN

PEOPLE WERE COMING AND GOING FROM THE EMBASSY, just as they always did. It was one of the most busy places in all of Sydney, due mostly to the fact that so many governmental operations were dependent on a good relationship with the United States. As a result, the security was accustomed to seeing many faces show up at the front gate every day, and a number of them had become familiar enough to cause the security to be less than thorough.

Corporal Darrell Garrett stepped out as the car pulled up to the gate and leaned down to look inside at the driver. He smiled when he saw who it was.

"Mr. Hanover," he said. He glanced cursorily at the ID that the driver held up, then looked at the man again. "Wasn't sure if we were going to see you today, after what happened last night. Real shame about Mr. Wentworth, wasn't it?"

"It was indeed," Hanover said. "He was a good man."

Corporal Garrett nodded and stepped back, then reached through the window and hit the button to raise the gate. He waved Hanover ahead and the car proceeded on through.

Jonathan Hanover was the embassy liaison with the Australian government. A member of ASIS, he was primarily concerned with ensuring that any spying that went on at the embassy would not endanger Australian sovereignty or security, and while he was extremely capable at his job, he was also very well-liked by most of the embassy staff. He was a jovial man, slightly overweight, but far more physically fit than he appeared.

He parked his car in his assigned space and got out, then walked quickly into the building. He didn't bother going to his own office, but presented himself to the ambassador's receptionist.

"Is Mr. Jamison in?" he asked.

Janine looked up and smiled. Like most of the staff, she found Hanover to be a delight to deal with.

"He is, sir," she said. "If you'll take a seat, I'll see if he has time to see you."

"Yes, please," Hanover said with a smile. He took a seat in one of the comfortable chairs in the waiting area, and it was only a moment later that Janine told him he could go on in.

Ambassador Jamison looked up from his desk, but the smile on his face seemed forced. "Jonathan," he said. "Good of you to come. Can you give me any idea what's happening on your end of this mess?"

Hanover walked directly to the desk. "Actually, I'm afraid I have some bad news," he said. "Our people seem to think that yours might be behind the fiasco that happened last night."

Jamison's eyes went wide. "You've got to be kidding," he said. "What possible reason could we have wanting any harm to come to McNealy?"

"That's not what I'm referring to," he said. He reached into a pocket and produced a small pistol that had a silencer attached to it, which he pointed directly into Jamison's face. "The fiasco I'm talking about is the one that kept me from accomplishing my objective."

Jamison stared at the pistol for a moment, then raised his eyes to look into those of the man holding it.

"You're not Jonathan Hanover," he said softly.

The pistol coughed once and Jamison fell backward into his chair, a small, red hole appearing in his forehead while a large one spewed blood and brain matter out the back of his skull.

Dawson stepped around the desk quickly and began typing on the keyboard to Jamison's computer. He continued looking through various screens for several moments, then cursed softly when he couldn't find what he was looking for.

He glanced down at the deceased ambassador and then turned away. He walked over beside the door and then spoke in a voice that was very much like the ambassador's.

"Let me know if I can be of any service," he said, and then he opened the door and stood in the doorway, looking back toward the desk.

"I'll be sure to do that, mate," he said. "Give my best to Beulah." He pulled the door shut behind him, then nodded at Janine as he walked past her desk and through the door. Five minutes later, he was back in his car and out through the same gate where he had come in. As soon as he was out of sight of the guard shack, he reached up and pulled the mask off and tossed it into the floorboard.

"Damn things are so hot," he said.

———

NOAH HAD FINISHED up with Captain Reynolds and told Gary to tell Mr. Montoya to step inside the conference room. The man came in and took a seat, and Noah looked him in the eye.

"Mr. Montoya, thanks for coming," he said. "I wonder if you can tell me what you know about Dermot Calloway."

"Mr. Calloway? He's a businessman, I know that. He has a tendency to be a little bit on the pushy side, sometimes. Mr. Wentworth had to deal with him as technology attaché, and there were times when the exchange would leave him rather angry, but in general, I think they got along pretty well."

Noah nodded. "Do you think he is an honest man?"

Montoya's eyebrows rose slightly. "Honest? I'm not really sure that would be an accurate description, though I would be hard-pressed to put my finger on anything specific that would make it a lie. He's certainly a determined individual, and he doesn't like to take no for an answer."

Noah looked over at Neil. "How much can I say?" he asked.

Neil's fingers flew over the keyboard, and then he looked back at Noah. "Mr. Montoya has sufficient clearance," he said. "I don't know if he was privy to Wentworth's association with our bosses."

Noah turned back to Montoya. "Are you aware of an organization known as E & E?"

Montoya nodded. "I'm aware that Mr. Wentworth was connected to them in some fashion, and I know what they do. Is that important somehow, with regard to Mr. Calloway?"

"My team is part of that organization," Noah said. "Our mission is to determine the identity of a particular international crime lord, and we are beginning to believe that Mr. Calloway might be the man we're looking for. Did Mr. Wentworth confide in you about any of his work with our people?"

Montoya shook his head. "No, sir," he said. "In fact, he specifically warned me against asking any questions about it. The only involvement I ever had was when he needed something delivered to one of your people. I would be given a box and told to take it to a specific person, then leave before the box was opened."

Noah started to say something else, but a sudden commotion outside the room went from a low buzz to a loud roar. He glanced toward the door, then got up and quickly snatched it open to find people running toward the ambassador's office up the hall.

Noah hurried to follow. The receptionist, Janine, was sitting at her desk in tears, and several security personnel were entering the ambassador's office. Noah spotted Captain Reynolds and caught his attention as he was about to step through the door.

"What's going on?" he asked.

Reynolds turned and looked at him for a moment, his face set in an angry, stony expression.

"Ambassador Jamison has been murdered," he said. "And the last person to see him alive was the Australian Intelligence liaison."

"I need to see security video," Noah said. "Get my intelligence man access to it on his computer, now."

Reynolds stared at him. "Who do you think you are?" he asked. "You don't come in here and start ordering my people around like..."

"Condition Delta Theta two seven," Noah said, providing a code that only a high ranking government agent would know. "I'm E & E, and I have reason to believe that the killer might not be who you think it is. Give me that access, now."

Reynolds' eyes were wide, but he nodded instantly. "Yes, sir," he said. He took a cell phone out of his pocket and made a call, then scribbled down a code onto a piece of paper from Janine's desk and handed it to Noah. "That'll get you in," he said. "Sir, please let me know if you learn anything."

"I've got a better idea," Noah said. "Why don't you come with me?"

He hurried back into the conference room with Reynolds following. Neil, Jenny and Gary were sitting where he had left them, as well as Montoya. He passed the paper to Neil and told him to get access to the security video for the embassy, specifically for the hallway around Jamison's office.

Neil's fingers flew over the keyboard and the video opened a moment later. They watched as a man came up the hall, and Reynolds said, "That's Mr. Hanover. He's the Australian Intelligence man I was talking about."

"Gary," Noah said, "take a look."

Gary leaned close and looked at the monitor, then asked Neil to back it up and run it again. After the third time, he looked up at Noah.

"I don't know who that's supposed to be, but it's Dawson. I had plenty of opportunities to watch him walk, and that's him."

Noah nodded. "I thought so," he said. "Neil, see if you can trace him out of the building."

"Easy," Neil said. They watched the monitor as the view changed from camera to camera, keeping up with Dawson until he exited the building. A moment later, Neil found the camera outside that showed him getting into a car. He zoomed in to get the tag number and Reynolds scribbled it down.

"I've got to get this to the police," he said, and started out of the room.

"Go ahead," Noah said, "but they will only find the car abandoned somewhere not too far away. Neil, any chance you can track him down?"

Neil shook his head. "None that I can imagine," he said. "I just can't figure out why he would risk coming back into the embassy to kill the ambassador. That doesn't make any sense at all, not to me."

"Of course it does," Jenny said. "There's a computer on the ambassador's desk, right? I would just about bet it has access to everything that has to do with embassy operations. He came in looking for information, and he didn't have time to try to con it out of anybody. The simplest way was to go straight to the computer that would be able to access it and silence the only person who would be in the way."

"I think you're right," Noah said. "Neil, can you tell what he might have gotten into?"

"I'm on it already," Neil said. "I had a subroutine running on my computer to hack the network here when we came in this morning, just in case we needed any information out of it that somebody didn't want to give us. Give me a moment to find the ambassador's terminal—okay, got it."

A new window opened on the monitor and Neil began scrolling through hundreds of file folders. He typed a command into a search box, and one of those folders suddenly opened up.

"Oh, boy," he said. "Noah, for some reason I can't figure out, ASIS sent Ambassador Jamison an email this morning giving him the location of the safe house where they took McNealy. That's what he got into."

"Get the address," Noah said. "Let's go. That's where we'll find our friend Dawson."

———

Dawson had ditched the car only a few minutes after leaving the embassy, leaving it in a parking lot where he had stashed another vehicle the night before. His hunch had paid off and he knew where Patrick McNealy was being kept, supposedly safe. It was time to teach the Australians a lesson about that subject.

He switched cars and headed toward the safe house, pulling up and parking the car a couple of hundred yards away. He climbed out of the vehicle and reached into the back seat for a cane, then leaned on it as he walked along the edge of the street. The house was just up ahead, and was easy to spot because of the two men who seemed to be lounging nonchalantly in the front yard.

Both of them watched him as he approached, and he gave them a friendly wave and smile. They both waved back, and that's when the cane snapped up and belched twice. The built-in silencer made it sound more like a piece of meat hitting the ground than a nine millimeter slug leaving the barrel of a specially built rifle, and one bullet took each of the two men through the bridge of the nose. They both dropped instantly, and Dawson dropped the cane—it only had two shots available, anyway—and snatched out a pair of pistols as he ran up the stairs and kicked in the front door.

Two more guards inside, a man and a woman, fell instantly. McNealy was sitting on the couch watching television, and let out a scream as Dawson approached him.

"But why?" McNealy begged. "What'd I do?"

"Nothing," Dawson said. "You were just in the way." The

silenced pistol in his right hand coughed, and McNealy stopped worrying about why this stranger wanted him dead.

———

NEIL TYPED for a couple of seconds and the address suddenly chimed on Noah's cell phone in a text message. He slammed the computer shut and jumped to his feet, with Jenny and Gary following. They hurried out the door and out of the building, got into their car and were gone only moments later.

The safe house was near Croydon Park, and it took Noah nearly twenty minutes to get them there. By the time they arrived, it was obvious that they were too late. The place was surrounded by police cars, and there was a pair of sheet-covered bodies in the yard in front of the house.

"We're too late," Neil said. "He had a ten minute head start on us, at least."

"He hasn't gone far," Noah said. "He's not that far away yet." He closed his eyes and tried to think for a moment, putting himself into the killer's shoes. A couple of seconds later, his eyes snapped open, and he looked up and down the street.

A car was pulling away at the opposite end of the block. Noah took his foot off the brake and pressed the accelerator, making the car lurch ahead and launch into pursuit.

"That's him," Noah said. "Be sure to get a grip on something, because the ride is about to get rough."

NINETEEN

THE HOLDEN COMMODORE AHEAD OF THEM WAS whipping through the streets, and it didn't take Noah long to realize the car was not the standard model. Fortunately, neither was the Toyota that Noah was driving, and the four hundred horsepower V6 engine was screaming as Noah gave chase.

In the passenger seat beside Noah, Gary was clinging to the grab handle over the door, while Neil and Jenny were bouncing around in the back seat.

"Are you sure that's him?" Gary asked.

"It's him," Noah said. "He was watching us from the moment we arrived. When he realized I was looking around for him, he took off."

The Holden fishtailed around the corner and Noah followed in the Toyota. The Holden was a heavier car, and while it had a bigger engine than the Toyota, the power to weight ratio gave Noah's car the advantage. Bit by bit, he was gaining on the Commodore.

Dawson, looking in the rearview mirror, realized that as well. He made another left turn and then spun the car around, so that it was facing back the way it had come. He slammed it into reverse and floored the accelerator, keeping it moving at a fair percentage of its original speed, driving backward by using the rearview mirrors.

With one hand on the wheel and his eyes bouncing between the mirrors and the Toyota that was coming straight at him, he powered down the driver side window and lifted the pistol from his lap. He aimed it out the window, pointing it directly at where he expected Noah to be sitting and squeezed the trigger twice.

The windshield of the Toyota had a significant slant to it, and Dawson's bullet bounced off. Noah jerked the wheel to the left, and then back to the right, as Jenny let out a screech in the back seat.

"That son of a bitch!" she shouted. "How dare he shoot at us!" She quickly unfastened her seat belt and powered down her own window, then leaned out with a pistol in each hand and began returning fire.

Dawson's windshield was more vertical, and one of the bullets passed through it and barely missed him. His eyes shot open wide and he ducked as low as he could while still being able to see the mirrors, then whipped the wheel to the right and spun the car around again, slamming it back into drive. His foot slammed down on the accelerator once more, and he kept his head low as three more bullets came through the back window of the car.

One of them was low and nicked his left ear, and the sudden shock caused him to duck even lower. He instantly realized that he'd made a mistake, but by the time he popped back up over the dashboard, it was too late. The right front corner of the Holden clipped a car and he went into a spin that ended with the back of his vehicle smashed against a tree at the edge of a park.

Noah slammed on the brakes and slid to a stop just in front of Dawson's car, and Jenny kept both pistols trained on the killer as Noah got out and ran toward him. Dawson had one hand on his bleeding ear, and the other was still clinging to the steering wheel. He had dropped his weapon in the middle of the spin.

Noah snatched open the door and grabbed him by the front of his jacket, pulling him out of the car.

"Hello, Mr. Dawson," he said. "I have a young lady who wants to have a talk with you."

TWENTY

IT HAD ONLY TAKEN NEIL A FEW MINUTES TO FIND AN abandoned building listed online, and it wasn't far away. With Dawson sandwiched neatly between Noah and Jenny in the back seat, Gary drove them to the location as quickly as he could. The ride lasted almost half an hour, but the building was perfect. It was isolated, and had a large bay door that allowed them to drive the car right inside. Noah had the lock picked within seconds and the door was closed behind them only a minute later.

Noah climbed out, dragging Dawson behind him, then led the man to a post and held him while Gary secured his wrists behind it. Dawson was still doing his best to appear unconcerned, but there was a stiffness in his muscles that belied his nonchalance.

His composure began to crack, however, when Jenny stepped up in front of him. The twin karambit daggers in her hands were twirling, spinning so fast that the blades were almost invisible as she whirled them around her fingers, but it was still possible to see what they were.

"Jenny is my interrogation specialist," Noah said. "I'm going to ask you a couple of questions, and I want straight answers. If you give them to me, I won't turn her loose on you. If you don't, she's going to enjoy herself."

Neil had stepped out of the car and was standing beside Jenny. "Here's a tip," he said to Dawson. "There is nothing you want to see less in the world than her smiling when she has those knives in her hands. Trust me on that."

Dawson shrugged, his lips curving slightly in a grin. "You're going to kill me in any case," he said. "What makes you think you're going to be able to make me talk beforehand?"

"I haven't failed him yet," Jenny said, licking her lips. "You can save yourself a lot of pain and suffering if you answer his questions, but..." She paused, licking her lips again. "I really hope you don't."

Dawson blew her a kiss, and Noah reached out and took hold of his chin, turning it back so he could look the man in the eyes.

"Spear," he said. "Tell me who he is and where he is."

"Now, what kind of a man would I be if I did that? One of the most important things a guy like me offers to his clientele is anonymity. If I go giving them up, nobody's gonna want to hire me in the future."

"As you mentioned a moment ago, you do not have a future," Noah said. "Or I should say that your future is not very long. You can avoid making it extremely painful by answering my questions. Who is he and where is he?"

"He's the devil, and he lives in hell," Dawson said. "And I'll be sure to tell him hello for you when I get there."

Noah stepped back and released his face, then nodded once at Jenny. One of the daggers flashed and the tip of it sliced just underneath Dawson's bottom lip.

"UNGH," he said, shaking his head at the sudden burst of pain. "Geez, woman, are you crazy?"

"Damn right," Jenny said. "And I'm just getting started. Did you know that the lips are one of the most sensitive areas on the body? They're not the most sensitive, contrary to popular opinion, however. Would you like to guess where that is?" The tip of one of her daggers snagged in the crotch of his pants.

"Sure, go for it," Dawson said. "Like I said, I know I'm going to die. I'm just going to enjoy the look on your faces when you don't get the information you want."

Jenny pulled upward on the dagger and the sharp inner curve of the blade sliced through the fabric. She was careful not to let the blade touch his skin just yet, but his underwear was suddenly visible through the gap.

Dawson swallowed hard. "That's gonna suck," he said, "but it's not going to make me talk."

"Then how about this," Noah said. "How about a chance to stay alive?"

"Noah?" Neil asked, with Gary gasping beside him. "Are you nuts?"

"No," Noah said. "And we can always use someone with Mr. Dawson's talents. How about it, Dawson? You tell us what we want to know, and we not only won't kill you, we'll keep you in the line of work you enjoy. There's always room for someone like you in our organization."

"Organization, huh? You're an American, so that tells me you probably work for E & E. What makes you think I would believe they would have any use for me?"

"I have enough influence to guarantee it," Noah said. "Even though you killed Mr. Jefferson, your cooperation right now could get you a reprieve. If you come to work for us and don't get stupid, you could have a lot more years left in you."

Dawson's tongue shot out and tasted the blood that had splattered onto his lips from Jenny's cut, and then he looked at Noah again.

"I know little bit about your organization," he said. "Most of your torpedoes are rank amateurs, but you do have a couple of serious talents among you. Thing is, there's only one that I've heard of who might have that much influence with the Dragon Lady who runs the place." He grinned when Jenny's eyes went wide. "What? You didn't think that moniker got out about her? Most of the intelligence community knows who Allison Peterson is, and anything they know trickles down to people like me."

"In that case," Noah said, "you will know the name of that one assassin who could keep you alive. Does Camelot sound familiar?"

Dawson's eyes darted back to meet Noah's. "Are you saying that's you?"

"I'm saying that's us," Noah said. "Team Camelot. These people work with me, and you can have a team just like them to help you accomplish your missions."

Dawson looked into his eyes for a moment longer, then shrugged. "I won't say it isn't a tempting offer, but what makes you think I would believe it? If you know I killed Jefferson, you probably want my head as badly as the Dragon Lady herself does. I understand she had a little bit of a thing for him, is that right?"

"You watch your mouth," Jenny shouted, but Noah waved a hand to tell her to stop.

"We all do," Noah said. "That doesn't change the fact that your talents and experience could be useful to us. If you cooperate in helping us to shut down your employer, Allison will honor my promise to keep you alive and put you to work."

Dawson stood silent for several seconds, then cocked his head to one side. "If I go along with this," he said, "half of the professional killers in the world will be looking for me. If they find me, you lose your new associate. How do you plan to handle that?"

"A new identity," Noah replied. "Caleb Dawson, or whoever you really are, will be found dead. You become someone else, and your appearance can be altered enough to keep anyone from ever recognizing you."

Dawson licked a bit more of the blood. "That leaves us with only one serious problem." His eyes flicked to Jenny. "I don't necessarily think you have enough control to keep her from finishing what she started with my lip."

Noah looked at Jenny. "How about that?" he asked. "If I tell you to stand down, are you going to do it?"

Jenny glared at him for a moment, then lowered her eyes. "I won't like it," she said, "but I'll do it."

Noah looked at Neil and Gary. "What about you? Do you obey my orders?"

Neil nodded. "I always do," he said, but Gary just looked at him for a moment.

"Donald Jefferson is the one who brought me into this business," he said. "He was not only a mentor, he was a friend. If you do this, Noah, I'll go along with it, but I don't ever want to work with this son of a bitch."

Noah nodded once. "Fair enough," he said. He turned back to Dawson. "I'm becoming impatient. You can either accept my offer now, or I'm going to tell Jenny to go ahead and get the information her way."

Dawson glanced at Jenny and blew her a kiss. "All right," he said. "I'll accept. You want Spear? The first thing you need to understand is that it's not one man. Spear is a group, and the man who runs it is called the Director."

"Our understanding was that Spear was an individual," Noah said. "There's been no indication that it was a group of any kind before now."

Dawson shrugged. "Then perhaps your intelligence was wrong."

"Tell me who the director is, then," Noah said. "How do we find him?"

"I don't actually know his name," Dawson said. "I've met him a few times, but only as the Director. He's never given me any other name."

Noah stared at him for a second. He had been almost convinced that Dermot Calloway had to be the man he was after, but this information was throwing them in a whole new direction.

"Then how do we arrange to meet him?" Noah asked. "How do you make such an arrangement when you need to?"

Dawson grinned. "I make a phone call," he said. "That's all it takes."

Noah cocked his head to the side and looked at him. "And who do you call? Who is the person you contact who relays the request?"

"There are several numbers I can call," he said. "My primary contact is a man named Joshua, in Atlanta, but there are several others I can reach."

Noah looked him in the eye for a moment. "And you are willing to make an arrangement, to bring him to where we can get to him? Is that what you're telling me?"

"Considering the alternative," Dawson said, "I think that would be prudent on my part. The only condition I want to put on this is that I get to be the one to take him down. If anything goes wrong, I'll be looking over my shoulder the rest of my life, no matter how short it might be. If he's got to be taken down, I want to make certain it's done properly."

"I'll consider it," Noah said. "If you want to kill him so badly, why have you never done it before?"

"I never had a reason," Dawson said. "On the other hand, if I'm going to come in out of the cold, I want to be absolutely certain he can never tell anyone that I'm still alive. I don't care how much you make it look like I just disappeared, there are plenty of people who would believe him if he said I was still running around. I'd never be able to escape one of them finding me, sooner or later. I'll take your deal, but I have to be the one to make certain that he is dead. That work for you?"

"I'll kill him myself," Noah said. "But you can be with me when I do it."

Dawson shook his head. "Not good enough," he said. "I want to be close enough to see the light go out of his eyes. Those are my terms, take it or leave it."

Noah hesitated again, looking him in the eye once more. "When did you last see him?"

Dawson grinned. "Just last night," he said. "He was at the embassy when all the fun went down, but he'll be gone by now. I'm sure he probably had a flight scheduled already, so his departure won't look suspicious."

"Then he could be at the airport," Neil said. "Come on, Noah, we don't need this bastard. I can figure out who it is."

"I don't go back on my word," Noah said. He pointed at the bloody wound just below Dawson's lip. "Gary, see what you can do about that cut. We need to go catch a plane."

Gary spat on the ground, but then he opened the trunk of the car and got out a first aid kit. The cut wasn't as bad as it looked, only about an inch long, so he smeared antiseptic cream on it and then covered it with a thick adhesive bandage. It looked silly, but at least it stopped the bleeding.

They got back into the car and drove out of the building, then headed toward Sydney Airport, the international airport that served the area. It was almost forty-five minutes away, and they resumed their original positions, with Gary driving and Jenny and Noah serving as bookends around Dawson.

"I'm simply curious," Noah said as they drove along, "but who are you? Your real name, I mean."

"I'm not sure I even know anymore," Dawson said. "I was Rodney Kirkman when I was a kid, growing up in southern Illinois. I had that name until I joined the army, and then I got recruited by the CIA. I liked the work, but I didn't like the orders. After a couple of years, I decided to go out on my own, started out just hustling intelligence between rival nations, but then I developed an affinity for wet work. I've been changing names and doing this sort of thing ever since then."

Noah nodded. "I guess that makes some kind of sense," he said. "How did you get mixed up with Spear?"

Dawson chuckled. "Don't get the wrong idea, Camelot," he said. "I don't really give much of a damn whether you like me or not. I'm only going along with this because I'm not quite ready to die just yet, and it's the only shot I got at staying alive. I'll work for the Dragon Lady, but only because the alternative is being turned into shredded beef by this crazy bitch."

Jenny gritted her teeth, but said nothing. Noah looked at her for a second, then turned back to Dawson.

"I didn't even mean to imply that I liked you, or that I would ever want to. I was just curious how you came to be who you are."

With a sigh, Dawson looked at him again. "I got recruited, same as anybody else," he said. "Somebody in the organization found out who I was and that I would kill for hire. I was offered pretty lucrative contracts, more money than anybody else was ever going to pay, and each target was presented with most of the details already mapped out. Seemed like an easy way to keep the money rolling in."

He turned and looked out the window, and they rode the rest of the way in silence.

Neil, in the front seat, had been working on his computer during the ride. As they approached the airport, he turned and looked over his shoulder at Noah.

"I've got three distinct possibilities," he said. "Robert Fleishman is scheduled to fly out in about twenty minutes on a commercial flight, and he was on the guest list last night. His ticket was purchased more than two weeks ago, so he didn't come up on my earlier search for people hurrying to leave the country. Next is Michael Morgan, he's a British national with some known underworld ties. Like Fleishman, his ticket was bought well in advance. The third one is Larken Mitchell, retired Senator from Alabama. He's been seen at a lot of international events lately."

He held up his computer and showed photos of the three men. Noah nodded toward the monitor and then looked at Dawson. "Which one?" he asked.

Dawson shook his head. "It's none of those," he said. "The guy we're looking for is about six foot two, roughly fifty years old and with dark hair that's graying on the sides. When I saw him at the embassy, he was carrying a tray of drinks around."

Neil snapped his head around and looked at Dawson again. "And you couldn't offer that little detail before now? Noah, this guy is playing us."

"I'm not playing at anything," Dawson said. "You need to remember that nobody asked me any questions about what he looked like. You guys are holding all the cards, I'm doing exactly what you tell me to do and nothing else."

Neil muttered something under his breath and turned back to his computer. "I don't know how I'm supposed to find anything on the waiters," he said. "I would bet just about anything this guy isn't going to be on the list of catering staff."

"You're probably right," Noah said. He turned to Dawson. "Is this something that's common for him? To disguise himself as a simple staff member or something?"

"He can be whoever he needs to be," Dawson said. "He shows up where he wants to and then he leaves when he's ready. As far as I know, he's never left any kind of trail behind him. If we don't spot him here at the airport, then our next best move is to let me set up a meeting." He looked knowingly at Noah. "That's probably the best move in any case. Somehow, I don't think he's going to be easy to spot wandering around an airport this big."

Noah looked at him for a long moment, then turned his face forward again. "Gary, pull us over. Park someplace out of the way. I don't think there's much point in continuing toward the airport."

Gary spotted the parking lot of a restaurant and pulled in, finding a place away from the building where they would go unobserved. He put the car into park and turned to look at Noah.

Noah turned back to Dawson. "It's time for you to make that phone call," he said. "Set up a meeting, and don't even think about trying to play games. You let us go on a wild goose chase when we should have been concentrating on setting a trap. Pull that again, and you cancel our deal. Do you understand me?"

Dawson looked into his steel blue eyes for several seconds, then nodded his head. "Understood," he said. "In that case, we need to go back to my hotel. I have a dedicated phone that I use to call in, and I won't get anywhere if I call from a different number."

"That's bull," Neil said. "What if your phone dies, or gets lost or stolen?"

Dawson let out a sigh. "Then I know better than to call in until I get it charged or replaced. Believe me, it's the only number I can make the call from."

"Which hotel?" Noah asked.

Dawson told them, and Noah nodded to Gary. He started the car once more and put it into gear.

TWENTY-ONE

THE RIDE DID NOT LAST LONG. WHEN THEY ARRIVED AT the Royal Embassy Hotel, Noah and Jenny accompanied Dawson inside. Noah told Gary and Neil to go back to their own hotel and gather their things, because they were probably going to be leaving Sydney. They walked through the front door of the hotel as the Toyota drove away.

Dawson stopped at the front desk and asked for any messages, then thanked the clerk when he was told that there weren't any. As they walked away from the desk toward the elevators, he said solemnly to Noah that he had done so simply to stay in character.

They rode the elevator to the ninth floor and got out, and Dawson punched in the code that opened the door to his room. Jenny stepped inside first to make sure no one was waiting, then nodded for Noah and Dawson to come in.

"Where's the phone?" Jenny asked, and Dawson pointed toward a carry-on bag sitting on one of the beds.

"It's in there," he said. "There are five of them. You want the blue one, none of the others."

Jenny glanced at Noah, who nodded. She opened the bag and found the phones, then took out the blue one and looked it over carefully. After making certain that it was not some sort of concealed, disguised weapon, she handed it to Dawson.

"Thank you," he said politely, but Jenny only growled at him. He touched a button to power on the phone, then waited while it went through its start up routine. A moment later, he started punching in a phone number from memory, and put the phone on speaker when it began to ring.

"Mr. Lancaster?" said a man's voice.

"Hello, Joshua," Dawson said. "I'm sure you've heard about the fiasco here in Sydney."

"There have certainly been some interesting comments," Joshua said. "However, I was told just moments ago that the assignment was completed successfully this morning. Is that correct?"

"It is," Dawson said. "However, there have been some complications. I need a meeting with the Director, soon as possible."

"And what are the natures of the complications?"

Dawson looked sideways at Noah, then winked. "Remember that young lady who was with me? Turns out you were right, she was an American agent. I thought I had her under control, but she escaped and it almost got me caught. I need to speak with the Director about how we handle the situation, because she's got far more information than we want her to have."

Joshua was quiet for almost a minute. "I shall make contact with the Director and pass on your request," he said. "Call me again tomorrow at this time and I will have an answer."

"Yeah, that's fine, but give me some idea of where I will be going. Was he headed back to Atlanta?"

Once again, Joshua hesitated. "The last communication I had from him indicated that he was going to meet with another of his people in Rio de Janeiro. I expect he will be there for at least a few days, if you would like to visit the city."

Dawson chuckled, but there was little humor in it. "That figures," he said. "You guys know how much I hate the hot weather."

"Yes," Joshua said, "but I understand they have excellent air conditioning in the hotels there. Call me tomorrow."

The line went dead and Dawson powered off the phone again. He handed it back to Jenny and looked at Noah.

"You heard the man," he said. "Sounds like we need to head for Brazil."

Noah looked at him and nodded slowly. "Jenny," he said. "Dump out all of Mr. Dawson's bags and check them for any kind of weapons. We can't have the man traveling without a change of clothes."

Jenny grinned and then dumped out the carry-on bag first. In a false bottom, she found a couple of pistols and an assortment of knives. She picked up a couple of them and eyed them appreciatively, then tucked them into her pocket. "You won't be needing these anytime soon," she said. "They'll make a nice addition to my collection."

Dawson shrugged. "Be my guest," he said. "Just don't use them on me, that's all I ask."

Jenny smiled and winked at him. "Oh, why not? I keep hoping you give me a reason."

She found a couple of suitcases and searched them quickly, but there were no more weapons to be found. She double checked the drawers in the dresser, and then stood back and watched as Dawson began packing his clothes and toiletries.

"It's possible they'll be watching me," he said to Noah as he worked. "Not directly, but watching my travel cards and such. If I don't buy a plane ticket, it could look suspicious."

"Then you'll buy a ticket," Noah said. "But you'll fly on the Gulfstream with us. By the time anyone realizes you're not on the flight you bought the ticket for, this should be over."

"That's where you're wrong," Dawson said as he folded a shirt into the suitcase. "We may take out the Director, but someone else will simply take his place. This thing is like a giant spider, and its web spans the entire world."

"Then you have a lot more to tell us," Noah said. "Luckily, we have a nice, long flight ahead of us. You can do a lot of talking in a comfortable jet like the Gulfstream."

Dawson grunted and continued with what he was doing. A few minutes later, with all of his things packed and his weapons stuffed up under the mattress of the bed, they left the room and went down to the restaurant off the lobby. They sat down and ordered coffee while they waited for Gary and Neil to return.

Thirty minutes later, the Toyota pulled in and they walked out of the hotel. Gary opened the trunk of the car for the bags and then they all got back inside.

"Neil, Mr. Dawson needs a ticket to Rio de Janeiro. He'll provide you the credit card number."

Dawson glanced at Noah, then reached into the inner pocket of his jacket and produced his wallet. He took out a credit card and handed it over to Neil, who brought up an airline webpage and quickly purchased a first-class ticket with it.

"Done," Neil said. "Your flight will arrive tomorrow afternoon, twenty-three hours from now. I hope your expense account can handle first-class."

"I always fly luxury," Dawson said. "It's so much more comfortable that way."

"Where to, boss?" Gary asked.

"Let's head back to the airport," Noah said. "I'll call ahead and arrange for the pilots to get a flight plan filed to Rio. They should be ready to leave by the time we get there."

Neil glanced back at him. "That'll put Dawson in the city several hours before his commercial flight is due to arrive."

Noah nodded. "That's exactly what I'm counting on. We need to know if anyone is watching for him to arrive, and that's how we'll spot them."

Gary pulled out of the parking lot and headed back toward the airport. Noah was right, and by the time they arrived, the Gulfstream was fueled and ready. They all walked up the ramp together as the flight crew loaded their luggage.

Noah sat down beside Dawson, while Jenny and Neil took the

seats facing them. Gary took the single seat on the other side of the aisle, where he could hear the conversation that was about to take place. Noah logged his subcom on to the built-in Wi-Fi of the airplane and made contact with the server, then put a call through to Allison.

Back in Kirtland, Allison saw the caller ID register the number from the server that was assigned directly to Team Camelot and answered instantly. "Camelot, report," she said.

"We have taken Caleb Dawson prisoner," Noah said. "It turns out that Spear is not a single individual after all, but an organization that uses many people like Dawson to achieve their purposes. In return for assisting us in taking out the current director of the organization, I have agreed to give Dawson a chance to come to work for E & E. I'm about to debrief him on the organization, as we are on the plane headed toward Rio de Janeiro. It's currently expected that this is where we will find the Director."

Allison was quiet for a few seconds, then she let out a sigh. "As much as I hate it, it might be worth it. None of the agencies have been able to get any real information on Spear, so this could be a windfall." She paused for a second. "Do you have any way to record the debriefing? I'd like to hear it, later."

"Actually, yes," Noah said. "The server that routes our phone calls can also record what comes through the subcom. It's a new feature, but I'll set it up now."

"Do so," Allison said, and then the line went dead. Noah told the server to record and heard a voice that sounded a lot like the technician who designed the system say, "Recording activated."

He turned to Dawson, who had been staring at him while he seemingly spoke to nobody. "All right," he said. "Start talking."

Dawson shrugged. "What do you want to know?"

"Everything you can tell us about Spear. I want names, places, situations—absolutely anything you know that might help us take this organization down."

Dawson sighed deeply. "I don't have a clue how many people are involved," he said, "but it's got to be quite a number. They have a ruling council that plans their operations, and I know some of the people involved in that. Doctor Harold Simpson was one of them, but he's met with an untimely end." He looked at Noah and raised an eyebrow. "I have a feeling that might have been your work?"

"It was," Noah said. "Keep going."

"Okay," he said. "There are a few names on the Council you're likely to recognize. Senator Larken Mitchell is one of them, the retired senator from Alabama. There's also Philip Gates, he's a current congressman from the Philadelphia area. Arthur Adams, the Deputy Attorney General, is another one. Lord William Struthers, he is a member of Parliament in England. I think those are the only names I know for sure, but I've met a few others and could probably identify them if I saw them again."

"Wait a minute," Neil said. "You're telling us that all of these people are involved in this organization to manipulate different governments?"

"Oh, yes," Dawson said. "Do you have any idea how much money can be made in financing wars and conflicts? The organization is all about that, all about making money by deciding who is going to win and who is going to lose. Ironically, it's the losers who end up paying the most."

"Then what about all the terrorist actions?" Noah asked. "Why do things like the stuff that happened in Berlin? All that's done has been to limit what Germany can accomplish."

"That's how you see it," Dawson said. "To the organization, it has put Germany in a position of needing assistance from the rest of the EU, which will lead eventually to an economic collapse of the entire union. When the euro falls apart, there's going to be a run on the banks throughout Europe. Like I said, the organization is all about making money. When the banks over there start to collapse, you can expect several of those countries to suddenly erupt in border wars. They will all be handing over whatever they have in the form of gold or other precious metals to get their hands on the weapons and supplies they need to survive the conflicts." He grinned. "Don't feel too bad for Germany," he said. "I happen to know that the Director has already set it up for Germany to come out on top of the entire European Union when the dust settles. In fact, it's likely that several of the smaller countries will be absorbed right into them."

"Won't that lead to another world war?" Jenny asked. "The rest of the world isn't going to stand by and watch Germany take over Europe again."

Dawson turned to her. "If it was a matter of German aggression, you'd be correct. In this case, however, it's going to be a matter of Germany coming to the rescue of those other countries. They are actually going to be the one that stays out of fights, and the money that the organization will funnel into Germany, money that will be carefully laundered through several other countries, will enable them to offer humanitarian aid. A lot of those smaller countries are going to be grateful just for the chance to survive, so becoming part of the Fatherland isn't going to be nearly as bad as extinction."

"And how do we stop this from happening?" Noah asked. "Taking out the Director surely won't be enough. What will we have to do to prevent it?"

"I sincerely doubt you can," Dawson said. "This is the culmination of a plan that has been in the works for more than twenty years. Spear has been around a lot longer than you might think; I've even heard rumors that Henry Kissinger was one of its founders, and when you think about some of the things he said, it's believable."

"Give the world a common enemy, and they will happily surrender their liberties," Gary said softly. "That was one of the things Kissinger said."

Dawson nodded. "Exactly," he said. "In this case, the common enemy will be each other. There's a corollary to that, however, and that is the fact that when you have a common enemy, you also need a common savior. Germany will be the one to come to the rescue of all the other European nations. That's how they come out on top, and the world will be introduced to a new world superpower."

Noah shook his head. "There has to be a way to stop it," he said. "How can we identify the rest of the major players in the organization?"

Dawson grinned and looked at Jenny. "Turn her loose on the people I've already named," he said. "Most of them are politicians, they're not going to have the strength to resist serious interrogation." He winked at Jenny. "Especially her style."

Noah glanced at Jenny, who was trying to stifle a grin at the prospect. "We may have to do exactly that," he said. "What about their current plans? What's the next big thing they're up to?"

Dawson leaned his head back for a second, as if thinking. When he looked at Noah again, he was grinning. "There's a move coming that's going to be pretty devastating to most of the West," he said. "The Director has been working for quite some time to get certain people in position where he wants them, so that he can have people under his control in powerful offices. I can't give you exact details, but I know that there are at least a few Western world leaders who are going to be replaced in the near future. Some of them will be assassinated, some will be lost to accidents, and a few of them are simply going to be taken out of office after being exposed in some sort of scandals. The organization has long reach, and they can definitely touch anybody. When it begins, it'll be like a string of dominoes toppling over; one right after the other, and it'll happen too fast for anyone to stop it."

"And what's the goal? Simply to have his own puppets in place?"

"Tell me, Mr. Camelot, how much control would you have over the world if you could pull the strings on five or six of the most powerful world leaders? We're talking about enough power to essentially rule the whole planet, simply by making sure the most powerful nations do things the way you want them done."

Neil stared at him, and then he sneered. "Another bid to rule the world? Do you know how many of those we already stopped?"

"Did you?" Dawson asked. "Some of the earlier attempts to reach that kind of power had been absorbed right into this one. And before you get all cocky, you might as well understand that if this one were to get taken down, parts of it will still survive. The basis of any attempt to take over the world is always going to be a philosophy, and the philosophy in this case is one that has been around for centuries. It's based on the idea that the majority of the people are simply too stupid to know what's good for them, so they need a government that's going to make those decisions on their behalf. As long as there are politicians being voted into office, this philosophy is not going to die out."

"I don't think there's much chance of eliminating the democratic process," Noah said. "The best we can do for now is simply to eliminate the threats as they appear." He cocked his head and looked closely at Dawson. "Tell me something," he said. "Why are you being so cooperative? I get the feeling there's more to it than just a hope to stay alive a little longer."

Dawson grinned at him. "Did you ever have a job you didn't like?" he asked. "Just because I took the money doesn't mean I agree with everything they want to do. Spear lost a few people over the last couple of years, and the losses were just enough to slow them down a bit. If it hadn't happened the way it did, a lot of this would already be happening now."

"And you are behind those losses?" Noah asked.

"Some of them, yes," Dawson said. "A few of them were not mine, but I suspect there might be someone else within the organization who feels like I do. We can't stop it, we're too small. The best we can hope to do is slow them down, or at least that's what I was trying to do."

"And you don't know who else might have been working against them?" Jenny asked.

He looked at her. "I'm afraid not," he said. "If I did, I'd probably pretend I didn't, anyway. I'm pretty sure I wouldn't want anybody else inside the organization knowing what I've done, if you know what I mean. Whoever else was working against them probably wouldn't take kindly to me dropping in and offering to help."

"I can see that," Noah said. "So, at least one or two of you decided you didn't want to see their plans materialize. Do you think there's any way we can spread that further into the organization?"

Dawson sucked his bottom lip for a second. "I don't know how you could," he said. "One thing you can be sure of is that nobody inside the organization actually trusts anybody else. If someone had come to me and said they were trying to recruit from within to put a stop to what they were doing, I can guarantee you my first move would have been to let the Director know who approached me. The chance that it was a test would be too great a risk."

"Of course," Noah said. "You really wouldn't have much of a choice. All right, so there's not much hope of infiltrating the organization and taking it down from the inside. What we're going to have to do is identify the most powerful players one by one. You've given us a few names, and we can build on that list. Excuse me for a few moments."

He got up out of his seat and moved to another part of the airplane, then put a call through to Allison once again.

"Camelot, report."

"It turns out Spear is a lot more ambitious than we thought," Noah said. "I recorded everything on the server, so you can download it for analysis. In the recording, Dawson gave us the names of several people who are involved in the organization council. I would very much like to get the lot of them together, where Jenny can have a talk with them."

"Jenny? This must be pretty serious. All right, Noah, I'll get on it. I'll call you when I've got things arranged."

"All right," Noah said. "We'll be landing in Rio several hours from now, and hopefully we will be able to take out the Director by the end of the day tomorrow. The people Dawson gave us will know more of the names, and we are going to need to take each of them out as quickly as we can. The organization has plans that are going to be devastating to the world if they don't get stopped quickly."

"Very good," Allison said. "I'll be sharing this information with the rest of our own agencies, and possibly even some of our allies."

The line went dead again, and Noah leaned back in his seat. With Jenny watching him, Dawson wasn't going anywhere. It was time for a much-needed rest, but first, he had one more call to make.

"Noah to Sarah," he said, and the delight in his wife's voice almost made him smile when she replied.

TWENTY-TWO

GALEAO INTERNATIONAL AIRPORT SERVES THE RIO DE Janeiro area, and is one of the busiest airports in that part of South America, serving over fifteen million passengers per year. The Gulfstream touched down on the runway at just before noon local time, and taxied toward the terminal.

Noah had been notified two hours earlier that Molly had already arranged for their transportation and accommodations. When they came off the plane, the local E & E liaison was waiting for them.

"Mr. Wolf," the man said, "my name is Emanuel Garza. Welcome to Rio de Janeiro."

Despite his name, Mr. Garza's accent bore no trace of local flavor. In fact, he sounded like someone who had grown up in the southern U.S.A. Noah shook his hand and smiled. "Good to meet you," he said.

"And you, sir. We've heard a lot about you, and it's a pleasure to finally shake your hand. Please, all of you follow me. I have cars waiting for you, so you don't have to put up with all the BS at the rental counters."

"What about customs?" Noah asked.

Garza grinned. "All taken care of," he said. "One of the nice things about being in South America is that it's absolutely amazing how easy it is to cut through red tape with a little green paper. Just about everybody here is open to what we call 'negotiable cooperation.' We try not to think of it as bribery, but hey, whatever works, right?"

"My kind of people," Neil said. "Who needs red tape when there's a little money to throw around?"

They followed Garza through the terminal and Noah noticed that some of the police officers standing around seemed to pay a little attention to them, but no one moved to stop them. A moment later, they stepped out through the front doors and found a pair of Range Rovers waiting for them. Both of them were silver, and guards handed keys to Noah and Neil.

"Ms. Hansen said we were supposed to provide you with weapons," he said. "You'll find them in the back of each car, but I'm afraid the best we could do is some Beretta handguns."

"That's all right," Noah said. "We brought some with us, as well."

Garza's eyebrows rose. "And you were planning to take them through customs?"

"False bottoms," Noah said, tapping his suitcase. "These are good enough they've never been spotted before."

The liaison whistled and rolled his eyes. "You're a braver man than me," he said. "You wouldn't believe what they do to people who try to smuggle weapons into the country here. Anyway, you'll find a file in each car telling you about your hotel. Rooms are already arranged, and there is also a healthy supply of local currency. My direct cell number is in the file, so if you need anything else, all you have to do is call me."

Noah thanked him and he walked away. Noah, Gary and Dawson got into the first Land Rover with Dawson riding shotgun and Gary in the back seat. Neil and Jenny took the second, though it took Neil a moment to get the seat back far enough for him to get inside and drive.

Noah glanced into the file and found the name of the hotel,

the Hilton Copacabana, along with its address. The car had a GPS system, so he punched it in, then followed the directions to get to it. They checked in and went to their rooms, with Noah, Dawson and Gary sharing one room while Neil and Jenny had another to themselves. Once they were settled in, they all gathered in Noah's room and Noah nodded to Jenny.

Without a word, she produced Dawson's blue cell phone and handed it to him. He turned it on and waited until Neil gave him a nod before dialing Joshua's number. Neil had his computer out and was playing a background noise that sounded like the interior of a commercial jet. The muted roar of jet engines could be heard, along with the random chatter of passengers and flight attendants.

He hit the dial button and waited for the call to connect. A moment later, Joshua's voice came on the line.

"It's me," Dawson said. "Did you get hold of him?"

"There's a lot of background noise," Joshua said. "Are you still on the plane?"

"Of course," Dawson said. "We don't land for a few more hours, but it was time to call in. Did you make the arrangements?"

Joshua hesitated for a second, and Dawson's eyes narrowed.

"I did," Joshua said finally. "I can tell you that he was not pleased that you wanted to meet so soon, but if you are going to Rio, you can find him at the Marriott on the beach. He'll be in room six fourteen, but don't go there. Call him and he'll meet you in the restaurant."

"All right," Dawson said. "If you hear from him, tell him I'll be in touch in a few hours."

He ended the call and handed the phone back to Jenny, who stuck it back in her pocket, then turned to Noah.

"Room six fourteen at the Marriott," he said. "If we move now, we could get this done before they even know I'm in the country."

"Not just yet," Noah said. He looked at Neil. "Can you confirm?"

Neil already had his computer set up on the table and was tapping away on the keyboard. "First, I need to find a way into the Marriott security system," he said. "That shouldn't take long, and then I can check the video feeds around that room." He continued what he was doing for another couple of minutes, then said, "Bingo! I'm in. Now, let me see—here we go, sixth floor. I've got the video feeds from twelve cameras on the sixth floor, but I can't see the room numbers. Hang on another moment." He opened another window and typed for several seconds, and then clicked on a link that showed him the layout of the building. He identified room six fourteen, then went back to the other window and found the camera that had it in the best view.

Suddenly, people appeared on the monitor, but they were moving much faster than normal. They were also moving backward, as Neil ran the recording back until the hallway went dark. At that point, he moved it forward again, taking ten second jumps. Each frame that appeared on the monitor stayed for about a second, and then switched to another. Whenever someone could be seen in the frame, he quickly hit a button to freeze it. Dawson would lean close to see if he recognized the person, but each time, he shook his head.

Most of an hour passed by while they were scanning the security feed, but then another person appeared and Dawson said, "Wait. Let me get a better look."

Neil switched to another camera view that looked down the hall and managed to zoom in on the face of the person.

Dawson grinned. "That's him," he said. "That's the Director."

"It looks like he just checked in this morning," Noah said. "Neil, can you tell if he is still in the room?"

Neil went back to scanning ahead on the video, and fifteen minutes later, he turned to Noah with a grin. "At the moment, I would say he's there," he said. "Nobody has left that room since he entered earlier."

Noah looked at Dawson. "Are you ready?"

"I work for you, now," Dawson said. "You give the orders, I follow."

Noah nodded. "Let's go, then. Jenny, you're with us."

The three of them walked out the door and went straight to the elevator. The Marriott was only a kilometer away from the hotel they were in, and would only take a few minutes to get there. Noah kept his subcom on, so that Neil could warn him if the Director was to suddenly appear in the hallway.

They got into Noah's Range Rover and he drove quickly to the Marriott, parking the car out of sight of the main entrance. The three of them walked quickly toward the door and inside, then acted as if they belonged there as they went to the elevator and took it to the sixth floor. As they stepped out of the elevator, Noah checked in with Neil.

"Neil to Noah," he heard. "No activity at the door. If he's left that room, he did it out the window."

"All right," Noah said. He turned to Dawson and reached up under the back of his jacket to hand over a pistol. "One wrong move and you die instantly," he said. He let Dawson see the small Russian PSS silent pistol that he held in his hand.

Dawson glanced at it. "Sweet," he said. "No sound at all, right? Just a click?"

"Behave yourself and you won't find out," Jenny said.

Dawson grinned at her and turned toward room six fourteen. "How do you propose to get him to open the door?" he asked Noah.

Jenny stepped past him and walked ahead a few feet, stopping at the door and knocking on it. She put a smile on her face as she looked at the peephole. "*Serviço de quarto*," she said in impeccable Portuguese. "*Por favor?*"

The light blinked out through the peephole and Jenny kept the smile on her face, and a moment later they heard the lock click. The door swung open and all three of them rushed through it, dragging the man behind the door into the room with them.

"What the hell?" he yelled, and then he got a look at Dawson. "Lancaster? What is this?"

"I'm afraid, Director," Dawson said, "that it's the beginning of the end." He raised the pistol in his hand and pointed it into the man's face, but Noah reached out and pushed it up toward the ceiling.

"Not just yet," Noah said. He looked at the man who was now sitting on the bed, leaning back on his hands and his eyes wide. "First, we need some information."

"Lancaster? You've turned on us?"

"Yeah, well, it seemed like a good idea. It was either that or die, and I'm kinda fond of living." Dawson grinned at him.

Jenny picked up a jacket that was laying on the bed and found the wallet in the inner pocket. She opened it up and found an American driver's license from Florida, which she handed to Noah.

"David Garrity," Noah read. "Well, Mr. Garrity, I think you can figure out what's going on. Mr. Dawson, or Lancaster or whatever his name is, has decided to terminate his employment with you. He's coming to work for us, and part of the negotiation for his agreement was to allow him to terminate you personally. Before he does that, I wanted to give you a chance to negotiate for your own life."

Dawson's eyes went wide and he spun on Noah. "Wait a minute," he said. "We had a deal, remember?"

"Every deal is subject to renegotiation," Noah said. He reached out and took the pistol away from Dawson, then handed it to Jenny. She held it carefully, standing back out of reach as she kept both of the men covered. "If Mr. Garrity was to give us sufficient information, we might make another arrangement for him. I understand there are couple of fairly comfortable cells available in a special prison that we use just for people like him." He turned back to Garrity. "Well?"

The man looked from Noah to Dawson and back. "That's my choice? Spend the rest of my life in a cell or die here and now?"

"Yes, that's it," Noah said. "If you give us information that helps to take down your organization, you can stay alive. If not, then you are of no further use to us and I can let Mr. Dawson have things the way he wants them."

"Unbelievable," Garrity said. "I never would have believed that you would turn on me." He shook his head, then turned to Noah. "I'm sorry, but this thing is bigger than I am. You can kill me if you wish, but it won't make any difference in the long run. Everything we have put into motion will proceed as it's supposed to, and there's nothing you can do to stop it."

Noah looked at the man for a second, then handed the silent pistol to Dawson. "Go ahead," he said. "This one is actually loaded."

Dawson glanced at the pistol in Jenny's hand and she pointed it at Garrity and squeezed the trigger. Nothing happened, and Garrity suddenly looked relieved. The relief banished from his face a second later when the PSS made a distinctive click and a hole appeared in his forehead. Blood and brain matter sprayed the bed and the wall behind it, and the Director of Spear fell back dead.

Dawson glanced at Jenny again and saw that she had produced another pistol, which was aimed carefully at him. He grinned at her and winked, then handed the PSS back to Noah.

"We good?" he asked.

"We're good," Noah said. "See if we can find any intelligence here." He slipped the pistol into his pocket, and the three of them began going through everything in the room. Jenny found Garrity's cell phone and a computer, while Dawson came up with a notebook filled with what looked like some sort of coded scribbles.

"All right, let's go," Noah said. "Our work here is done, but we still need to get back to Kirtland."

"Kirtland, Colorado," Dawson said. "I finally get to meet the Dragon Lady." He winked at Jenny again. "You can't believe how much I'm looking forward to it."

"I'm not too sure you should be," Jenny said. "She might just decide to turn you over to me after all."

Dawson lost his grin, but he followed Noah out the door without another word.

————

THEIR COPILOT HAD COME DOWN with a mild fever, so the entire flight crew was taken out of service. As a result, they were forced to spend the night in Rio while another flight crew was brought down from Houston. Noah and Gary took turns watching Dawson, but he made no effort to slip away. As far as Noah could tell, he was committed to doing whatever Noah wanted, as long as it meant he could stay alive.

They were called at four a.m. to tell them that the flight crew had arrived and the plane was ready to go. It took them only a short time to get checked out and then they dropped off the Range Rovers at the rental lots and made their way toward the charter gate.

The plane touched down at Kirtland at just before two p.m. local time, and a team of men was waiting to take charge of Dawson. Noah watched as he was loaded into a van and driven away, and then walked over to where Allison stood on the tarmac, waiting for them.

"Debriefing first," she said. "We're going to milk him for as much information as we can get, and then we will decide whether he's worth trying to salvage." She looked up at Noah. "I can't believe you made a deal for me to hire the very son of a bitch who killed Donald."

"Spear has been able to manipulate things on a global scale for a long time," Noah said. "From what Dawson has told us, they have probably been around since the sixties or seventies. I felt that gaining intelligence about them might be worth the trade-off."

"And as much as I hate it, you were probably right. From what we've learned from Renée over the last thirty hours, he knows a fair amount about the organization. If I don't sanction him, I'm probably going to give him a team and send him out after as many of their people as he can find, but the team is going to have orders to terminate him if he goes off script even once."

Noah nodded. "I think that's a good idea. Let him clean up the mess."

"Exactly." She watched as the van drove away, then turned back to Noah and the others. "This has been a pretty busy airport, today. Four other planes have come in, and each of them had one of the people Dawson told you about. We have them in an interrogation facility out behind R&D." She looked at Jenny. "Do you want to rest up first?"

"Oh, hell, no," Jenny said. "Do you have any idea how much stress I got built up inside me? I need to let it out, and these are exactly the kind of people who need to help me relieve my stress."

"Yes, I thought you would feel that way," Allison said with a grin. She turned toward a young man standing nearby and clicked a finger at him. "This is Darrell," she said. "He'll drive you out there."

Jenny smiled, and then she and Neil got into the car Darrell was driving. It pulled away a moment later, leaving Noah and Gary standing alone with Allison.

"When she gets done," Allison said, "you're going to have an awful lot of work to do, Noah."

"I know," Noah said. "But first, there are couple of things I'd like to take care of here at home."

"Oh, really? A visit to your wife, maybe?" Allison smiled.

"Definitely," Noah said, "but first I need to make a stop at the cemetery."

———

NOAH STOOD AT THE GRAVESITE, noticing that the ground still looked freshly turned. It would take a while for the dirt to settle back in and smooth out, but that didn't matter.

"I got him, Donald," he said. "I got the man who ordered your death, but not the one who actually caused it."In his mind, he heard Jefferson answer. "It's all right, Noah," the imaginary voice said. "Sometimes you have to make a trade. The nice thing about this life is that each and every one of us will eventually get what's coming to us. He who lives by the sword will die by the sword, isn't that what they always say?"

"Yes," Noah said. "I suppose they do."

"Then don't worry about it. Dawson will get justice someday. Don't let it eat at you until he does. You have too much work to do, Noah. And from everything I've been hearing, it's probably just beginning."

Noah turned off his imagination and walked away from the grave. He climbed back into the car Allison had driven him there in and looked at her.

"All done?" she asked. "Ready to go home?"

"For the moment," Noah said. "I could stand a decent night's sleep."

Allison patted his arm. "I'm pretty sure there's a little blonde waiting to make sure you get one." She put the car in gear and drove away, heading out of town toward Temple Lake Road.

TWENTY-THREE

NEIL WASN'T A FAN OF WATCHING JENNY WORK, SO HE decided to visit R&D while she went to the interrogation facility. Being technically minded himself, he was always welcome there and Wally was delighted to show off some of his new toys.

Jenny didn't mind. She knew that he could be squeamish at times, and she didn't want to have to think about him while she was enjoying herself this way.

Senator Mitchell was first. He was sitting in one of the interrogation rooms, looking slightly bewildered when the diminutive blonde walked in.

"Are you here to tell me what's going on?" he asked. "Because I don't have any idea what this is all about, and it's getting a little old just sitting here."

Jenny grinned at him. "I guess you could say that," she said. "Actually, I'm here to ask you a few questions. If you answer me properly, then you get to have a good day. If not, then I get to have a good day."

Mitchell narrowed his eyes. "Young lady, what the hell are you talking about?"

"I'm talking about Spear," Jenny said, and she watched his

face for a reaction. She saw it, just a split second of pure terror that crossed his face before he managed to get it under control.

"Spear? What is that?"

"Now, see? That's exactly the kind of wrong answer I was expecting." She reached behind herself and pulled out a couple of the karambit daggers, hooking her index fingers into the rings and giving them a spin as they came into view. "Next time you give me a wrong answer, I'm going to demonstrate just how much I love these little toys of mine."

Mitchell got up out of his chair and stood warily, watching her like a hawk. "Now, see here," he said. "This isn't legal. I don't know where you and I are, but this is..."

"This is the place where you can either tell me the truth or I can skin you alive, one square inch at a time, and nobody is going to get the least bit upset about it." She giggled. "Especially me, I love this stuff."

Mitchell swallowed hard. "But I'm telling you, I don't know anything about..."

Before he could even react, she had spun herself around and dragged the tip of one of the blades across his chest. The blade was sharp, cutting through his shirt and the skin underneath as if both of them were made of tissue paper. It happened so quickly that Mitchell didn't even register that he had been cut until the warm blood began to flow down onto his belly, making him look down.

Suddenly, it hurt like hell, and he screamed.

"Tell me about Spear," she said. "I want names, places, all of it."

Mitchell clapped his hands onto his chest, trying to hold the flayed skin together, but the blood was oozing between his fingers. The cut wasn't terribly deep, but it was bleeding rather profusely.

"But I don't know," he said. "I swear to you, I don't know what you're talking about!"

The second blade flashed and a piece of his earlobe fell to the floor. This time, he felt the pain as soon as it happened, the white hot pain that came with the removal of a piece of useless but sensitive skin. He howled out loud, and tried to keep one arm over the wound in his chest while he slapped the other hand onto his ear.

"Two for two," Jenny said. "I'll bet you that I can take the other ear off completely, what do you think?"

Mitchell clamped his mouth shut and swallowed again, then took a deep breath and looked at her. "Okay! Okay, I'll tell you whatever you want to know. Just stop that, you're going to make me bleed to death."

Jenny lowered the knives and looked at him, and an expression of disappointment came over her face. "Hell, you're no fun," she said. She turned and looked at the mirror on the wall. "Okay, he's all yours," she said.

The door opened a moment later and two men came in. They stood there and looked at Mitchell as Jenny walked out of the room, noticing that each of them was wearing a pair of the deception detecting glasses Wally's people had developed.

Another man was standing in the hallway, waiting for her. He pointed toward another door and she stepped through it. Arthur Adams, Deputy Attorney General of the United States, looked up from his chair by the table.

"Well, hello," he said with a smile. "Are you going to tell me what's going on?"

Jenny returned the smile. "You could say that..."

———

SARAH WAS delighted when Allison dropped Noah off at the house, and it didn't take her long to drag him into the bedroom. First, he let her know just how much he had missed her. Then, since he had spent most of the last two days awake, keeping track of Dawson, he curled up close to her and went to sleep.

Neil and Jenny arrived back at the trailer around six, and Neil came over to the house. Sarah had heard him pull in and slipped out of bed to tell him that Noah was sleeping, and seemed to need more rest. Neil nodded and whispered that he would see them in the morning, then made his way back over to the trailer, where Jenny was showering off the blood that was coating her when she had gotten back to him.

Noah awoke at six a.m. and made his way to the kitchen to start coffee before Sarah got up, then went back to the bedroom and went to the shower. He was trying to rinse the shampoo out of his hair when the shower door opened and Sarah climbed in with him.

"Need some help?" she asked.

"You can wash my back," Noah said. She did so, then turned him around and proceeded to wash the front of him just as thoroughly. By the time they were finished in the shower, the water was getting cold.

They climbed out and toweled off, then slipped into casual clothes and headed for the kitchen. Noah poured them coffee while Sarah started bacon frying and got out the eggs she was going to scramble into an omelette. The bacon was just beginning to sizzle when Neil and Jenny knocked on the door.

"How did it go?" Noah asked Jenny.

"Kinda boring," she said. "The Englishman was the most entertaining of the bunch, but even he caved in before I could really start cutting deep."

Noah nodded. "Did you learn anything good?"

"I didn't," she said. "I left the real interrogation up to Allison's people. I guess they just wanted me to soften them up, let them know what would happen if they didn't cooperate."

"That was probably an effective technique," Noah said. "I doubt any of them wanted to see you again anytime soon."

"What's going to happen to them now?" Sarah asked. "After Jenny gets done with them, do they just send them off to prison or something?"

"Maybe the special prison," Noah said. "The one they kept

Allison in for a while is used when a high-ranking official needs to be kept on ice. Either that, or they end up in the potter's field." The potter's field was the cemetery where those who were terminated by E & E locally were buried. None of the graves had names on the markers; they had numbers only, so that it would be possible to identify who was buried where, should the situation ever be necessary.

Only Neil showed any remorse at the thought that these traitors might be terminated. He shuddered once, but didn't say anything.

Noah's phone rang at that moment, and he saw that it was Allison calling. He picked it up and hit the speaker button as he answered.

"Camelot," he said.

"It's Allison," she said, unnecessarily as ever. "My office, nine a.m. Bring everybody, even Sarah."

Sarah's eyebrows shot upward, but she didn't say a word.

Noah answered, "We'll be there," and the line went dead.

"Why me?" Sarah asked. "Is she going to send me out with you after all?"

"I don't know," Noah said. "I suppose it's possible." He dialed Marco's number, also on speaker, and wasn't surprised when the man answered instantly.

"Noah? Are you back?"

"We got in yesterday," Noah said. "I just needed to get some rest. Thing is, Allison just called and said to bring everyone to the office at nine. How's Renée doing?"

"She seems perfectly normal," Marco said. "Doc Parker says he wants to talk more with her, but that he thinks her biggest problem now is just feeling like she let the team down. I keep telling her it wasn't her fault, but you know how women are."

"No," Jenny said. "Tell us how women are, Marco."

"Hi, Jenny," Marco said, chuckling. "You know what I mean, she just keeps trying to blame herself."

"It could be worse," Neil said. "She could blame you."

"I wouldn't mind, if it would bring her out of the funk. No, really, she seems to be doing okay most of the time. Like I said, she just feels like she messed up."

"Well, if Doctor Parker is comfortable that she's all right, she may get a chance to prove herself. We brought in Dawson, and between him and some other people that were rounded up, I gather we got some intel on others involved in this whole conspiracy. I suspect we're getting ready to go out on another mission, so I hope you enjoyed the couple of days you had off."

"I'm up for whatever we need to do," Marco said. "Nine a.m., right? We'll be there."

"See you then," Noah said, and he cut off the call. He dropped the phone on the table and dug into the omelette that Sarah put in front of him.

She put a couple more plates in front of Neil and Jenny, then made one for herself and sat down. "I figured you guys would be over," she said. "I think Neil can smell the bacon as soon as I put it in the skillet."

"Hey," Neil said. "I didn't smell it until we got into your driveway."

They ate breakfast together, something they did fairly often, and then Neil and Jenny sat at the table drinking coffee while Noah and Sarah went to dress properly for the day. By the time they returned to the kitchen, Jenny had already made a second pot of coffee. Noah and Sarah got another cup each and sat down, and Noah let Neil and Jenny fill Sarah in on how the mission had gone.

"I hope I get to go with you this time," Sarah said. "I'm not even showing yet, not really. I can still drive."

"We'll find out when we get there," Noah said. "Although, I can't say I really like the idea of you going out on a mission. If it's up to me, I think you need to stay here."

Sarah stuck her tongue out at him. "In that case, I'm glad it's not entirely up to you."

THEY ARRIVED at the offices of Brigadoon Investments a few minutes early, all of them riding in Neil's big Hummer. He parked it in the underground garage and they took the elevator up to the top floor, where Allison's office and conference room were. The receptionist, a new girl they hadn't seen before, told them to go on to the conference room.

They walked in to find Marco and Renée already there, along with Allison and Molly. Neil went to the side table and grabbed a couple of donuts and coffee, but the rest of them just sat down around the table.

"Molly?" Allison said. "Go ahead."

Molly, who had been Noah's childhood friend, cleared her throat and pointed to the video screen behind her. A remote in her hand clicked and a number of photographs appeared on the screen.

"After interrogation of all the prisoners last night, we identified more than fifty individuals involved in the Spear organization," she began. "Almost all of them are ranking political officials in various countries and they are being rounded up, but there's one person we've yet to locate." She waved the remote again and the collage of photos disappeared, to be replaced by one image that made all of them stare at the screen.

"That's not possible," Sarah said. "He's dead, I killed him myself!"

The image they were looking at was that of Nicolaich Andropov, the former Russian superspy who had gone rogue and kidnapped Sarah twice in attempts to trap Noah and kill him.

"You're right," Molly said. "This is not the man you think it is. This is Gregor Sokolov, but he may be a close relative of Andropov's. I admit, the resemblance is uncanny; Allison showed me photos of Andropov, and I would almost swear it was the same man myself."

"All right," Noah said. "How does this guy figure into our Spear situation?"

"That's pretty simple," Molly said. "From what we learned last night, he is next in line to take over as Director, and eliminating him is going to be absolutely necessary if we want to bring this organization to an end. Sokolov is currently wanted by Russian authorities for a number of crimes, including several assassinations. He is one of the highest ranking members of Spear, and it's imperative that he be terminated as quickly as possible."

"But we have no idea where he is?" Neil asked. He had also been abducted by Andropov at one point, and he was obviously still shaken by the resemblance.

"Not at the moment," Molly admitted, "but there is one person who might know his whereabouts. That person is his daughter, Yvonne." She clicked the remote and a photo of a young woman appeared on the screen. "Yvonne is a professional interpreter in Geneva, but we know that her father visits her there fairly regularly. You are being sent to Geneva today, to begin surveillance on her and watch for her father to appear. When he does, you will do whatever is necessary to terminate him with extreme prejudice."

"Whatever is necessary," Jenny repeated. "That makes it sound like this is not going to be an easy job."

"Unfortunately, that's correct," Allison said. "Sokolov commands a small private army, more than a dozen former Russian special forces troops that have sworn loyalty to him. Besides those, he has more than a hundred other people working with him, and all of them are known to be proficient with weapons. Taking him out may involve a lot of collateral damage, but it's absolutely necessary. If he is allowed to assume control of Spear, the organization will be back up to full strength within months. We cannot allow that to happen."

Noah nodded. "All right," he said. "Mission identities?"

"You'll continue to use the ones you already have," Molly said. "None of them were compromised on this last mission, and we need you to be on the way to Geneva immediately. Because I knew you just got in, I took the liberty of having bags packed for you. They'll be waiting for you at the airplane, so you don't even need to go home to pack."

"Molly," Renée said. "I don't know if I'm really ready to go out again."

Molly turned to her, but before she could speak, Allison interrupted.

"Parker says you are," she said. "That's good enough for me." She turned to Noah. "You're also taking Sarah with you this time," she said. "Her identity was easy to create, so it will be in her bag at the airport. She is your wife, of course, so you'll be able to establish a cover as a tourist couple. In fact, each of you will maintain that cover until your target appears. At that point, Noah, you will have to determine the best way to carry out your mission and make it happen."

"All right," Noah said. "What about equipment?"

"I already thought of that," Allison said, "so Wally is waiting for you. You can stop at R&D and get whatever you think you need, then go on to the plane. I need you in Geneva by tomorrow morning, their time."

The dismissal was obvious, so Noah got to his feet and the rest followed. They went down the elevator together, then Marco followed the Hummer out to the R&D building.

"You just don't get a break, do you?" Wally asked. "You just got home, and now you're going out again. Any idea what you want to take with you?"

"I want one of the explosive printers," Noah said. "Also, I need some sort of a missile launcher. Something that can be accurate over distance, good enough to hit a target dead on."

Wally giggled. "Oh, have I got something to show you. Follow me!"

They all followed him down the hall, and he stepped into a large room that was set up like a firing range. It was almost 100 feet long, and there were four shooting lanes. A couple of technicians looked up as they entered and Wally motioned one of them to come closer.

"Noah, this is Lonnie," Wally said. "Lonnie, Noah Wolf. He wants to see the blaster."

Lonnie let out a grin and shook Noah's hand. "Sir, I've heard a lot about you," he said. "Come on, I'll show you what we came up with."

They followed him to a workstation and he picked up what looked like a simple plastic rod with a box on top of it. It was about three feet long and two inches in diameter, and one end had an opening that was about an inch and a half across.

"This is what we call the blaster," he said. "It looks pretty solid, but it's actually a single shot launcher for an AI-enhanced missile. The tip of the missile, which you can't see at the moment, has an extremely sensitive micro camera built into it. This little box," he said, pointing, "holds the video screen that lets you select your target. As long as you keep it pointed toward the target when you tell it to fire, that missile will do whatever it has to do to hit that target. If it has to duck around obstacles, it will, and it won't detonate at all until it hits its intended target. Come on, let me show you how it works."

He walked over to the firing range and hoisted the device up to his shoulder, holding it over his shoulder like a bazooka. He touched the box on top and it opened up to reveal a three inch video screen with crosshairs. The screen came to life and they watched as he moved it around, showing that whatever the weapon was pointed at was what appeared on the screen.

"Now, watch this," he said. "I'm going to put it on the bull's-eye of the target down there." He did so, and they saw the crosshairs light up on the bull's-eye. "Now, to make it lock, all I have to do is tap the screen once."

He reached up with one finger and tapped the screen, and the crosshairs began blinking. He moved the weapon to the left so that it was actually aiming into another firing lane, then tapped the screen again.

There was a soft *Whumpf,* and something shot out the open end. They saw a fiery tail as the missile took flight, and then watched as it curved around to go back to where it had originally been aimed. When it struck the target, Noah felt confident that it hit the bull's-eye dead on, and then it exploded into a fiery cloud that completely obliterated the target.

"That's perfect," he said. "Give me two of them, Wally."

TWENTY-FOUR

"THIS IS A BEAUTIFUL CITY," SARAH SAID THE NEXT day, when they got their first good look at Geneva. "You think we can get away with calling this a honeymoon?"

Noah shrugged. "Why not?" he said. "We don't know how long we'll be here, so we might as well enjoy it."

They were driving down the street, and Noah was enjoying the local architecture. They'd already seen the St. Pierre Cathedral and the United Nations building, and were driving toward the famous flower clock. In the seat behind them, Marco and Renée were also looking out the windows at the scenery, while Neil and Jenny were taking the first duty of watching Yvonne Sokolov.

The young woman had been easy to locate, and the intelligence agencies had told them that she was about as normal as any young Russian woman could be. Except for the fact that her father was a notorious criminal, there wasn't a single black mark on her record anywhere. She worked for the United Nations as an interpreter, and when she wasn't at work, she was usually at home.

That day happened to be her day off, and Neil and Jenny had her house staked out. They were sitting in a car just watching, waiting to see if the girl went anywhere or had any visitors, but so far, they'd seen nothing of interest.

Unfortunately, the first day set the tone for the next two weeks. They took turns watching Yvonne, and each of them spent some time in the United Nations building when she was on duty. Parts of it were open to the public, and they could conveniently keep an eye on her workspace most of the time.

Noah kept reminding them not to become lax. Just because Sokolov had not appeared, they still had to remain vigilant. Sooner or later, he was likely to show, because he rarely went more than a month without stopping to visit her. It had been almost a month since his last visit when they had arrived, so he was actually running late.

It was Marco and Renée who were on duty when he finally appeared, and Noah and Sarah were out sightseeing once again, with Neil and Jenny tagging along.

"Marco to Noah," Noah heard through the subcom. "Our boy just showed up. He drove up in a caravan of vehicles, and his security force is watching closely."

"Where are you?" Noah asked.

"Sitting outside the daughter's place. Daddy is headed inside the house now. What do you want us to do?"

"Just watch," Noah said. "We are on the way."

The rest of them arrived a half hour later, and Noah got a good look at the obviously armed security people who were standing around in front of the house. A couple of them had wandered around the back, according to Marco, but most of them were visible in plain sight.

"What's the approach?" Marco asked. "We could probably take him with a blaster when he comes out, but I doubt we'd have a chance of getting away afterward. Those people look serious."

"Undoubtedly," Noah said. "And the vehicles are probably armored, so trying to hit him in the car would probably be a wasted effort."

"I agree," Marco said. "Got any ideas?"

Noah sat behind the wheel of his van and watched for a couple more minutes. "He usually stays a couple of days," he said. "I think we'll keep watching for the moment, see what happens tomorrow. I want the rest of you to go back to the hotel, and take Sarah with you. I'm going to stay here and watch for the night."

Sarah looked at him. "Noah," she said. "You can't take them all alone."

"I don't have any intention of trying," he said. "I just want to be here if he decides to leave suddenly. If I can get a chance to take him out somewhere else, somewhere away from other people, that would be best. The trouble is going to be getting past his security guards. Even if the missile took out a few of them, it's not likely to get them all."

"Not even with both of them," Marco said. He looked at Noah for a moment, then said, "I can try a sniper shot. There's bound to be somewhere around here I can get a high vantage point."

"We might save that for a last resort," Noah said. "You can take a look around, see if you can find a spot that might work where you could see the front door. If you find one, let me know. Otherwise, just go on back to the hotel and get some rest. Somebody's going to have to relieve me in the morning."

Sarah leaned over and kissed him, then got out of the van and went to Marco's car. She, Neil and Jenny climbed into the back seat and Marco got behind the wheel and drove them away.

There was no sign of Sokolov through the night, and it was Neil who relieved Noah the following morning. Jenny came along with him, but Noah cautioned them to do nothing but watch. They were parked far enough down the street that the security guards were ignoring them, but close enough that they could tell if their target decided to leave the house.

At two o'clock that afternoon, Marco and Renée took over again. Neil and Jenny went back to the hotel, where Noah and Sarah were waiting for word that Sokolov was on the move.

An hour later, Marco called Noah by subcom.

"Marco to Noah, he's out. He's getting into his car, and his daughter is with him. Security guards are also loading up, so they're all headed somewhere."

"Good," Noah said. "Follow at a distance, try to keep them in sight. Give us a running account of where you go, and we'll catch up with you as soon as we can."

An hour later, Marco reported that the convoy had stopped at what appeared to be a floating restaurant on the Rhône. A couple of the security guards had gone into the restaurant with Sokolov and his daughter, but the rest were waiting near the cars.

"This might be our best opportunity," Noah said. "We'll be there in a couple of minutes, just keep an eye on the situation."

They arrived moments later and Noah saw the security guards standing around the vehicles in the parking lot that was across the street from where the floating restaurant was moored. He pulled the van in and parked, then he, Neil and Jenny climbed out. Sarah remained in the van, ready to pick them up in a hurry if necessary.

The three of them walked over to where Marco and Renée were sitting in their car.

"What you have in mind, boss?" Marco asked. "I know the Dragon Lady talked about collateral damage, but that's an awful lot of people in there. I'm not sure what we can do at this moment."

Noah leaned on his car door and looked over his shoulder at the restaurant. "I think I'm going to go inside and try to look the situation over," he said. "Our orders are to terminate Sokolov at the first possible opportunity, but I don't know if this is going to be it or not."

"If you're going in, so am I," Jenny said. "Besides, we'll look better as a couple. Nobody's likely to pay much attention to us if we're together."

Noah nodded. "I agree," he said. "Marco, I want you and Renée to drive down the street a bit. Just in case the security guys noticed you, I want you out of the line of fire if things get crazy."

"What about you?" Marco asked. "If things go crazy, you're going to be stuck inside there."

Noah looked at the restaurant again. "I think it's still worth taking a look. Sarah's got the van running, just in case we need a quick getaway. Be ready to run interference if we need it, okay?"

"Hey, wait a minute," Neil said. "What about me?"

"Just get in the car with Marco, pookie," Jenny said. "I want you out of the line of fire, too."

Noah turned and started toward the restaurant and Jenny followed. Neil stared after her for a moment, then got into the back seat of Marco's car. Marco started it up and put it in gear, left the parking lot and headed down the street away from the restaurant.

"Okay, Noah," Jenny said as they walked toward the front door. "What's our game plan?"

"For the moment, we're just going in to observe. I want to get a look at the target, see if there is any hope of accomplishing the mission this afternoon."

"Would've been nice if we'd known he was coming here," Jenny said. "We could have tried to set something up before he arrived. Maybe a nice cocktail filled with arsenic or something."

Noah glanced at her, then turned his face back forward. They walked through the door and were greeted by a hostess who seemed to speak perfect English.

Noah spotted Sokolov and his daughter near the back of the dining room as the hostess led them to a table that was only a couple of yards away. They sat down and picked up menus like any other tourists, but they were continuing to whisper to each other through the subcoms so that no one else would hear.

"I think we may have one play," Noah said. "He's sitting right near the entry toward the restrooms. If we could start some sort of distraction, something that will occupy the two security guards with him, then one of us might be able to get close enough to take him out."

"You take care of the distraction," Jenny whispered back. "I haven't gotten to kill anybody in weeks, this bastard is mine."

Noah continued looking at the menu for another moment, then whispered that he was going to make an attempt. He put down the menu and got up from his chair, then looked back at Jenny.

"I need to hit the head," he said. "Order me something to drink, will you?"

Jenny looked up with a smile. "Sure, babe," she said. She turned her face back toward the menu, but kept watching Noah from the corner of her eye.

Noah headed toward the men's room and watched Sokolov carefully as he passed by. Neither he nor his bodyguards seemed to pay much attention to him, so he went on to the men's room and made a show of flushing the toilet and splashing water around.

"Noah to Sarah," he said quietly.

"I'm here, baby," Sarah said. "Just be careful, please?"

"I think we have a chance at getting this done," Noah said. "I want you to leave the parking lot and drive down to where the bridge goes over the river. There should be somewhere there you can pull over and wait for us."

"Wait for you at the bridge? Noah, that's probably a quarter of a mile. How are you going to get away if the security guards come after you?"

"I've got that worked out," Noah said. "Now it's time for the distraction. Noah to Marco, are you listening?"

"You know it, boss. What you got in mind?" Marco's Cajun accent was coming out a little bit, the way it did when he was getting nervous.

"I want you to get out one of the blasters and hand it to Neil. Turn around and drive back past the restaurant as fast as you safely can, and then Neil, I want you to aim that thing at Sokolov's limousine. Try to hit it dead on, and that should keep everybody busy for at least a minute or two. Jenny, as soon as the blast goes off, you make your move and I'll take care of the body-guards inside. As soon as Sokolov is dead, then both of us go out the back and onto the deck. The water is our best escape route."

Jenny managed to giggle in her whisper. "I like the way you think, boss man. Neil, pookie, make your shot count."

"I'll do my best," Neil said. "Give us the word when you're ready for this to happen."

Noah reached for the knob on the bathroom door. "Now," he said. He opened the door and stepped out into the hallway, then made his way slowly back toward the dining room.

From outside on the street, the sound of tires squealing could be heard. A moment later, they heard people shouting outside as Marco drove rapidly back toward the restaurant, his engine racing as he raced along the narrow, two-lane road.

There was a sudden blast, and a flash of light came through the windows that faced the road. Sokolov's bodyguards leapt to their feet, snatching pistols out from under their jackets as they turned toward the door, and neither of them ever saw Noah pull the little PSS out of his pocket. It clicked twice, and people began screaming as blood and brain matter splattered across several tables.

Noah turned toward Sokolov, ready to take the shot if Jenny hadn't gotten close enough, but he focused his eyes just in time to see her grabbing the man by his hair and snatching head back as she dragged her curved karambit dagger across his throat. Sitting directly across from him, his daughter Yvonne began to scream, and Jenny looked at her.

The bloodlust in Jenny's face was obvious, but she jerked her eyes up to Noah. He shook his head once to tell her to leave the girl alone, and Jenny turned and ran through the curtain over the doorway that led out onto the deck. Noah pocketed his pistol and then followed Jenny through the doorway just in time to see her dive over the rail and into the water. He hit the water just behind her, and the two of them swam up under the restaurant. They surfaced between the floats and held onto the structure for a moment.

"Well," Jenny said softly. "That was fun. Do you think we have a snowball's chance in hell of getting out of this alive?"

"I think we are almost home free," Noah said. "Fill your lungs up good, because we need to stay under the surface for as long as we can. Just keep swimming toward the bridge, that's where Sarah will be waiting for us."

Jenny took several deep breaths, then nodded her head as she sank under the water. Noah did likewise, then the two of them swam under the surface for nearly a hundred yards. By the time they came out, sirens were screaming on the street beside the river and nobody was paying much attention to what was happening in the water.

Both of them were strong swimmers, and they made good time. Fifteen minutes later, they were able to climb out of the water and dive through the side door of the van. Sarah put it into gear as they closed the door and turned to cross the bridge.

"Noah to Marco," Noah said. "Where are you?"

"About two miles away," Marco replied. "I don't know who it was, but somebody tried to chase us down. I lost them, everything's okay. How did it go on your end?"

"Mission has been accomplished," Noah said. "Let's get back to the hotel. I don't know about anybody else, but I'm ready to go home and take a break."

"You won't get any arguments out of me," Neil said. "I just want to get back to my trailer. We haven't spent enough time around home lately, anyway."

On the floor of the van beside Noah, Jenny giggled. "You just want to get me alone again," she said. "I like it at the manor, but there's something nice about having the trailer all to ourselves."

Sarah, a grin spreading across her face, glanced back at Noah. "I think it might be nice to spend some time at the house, myself," she said. "Maybe we can get some time off, and just pretend to be normal for a little while."

Noah looked up at her and began to speak, but then a voice from memory made itself known in his mind.

"*Now might be a good time to ask for a vacation,*" it said. "*Maybe Allison will agree.*"

"*Yeah,*" Noah thought. "*I think she just might.*"

———

THEY FLEW HOME the following day and Allison met them at the airfield. She waited until they were all off the plane and were piling luggage into the Hummer and Marco's car, then motioned for Noah to step off to the side with her.

"Debriefing can wait until tomorrow," she said. "I just wanted to catch up with you now to say thank you. By exposing the real depth of Spear's operations and taking out Sokolov, you have at least given Donald's death some meaning. If he were alive, he would approve."

"Just doing my duty, ma'am," Noah said. "This is what you pay me for, right?"

Allison grinned. "Yeah, right," she said. "Like we could ever pay you enough for what you do. Noah, I don't know how to express what this really means to me, but I think you might be able to understand. Donald was more than a friend to me, I think you knew that. We could have been lovers, but neither of us was willing to let it go that far. Besides, he had a wife and a daughter. I may be a murderous bitch, but I'm no homewrecker."

Noah nodded. "I know," he said. "And I'm quite certain that Donald loved you, as well. I'm going to miss seeing him in the conference room."

"Yes, I'm sure you will. And, just so you know, there might be some other changes coming up. While you were gone on this last mission, I received a message from the president. He's asked me to consider another position, but only if I can find someone qualified to take my place at E & E."

Noah raised an eyebrow. "I hope it's some kind of promotion," he said. "Is it?"

"You could say that," she replied. "He's asked me to take over as Director of the CIA. The only problem is, who in the world could I put in charge of this organization that could run it properly?"

Noah shook his head. "I don't know," he said. "I don't know anyone else who could be trusted with that much power."

Allison looked him in the eye. "Don't you?"

Noah returned her gaze. "Me?" he asked.

"Well, who else could I trust? At least, in your hands, I would know that any sanction you authorized would have been carefully considered. Anybody else might just decide to use the position for political gain. God knows I was tempted enough times, but you wouldn't be. It wouldn't be logical, so you're the obvious best choice."

Noah looked at her for a moment, then slowly nodded. "If you want me to take the job, I will," he said. "The only problem is, that would leave me stuck here all the time."

"So? Jenny is capable, and you can let her have Neil and Marco and Renée. They would be a good team for her, don't you think?"

Noah glanced over at where the rest of them were waiting beside the vehicles. "I think they would be, yes. And it would mean Sarah wouldn't be going out on more missions, which definitely works in my favor." He turned his eyes back to Allison. "But what do I do about the missions that you always sent my team to handle? Who would I send?"

Allison grinned and bumped his elbow with her own. "You're not fooling me, Noah," she said. "You're just trying to make sure you could still take an occasional mission of your own. You're still the best, you know. At least, now, you'll be able to make your own decision on when you need to send Camelot out to save the world."

"Yes, I suppose so," Noah said, and then he cocked his head to the side and looked at her. "Would you like to be the one to tell Sarah?"

Allison's grin turned into a smile. "You bet," she said, and turned and started walking back toward the rest of them, leaving Noah to catch up.

Don't miss PACK LEADER. The riveting sequel in the Noah Wolf Thriller series.

Scan the QR code below to purchase PACK LEADER.

Or go to: righthouse.com/pack-leader

NOTE: flip to the very end to read an exclusive sneak peek...

DON'T MISS ANYTHING!

If you want to stay up to date on all new releases in this series, with this author, or with any of our new deals, you can do so by joining our newsletters below.

In addition, you will immediately gain access to our entire *Right House VIP Library,* which includes many riveting Mystery and Thriller novels for your enjoyment. Including a prequel novella to this series!

righthouse.com/email

(Easy to unsubscribe. No spam. Ever.)

ALSO BY DAVID ARCHER

Up to date books can be found at:
www.righthouse.com/david-archer

ROGUE THRILLERS
Gates of Hell (Book 1)
Hell's Fury (Book 2)
Ice Burn (Book 3)
Judgement by Fire (Book 4)

JACOB HUNTER THRILLERS
The Kyiv File (Book 1)
The Bogota File (Book 2)
The Havana File (Book 3)
The Amsterdam File (Book 4)

PETER BLACK THRILLERS
Burden of the Assassin (Book 1)
The Man Without A Face (Book 2)
Unpunished Deeds (Book 3)
Hunter Killer (Book 4)
Silent Shadows (Book 5)
The Last Run (Book 6)
Dark Corners (Book 7)
Ghost Operative (Book 8)
A Fire Burning (Book 9)
Dawnlight (Book 10)
Dead Ice (Book 11)

ALEX MASON THRILLERS
Odin (Book 1)

Ice Cold Spy (Book 2)
Mason's Law (Book 3)
Assets and Liabilities (Book 4)
Russian Roulette (Book 5)
Executive Order (Book 6)
Dead Man Talking (Book 7)
All The King's Men (Book 8)
Flashpoint (Book 9)
Brotherhood of the Goat (Book 10)
Dead Hot (Book 11)
Blood on Megiddo (Book 12)
Son of Hell (Book 13)
Merchant of Death (Book 14)
Extinction C-14 (Book 15)

NOAH WOLF THRILLERS
Code Name Camelot (Book 1)
Lone Wolf (Book 2)
In Sheep's Clothing (Book 3)
Hit for Hire (Book 4)
The Wolf's Bite (Book 5)
Black Sheep (Book 6)
Balance of Power (Book 7)
Time to Hunt (Book 8)
Red Square (Book 9)
Highest Order (Book 10)
Edge of Anarchy (Book 11)
Unknown Evil (Book 12)
Black Harvest (Book 13)
World Order (Book 14)
Caged Animal (Book 15)
Deep Allegiance (Book 16)
Pack Leader (Book 17)
High Treason (Book 18)
A Wolf Among Men (Book 19)

Rogue Intelligence (Book 20)
Alpha (Book 21)
Rogue Wolf (Book 22)
Shadows of Allegiance (Book 23)
In the Grip of Darkness (Book 24)
Wolves in the Dark (Book 25)
Olympus Must Fall (Book 26)

SAM PRICHARD MYSTERIES
The Grave Man (Book 1)
Death Sung Softly (Book 2)
Love and War (Book 3)
Framed (Book 4)
The Kill List (Book 5)
Drifter: Part One (Book 6)
Drifter: Part Two (Book 7)
Drifter: Part Three (Book 8)
The Last Song (Book 9)
Ghost (Book 10)
Hidden Agenda (Book 11)

SAM AND INDIE MYSTERIES
Aces and Eights (Book 1)
Fact or Fiction (Book 2)
Close to Home (Book 3)
Brave New World (Book 4)
Innocent Conspiracy (Book 5)
Unfinished Business (Book 6)
Live Bait (Book 7)
Alter Ego (Book 8)
More Than It Seems (Book 9)
Moving On (Book 10)
Worst Nightmare (Book 11)
Chasing Ghosts (Book 12)
Serial Superstition (Book 13)

CHANCE REDDICK THRILLERS
Innocent Injustice (Book 1)
Angel of Justice (Book 2)
High Stakes Hunting (Book 3)
Personal Asset (Book 4)

CASSIE MCGRAW MYSTERIES
What Lies Beneath (Book 1)
Can't Fight Fate (Book 2)
One Last Game (Book 3)
Never Really Gone (Book 4)

ABOUT US

Right House is an independent publisher created by authors for readers. We specialize in Action, Thriller, Mystery, and Crime novels.

If you enjoyed this novel, then there is a good chance you will like what else we have to offer! Please stay up to date by using any of the links below.

Join our mailing lists to stay up to date -->
righthouse.com/email
Visit our website --> righthouse.com
Contact us --> contact@righthouse.com

 facebook.com/righthousebooks

 x.com/righthousebooks

 instagram.com/righthousebooks

EXCLUSIVE SNEAK PEEK OF...

HIGH TREASON

PROLOGUE

POTUS WAS IN THE HABIT OF RISING EARLY EVERY morning, and this particular morning was no exception. The First Lady rolled over and mumbled something in her sleep as he rose, and he glanced down at her with a smile before heading to the bathroom for a quick shower and shave. Morning ablutions completed, he stepped into his dressing room and selected the suit he would wear for the day.

"Just one moment, Mr. President," said Mike Carrington, his current "Body Man." Mike's job was to make sure that POTUS constantly looked his best, and he carried a number of special tools for the purpose. One of them was a lint roller, which he quickly ran over the left arm of the president's signature blue suit.

Looking sharp, POTUS bypassed the residential dining room and stepped into the room he called his den. His favorite news channel was already streaming on the television mounted to the wall as he sat down in the recliner and picked up the note pad on the side table. He'd always found that analyzing the news each morning gave him a feeling for what would be coming throughout the day..

An hour later, satisfied that he fully understood each relevant news story, POTUS moved out of the residence toward the Oval

Office. For once, he was pleased to see that he didn't have half a dozen congresspeople waiting to waste as much of his time as they possibly could. His receptionist, whose name was Carly, but whom he always referred to as Carolyn for some reason no one understood, passed him a couple of notes as he entered the office, and Mike took a seat beside her desk.

"He looks like he's in rare form today," Carly said. "Something good on the news this morning?"

"Just the usual," Mike replied. "Some reporters are saying his fuss with Senator Friedman is a bit ridiculous, but I'm pretty sure he's accomplishing exactly what he wants."

Carly shook her head. "I don't always understand him," she said, "but I can tell you this. I've seen senators and congressmen and lawyers and judges come stomping in here, all ready to chew him out over whatever fight they've got going on with him, their panties all twisted up in a wad and spitting fire out of their ears, but after ten minutes in the office with him, they come out with their tails tucked between their legs and promising to give him something he's demanding. It's amazing, it really is."

Mike nodded. "He's devious, if you want my opinion. He's always got someone mad at him, on both sides of the aisle, but he doesn't back down. Somehow, he can always make certain people jump through the hoops that he's holding up for them. By the time they realize the corner he's backed them into, it's too late and they've already given him what he wants. They can't back down without looking like idiots, but they still fall for it every time."

"Well, today isn't going to be one of those days. He's got three teleconference meetings this morning, all of them over the trade war. Half the leaders of the world want to lynch him, and the other half are trying to get in his good graces to pick up some of the trade possibilities with the US. Everybody thought we were going to get hurt when China pulled out of the trade talks, but he's got other countries lining up to provide even better quality products at lower prices. This morning, on the way into work, I heard on the radio that the Republicans are screaming over the loss of six hundred jobs in New York because of the trade talks, but they're ignoring the fact that the overall economic outlook says we gained over a hundred thousand new manufacturing jobs in the last month, alone."

INSIDE THE OVAL OFFICE, the president was sitting at his desk, his chin propped on his fists and his eyes closed. This was the way he started every workday, by taking a few minutes to think through what he wanted to accomplish. According to him, this enabled him to plan everything he wanted to say and predict the objections he was going to face, so that he could have counter-arguments ready.

Precisely fifteen minutes later, he opened his eyes and tapped the intercom button.

"Carolyn? I'm ready for the first call."

"Yes, Mr. President."

A large monitor sitting on his desk lit up, and over the next few seconds it was populated with half a dozen faces. The commerce ministers and secretaries of Russia, China and four other nations stared out at him, their faces devoid of any expression.

"Well, good morning, ladies and gentlemen," POTUS said with a smile. "How can I make your days worse than they already are?"

"I doubt you can," said the Russian minister with his familiar scowl. "Mr. President, I intend to implore you once again to relax your trade demands on our allies. They are creating economic havoc in the eastern part of the world."

"I'll be glad to," POTUS said. "Just as soon as they agree to the trade equality package that I proposed, my objections can go away pretty quickly. Everybody ready to sign on?"

The Chinese minister scowled. "Your proposal is ridiculous, Mr. President. Trade equality with the United States is not even possible. Your country is the greatest consumer of our goods, but you make very little that our people want or need."

"That's only because you keep them afraid to admit what they want," POTUS replied. "If you could be a little more democratic, let the people make their own minds up, I think you'd find that we have a lot to offer."

The conversation continued in that vein for some time, and ended precisely where it had begun. The trade restrictions would remain in place, and POTUS invited each of the officials to reconsider his proposals.

The next teleconference was slightly more rewarding. The faces looked almost the same, but they were the African counterparts of their predecessors on the screen, and eagerly courting the president's approval for some trade resolutions that would be beneficial to both their own countries and the USA. With a few modifications, POTUS told them, he would be quite willing to ask Congress to approve those resolutions, so these faces were all smiling by the time the conference ended.

The third teleconference, which began just after a break for lunch, was considerably different. There were eight faces on the screen, each of whom was the chief executive officer of a multinational corporation. The trade fiasco was affecting their businesses, they said, and they wanted to negotiate some exceptions to the restrictions POTUS had put into place.

"Jeff," POTUS said, speaking directly to one of the people on the screen, "I know you make an awful lot of money from your Chinese connections, but the people in this country find the human rights violations involved in making those products to be reprehensible. I can connect you with countries that will produce even better products at better prices, and who are willing to allow oversight so that we can be sure none of those violations will be taking place in the future. Are you seriously going to complain about a few dollars you might be losing right now, compared to the millions you could make while also becoming a hero to those Americans who want you to support the people who actually make your products? If you move your production to countries that treat their workers more fairly, who don't make children work long hours every day or force people to work for slave wages, you're going to find your company becoming a lot more popular."

"Here in the US, sure," the man replied. "But what about our global market? Many of our products are going to China's allies, and we could lose billions each year in sales if they decide not to continue purchasing through us."

"That wouldn't last long, and you know it. The biggest thing your company does for all those countries is make shipping and product delivery a lot easier. They're not going to be able to go straight to China and buy all those things, not if they want them shipped as inexpensively as you can do it. You give them a couple of months to think about it, and they'll be right back on your websites and spending money faster than ever before."

"That isn't the point," said another man, whose company handled financial transactions all over the world. "We handle an awful lot of the transactional processing involved in trade with the countries you are restricting, and this is costing us hundreds of millions of dollars every month. There's no way this can continue, Mr. President. If it does, I'm afraid my colleagues and I are going to need to take some sort of action."

POTUS chuckled. "Are you honestly going to sit there and threaten me? Have you looked at my current approval rating? Almost a million new jobs in the last eighteen months, unemployment is lower than it has been in decades, I've thrown away tens of thousands of ridiculous federal regulations... I don't know what you think you can threaten me with, but I'm really not too worried about it."

"Oh, good grief," said yet another face. This was a man whose social media empire had more members than the populations of many countries. "We aren't going to get anywhere like this. Look, Mr. President, you are affecting all of our businesses, and I'm frankly quite amazed that you seem to discount just how important we are to your administration. Between us, we can effectively shape public opinion; do you really want to turn us into enemies?"

"Well, Mr. Feinberg, that is entirely up to you. You see, as long as your companies continue to work against the best interests of this nation, it is you who are the enemies, not me. My sworn duty is to protect and defend the people and the Constitution of this country, and that's what I'm doing. If you are honestly suggesting that you want to stop me from doing that, I might have to consider the possibility that your actions could be considered treasonous. Would you have anything you want to add to that?"

There was an excited uproar, as each of the people on the screen objected to the veiled accusation.

"All right, knock it off," POTUS said. "Here's the deal, folks. The trade equality treaty is going to happen, and if you want to play ball in the US, you're going to have to learn to live with it. I'm quite serious when I say there are far better opportunities available for you, so you can choose whether to lose some friends in the Far East, or lose a nation full of customers back here. Do I make myself clear?"

There was another outburst, but POTUS had had enough. He cut off the connection with the punch of a single button, then leaned back in his chair and closed his eyes for a few seconds.

AFTERWARD, he dealt with a few sudden calls from senators and congressmen, then leaned back in his chair to think. He had a trip to Florida scheduled for the next day, a chance to hit the links and knock some balls around with a few of the real movers in Congress; most of the real work of the presidency seemed to get done that way, and it made it a lot more enjoyable than sitting in the office all day.

———

"WHAT I WANT TO KNOW," POTUS said the next day, "is how the hell people managed to get close enough to the resort with a surface-to-air-missile to even be a threat to my aircraft. Somebody want to tell me what in the world this is all about?"

Steve Nichols, the head of the presidential security team, stood at attention in front of his boss. "Sir, there was actually no serious threat," he said. "Local police in Orlando had gathered intelligence that alerted us to the terrorist plans, and everything was handled before we even arrived."

"I'm aware of that, Steve," POTUS said. "My question is how they managed to get far enough in their plans without us being aware of it that they were arrested on the outskirts of the resort itself. You guys are doing a great job, but somebody has fallen asleep at the wheel. Terrorists should never be able to get that close to the president of the United States."

"I agree, sir," Nichols said. "Homeland Security is already reaming ass over this, and the FBI is conducting its own internal investigation to see how they managed to miss it. The only thing we have at the moment is some kind of rumor that the attack was funded by corporate interests, rather than political."

POTUS's eyes became a little wider. "Corporate? I guess I can figure that one out." He paced around his hotel room for a moment, hands clasped behind his back, then turned to Nichols again. "Get Stacy in here. I think there's a little business I've been putting off that I need to take care of."

Stacy Richardson was the president's executive assistant. She traveled everywhere with him, ready to make calls or arrange meetings on the spur of the moment. Her room was directly adjacent to his own, and she appeared less than a minute after he asked for her.

"Yes, Mr. President?" she asked.

"Stacy, a couple months ago you told me about this guy who took over for Allison Peterson when we moved her to CIA. What was his name again?"

"Noah Wolf, sir," Stacy replied. "He's been asking for a

meeting with you, so that he can officially receive his orders to take the position."

"Well, good," POTUS said. "Get him on the phone and then get him on a plane. I want him here within six hours."

Stacy ducked her head once in an affirmative nod. "Yes, sir," she said. She turned and walked out of the room instantly, returning to her own room to make the call on the secure cell phone that had been provided for her use.

———

NOAH WOLF SAT behind the desk that Allison had occupied for several years, reading through the files that had been dropped on it during the night. Molly Hansen, his director of operations, sat in her own chair beside the desk.

"The next one," Molly said, "is Alberto Gomez. Mr. Gomez is the current head of the Matagoros Cartel that's been operating out of Tijuana. They've been running drugs in to the Southwest for several years, but recent events have caused Gomez to step up a lot of their operations. With the increases in border security over the past couple of years, it is suspected that Gomez is trying to establish underground tunnels and Pacific water routes for bringing his drugs into the country. The DEA has not been able to get close enough to stop him, nor to get enough evidence to get the federals to cooperate. The sanction request came from the DEA, through DHS."

"He's not going to be an easy one to hit," Noah said. "I'm thinking Cinderella, with Pegasus for backup."

"I'm sure Jenny would be glad to get back into the field. But Pegasus for backup? Do you think Ralph is ready for an operation like this?"

"I wouldn't put him on lead, but I think his team can back Jenny up. Tell both teams to show up for briefing..." The phone on his desk rang suddenly, and he picked it up. "Yes, Danielle?"

Danielle Niemeyer was the secretary who had been working

with Allison when she transferred to the CIA, and Noah had seen no reason to replace her.

"Mr. Wolf, I have Stacy Richardson on line three," she said. "Ms. Richardson is the..."

"Executive assistant to the president," Noah said. "I'm aware of who she is. Thank you." He reached over and hit a button on the phone. "Ms. Richardson? Noah Wolf."

"Mr. Wolf," Stacy said, "thank you for taking my call. The president would like you to join him on his vacation outside Orlando this afternoon. Within six hours, he said."

One of Noah's eyebrows went up half an inch. "Orlando? All right, if that's what he wants. I'll get a flight arranged immediately and be there as soon as I possibly can. Is there anything I need to bring along?"

"I wasn't given any specific instructions, Mr. Wolf, so I will leave that to your discretion. I will let the president know that you are on the way."

The line went dead, and Noah replaced the handset on its cradle. He turned to Molly.

"I have to go to Orlando to meet with the president, right away. Would you like to make the arrangements for me?"

Molly smiled. She and Noah had been friends since childhood, and even went through a phase as teenage lovers, though it was more for camouflage than any other reason. Being devoid of emotion and operating on logic, Noah rarely considered romance to have any importance in his life, while Molly preferred to spend her time concentrating on her studies. Both of them were regularly teased about their lack of any sort of love life, so the idea of the pretense seemed to be the answer to a problem. Besides, as Molly had said, both of them had physical needs. Emotions or not, Noah could see the logic in learning more about sex and the physical pleasures, and Molly had proven to be an excellent study partner.

"I can have the Gulfstream ready within an hour," she said. "And I suggest you take your wife along."

"I was planning to," Noah said. He watched Molly get up from her chair and leave the room, then took out his cell phone and dialed Sarah's number.

"Noah? Hi, sweetheart," Sarah said.

"Hey, baby," Noah replied, using the pet name he knew she loved the most. "Do me a favor and pack a bag for each of us. Probably enough for one or two nights away from home. If we need more than that, we can get it while we're out."

"Out? Where are we going?"

"Orlando," Noah said. "I've been summoned to a meeting with the president, and I thought you might like to go along. We can do a little sightseeing while we're there, if you like, or maybe some shopping."

"Sightseeing and shopping?" Sarah asked. "Sure, and I know just the place. You, Mr. Executive Director, are taking your wife to Disney World."

CHAPTER 1

THE PLANE TOUCHED DOWN JUST BEFORE THREE P.M., putting Noah right on schedule to meet the president's request. As he and Sarah stepped off the Gulfstream, a Lincoln limousine pulled up beside it. A young woman stepped out of the front seat.

"Mr. Wolf? I'm Stacy Richardson." She opened the back door of the limo while the chauffeur came around to take the bags and load them into the trunk of the car. When Noah and Sarah had gotten inside, Stacy followed.

"I take it this is the meeting I've been waiting for?" Noah asked.

"And perhaps more than that," Stacy said. "Mr. Wolf, are you aware that there was an attempt to assassinate the president here earlier today?"

"I was not until now," Noah said. "May I ask about the particulars?"

"We really don't know a lot of details just yet," Stacy said. "A small terrorist cell that was operating out of Orlando managed to get several people on the work crew for property adjacent to the resort. Apparently, their IDs all checked out and no one had any reason to think they might be a threat, but the Orlando police stumbled across some intel that led to their capture. They had with them a pair of surface-to-air missiles, and apparently had intended to shoot down the president's helicopter. According to police interrogators, one of the terrorists has implied that they were actually hired for the job by someone representing multinational corporate interests."

"Interesting," Noah said. "Have they said who their employers were?"

"Not to my knowledge. However, I'm supposed to brief you that the president intends to speak to you not only about your new position, but about giving your organization the authority to investigate the situation. He will then expect you to do whatever is necessary."

Sarah glanced up at Noah, who was watching Stacy intently.

"Ms. Richardson, are you aware of what my organization does?"

Stacy swallowed. "I have heard rumors," she said. "However, I do not have sufficient clearance to confirm those rumors."

"That's a very good response," Noah said. "In that case, we shall need to discuss something else for the remainder of the ride."

Stacy seemed slightly relieved. "That's fine," she said. She turned to Sarah. "You are Mrs. Wolf?"

"I am," Sarah said, with a slight hint of menace in her voice.

"I'm delighted to meet you," Stacy said. "When we learned you were coming with your husband, I was instructed to do anything you need to make your visit here enjoyable." She leaned forward and lowered her voice to a stage whisper. "I personally recommend the spa here at the resort," she said. "It is absolutely divine."

Sarah broke into a smile. "That sounds good," she said. "Do they have a couples' program?"

"They do," Stacy said, "but unless you object, I was thinking that you and I could take it in while your husband is busy with the president. I was told to give them a minimum of three hours alone, and it's the perfect time for you and me to enjoy a massage, a soak and the most incredible hot stone treatment I've ever had."

Sarah grinned and glanced at Noah, who nodded. "Go ahead," he said. "I'll be busy anyway, for a while. Afterward, we can look into where to go for dinner."

"The restaurant here at the resort is one of the finest in the Orlando area," Stacy said. "Antonio, the chef, is considered one of the three best in the world. Of course, because you are here on business with the president, everything is covered under your organization's budget."

"We'll make that decision later," Noah said. "This is our first trip to Orlando, and we were hoping to get in a little bit of vacation while we're here."

"Of course," Stacy said. "If you're interested in visiting any of the theme parks, we have all-inclusive passes available for all of the president's guests. Just say the word, and I can get them for you."

"Disney," Sarah said. "I've always wanted to go to Disney World."

Stacy grinned. "Not a problem," she said. "Perhaps you'd like to spend the day there tomorrow? It'll probably be a little late by the time your husband gets finished up here today."

"That sounds great," Sarah said. She rubbed her belly. "It may be the last time we get to do things like this alone."

Stacy nodded. "How far along?" she asked.

"Almost six months, now," Sarah said. "Only three more months of misery and stretchy clothes to go."

The ride took about thirty minutes, and then the car pulled up in front of an incredibly impressive building. Stacy waited for the chauffeur to come around and open the door this time, and the three of them stepped out of the car. A bellman moved quickly down the steps to collect their bags and then followed them inside. Stacy took them directly to the front desk, where reservations were waiting.

"The president suggested we put you in the honeymoon suite," Stacy said. "It happened to be available, and it is rumored to be even more luxurious than his own suite."

She collected the key cards and handed them to Noah, then

led the way to the elevator. The resort had six floors, and the honeymoon suite was on the fifth. When they opened the door and walked inside, Sarah gave a small gasp.

The suite consisted of one large room, and the central feature was a large, heart-shaped bed. It was surrounded by water, in a horseshoe-shaped hot tub, and the bed was draped with towels. There was a small bridge over the water on each side of the bed, and the water seemed to be steaming slightly.

"That—that," Sarah said, "is the most incredible thing I have ever seen."

Stacy giggled. "Why do you think I didn't warn you? I was dying to see the look on your face when you got your first look at it. They tell me, though I've never tried it myself, that the bed is actually somewhat waterproof. It's designed so that even if you climb into it while you're still wet, it will dry you and absorb the excess water. I guess it works something like a diaper, to keep the moisture away from your body."

Sarah's eyes were wide, but Noah simply looked at the bed and the surrounding water.

"Looks relaxing," he said. "We'll have to give it a try later."

Sarah looked at him, and her eyes seemed to indicate that she wasn't too sure about this. "We're going to sleep in a giant diaper?"

Stacy laughed again. "Okay, that was probably a bad choice of words," she said. "I just meant that it pulls the water away from you, so you're not sleeping in a wet bed. I really don't know how it works."

"We'll find out later," Noah said. "For now, I believe the president is waiting for me."

"He is," Stacy said. "If you'll follow me, I'll show you to him, and then Mrs. Wolf and I can go get a massage."

"That," Sarah said, "is the best thing you've said since we got here."

They followed Stacy back down the elevator, and then to an office suite that was toward the rear of the ground floor. The

Secret Service agent stationed outside it checked Noah's ID and then opened the door for him. Sarah and Stacy waited until he was inside and the door closed, then turned in a different direction.

Inside the office, Noah found the president of the United States waiting for him. POTUS got to his feet and came around the desk in the middle of the room, his hand extended.

"Mr. Wolf," he said. "It's a pleasure to finally meet you. I'm sorry it's taken so long to get this meeting arranged, but I've been extremely busy the last few weeks."

Noah shook his hand. "I am at your service, Mr. President," he said.

The president invited him to have a seat, then took the chair directly in front of him.

"Let's get first things out of the way first," he said. "Allison Peterson tells me you are the ideal person to take over her position. Naturally, I've read through your file and I personally agree. However, I have learned it's always best to ask the person who's going to be in the seat whether they are comfortable in it. How do you feel about running E & E?"

"I don't actually feel anything about it at all, sir," Noah said. "If you've read my file, you'll understand what I mean. However, having said that, I believe that I'm capable of doing the job the way Allison intended it to be done. One of her greatest fears is that someone will eventually succeed her and turn the power of the office to personal gain. I don't believe I would ever be tempted to do so."

The president nodded. "That's what she told me you would say if I asked," he said. "Now, suppose someone kidnapped your wife and held her hostage in order to get you to order assassinations for their benefit. What would you do in that case?"

"My wife has been abducted before," Noah said. "I would do exactly what I did in each of those cases. I would kill the person responsible."

"And if that were impossible?"

"Then I would probably die in the attempt," Noah said. "However, I would not give in to the demands."

"You seem pretty sure of yourself. Why is that?"

"Because I operate primarily on logic, rather than emotion. My condition leaves me without the ability to feel emotion the way most people do, even to the point of being unable to recognize certain types of humor, or certain aesthetic values. To accede to the demands of someone who was threatening a person I care about would require me to set aside the moral code I have lived by since I was a child. I don't believe I'm capable of doing that."

"I would say I understand, but I don't. I'm actually quite an emotional person, myself, though I try my best to use it only to my advantage. I'm sure you've seen many of the news stories about my fights with Congress. Can you tell me your opinion of those stories?"

"I believe," Noah said, "that most of those fights serve as camouflage, or perhaps smoke screens. I've spent some time analyzing some of those arguments, and it looks to me that the whole time some senator or congressman is ranting and raving about whatever has them in an uproar, they are being subtly manipulated into a position that gives you an advantage. Considering how many of the opposition party have lately been declining to comment lately, I think some of them are beginning to understand that."

The president of the United States threw back his head and laughed out loud, then took a moment to get himself back under control.

"She told me you would say that, too. Mr. Wolf—may I call you Noah? Noah, I will officially confirm your assignment as soon as I get back to the Oval Office, but for now I need to talk to you about something else. Are you aware of the growing power of some of our international—no, let me rephrase that, our *multi*national corporations?"

"I'm aware that some of them do seem to have a surprising amount of influence in the world," Noah said. "Ms. Richardson just explained to me that the recent attempt on your life may have been engineered by some of them."

"That's the story we've been getting out of some of the people who were captured. If it's true, then it is my feeling that these people have crossed the line. Would you agree with me on that?"

"I would, sir."

"Suppose I were to tell you that I want you to find out which companies were behind the attempt, and then kill the people in charge of them. What would you say?"

"Mr. President, I would tell you to submit your request through the proper channels, along with all the documented evidence to support the necessity of a sanction. If I found that evidence to indicate that it would be more advisable to eliminate these people than to attempt to prosecute them, I would grant that request."

"And if not?" POTUS asked. "What would you do then?"

"I would reject the request and send it back through the channels. I would probably suggest that the situation be handled by the FBI, instead."

"Here's the problem," the president said. "The FBI and CIA haven't been able to get a handle on what these companies are actually up to, although Allison has some intel that may confirm things are worse than we imagined. Noah, based on Allison's recommendations and my own gut feeling about you, I believe that you can be trusted completely, and that you will make the appropriate decision about how to handle the people behind this attack if I simply leave it up to you. I'm not saying to you that I want them eliminated; I'm saying that I would prefer to let you make that decision, and that I would also prefer to have you take charge of the investigation."

"Yes, sir," Noah said. "Under those conditions, I would be happy to do so."

"Excellent. Now, let's talk about some other things. Is there anything you need from me in order to best perform your duties in this new office?"

"Yes, sir," Noah said. "A simple understanding. I believe you've already expressed your willingness to refrain from ordering me to authorize a sanction, so I would simply like to verbalize it. I will not accept any order that I do not believe to be in the best interest of the nation, or secondarily, of my organization and its people. In other words, I will refuse any order you give me to authorize a sanction, and will then make my own determination of whether I believe it is necessary. I will also refuse any order that I honestly believe puts my people in unnecessary jeopardy."

The president slapped his knee and laughed again. "My goodness," he said, "you can't imagine how nice it is to talk to somebody who can say that to me with a straight face. I have people all the time tell me they'll refuse to do what I want, but if you watch their eyes, you know they are only bluffing. They know damn well they're going to give in, because I'm the president, for goodness's sake." He leaned closer and looked Noah in the eye. "Not you, though. You say exactly what you mean, don't you?"

"I don't know any other way to be, sir," Noah said. "To me, except in the case of maintaining a cover during a mission, to be untruthful would be illogical."

Noah sat and watched the president for a moment, as the man seemed to be considering what he'd just said.

"Noah," POTUS said after a moment, "I have a feeling you and I are going to get along just fine. If you'll come with me, I have some people waiting to talk to you. The police officers who arrested one of the terrorists are waiting in another room to tell you what they know about the case."

They got up and left the office, and Noah noticed that a pair of Secret Service agents fell in behind them as they walked down a hallway. They stopped at a door and the president tapped on it gently.

A few seconds later, the door was opened by another Secret Service agent. He looked Noah up and down, then stepped aside to allow them to enter. Several men and a couple of women were sitting at a conference table, and all of them turned to see who had entered.

One man's eyes suddenly went wide. "Oh, you've got to be kidding me," Sam Prichard said. "You again?"

Scan the QR code below to purchase PACK LEADER.
Or go to: righthouse.com/pack-leader